RENEGADE SUMMER

BY

OTIS L. SCARBARY

Renegade Summer
Otis L. Scarbary
Copyright 2021 Otis L. Scarbary

ISBN: 978-0-9898648-6-2

First Edition

Layout by: Cheryl Perez – yourepublished.com
Front cover art: Carl Graves – extendedimagry.com

Also by Otis L. Scarbary:

Leo's Redemption

Ollie's Dilemma

Leo's Choice

Dedication

This book is dedicated to all young people growing up and trying to figure out life and love. Well, maybe also to those of us who somehow made it through the tough years and now take pleasure in remembering those times long ago.

First love is only a little foolishness and a lot of curiosity.

George Bernard Shaw

*Love is the most important thing in the world,
but baseball is pretty good, too.*

Yogi Berra

CHAPTER 1

Odell Sterling slouched in the assigned one-piece metal framed desk. His arms rested on its wooden top while he dreamed of tomorrow. He had honed the look of feigned attention to an art form even when he was somewhere else in his head. Summer vacation was here when this day was over, and he was ready for some fun.

Not that he minded going to school, but Odell relished the thoughts of sleeping a little later and playing lots of baseball. Some of the other guys in the neighborhood had already agreed they should play in the Macon Recreation League one last time in the fifteen and under division, and he figured they would have a good chance of winning the trophy. Participating in that league would not keep them from playing other organized ball since most of them were on either Pony or Colt league teams as well. A couple of the kids were still in Little League.

It might be the last year Odell would play the game he loved. One of his goals was to have a car to call his own, and his daddy had already told him there was only one way that would happen.

Odell would have to find a job to pay for everything associated with ownership including insurance, gas, and maintenance. He thought that was doable, but it would cut into being able to play his favorite sport.

Other thoughts of enjoyable things to do before September and the looming tenth grade of high school included going to Durr's skating rink on weekend nights, water skiing on the lake, watching movies in the air-conditioned comfort of a movie theater, and reading for the enjoyment of it rather than what was required for school. Odell loved books that opened doors to other worlds or that illuminated history in a way he could imagine himself as part of the times, and the summer vacation gave him plenty of time to expand those horizons.

Oh yeah, he thought, *and girls.*

Odell had always been a little shy around the fairer sex, and going to an all-male school didn't help matters. It had always been difficult for him to carry on a conversation with a girl. He couldn't help but think, however, about maybe even finding a steady girlfriend, if he could control his acne better. There were a few prospects in mind, but he wondered whether they knew he was alive. The cute ones his age seemed to have eyes on older guys. Even if they were a year younger, a couple of possibilities lived nearby and there were several who frequented Durr's.

The biology teacher, Mr. Hinson, had been a favorite instructor throughout his ninth-grade experiences because of his ability to make the subject relevant. But, Odell's mind wouldn't let up about the upcoming summer, so he didn't hear the teacher's question.

"What was the one thing you learned about biology this year that will stick with you?" Odell? Mr. Sterling? You've still got to get through this day to be promoted."

The teenager felt his face reddening probably causing the pimple on his nose to appear more inflamed. He prided himself on being attentive enough to whatever the teacher was saying so he could answer intelligently if called upon, unlike others who were less likely to care.

"Sorry, sir. I didn't hear the question," Odell stammered while adjusting his horn-rimmed glasses.

"I could tell, Odell. You've got glazed eyes telling me you're somewhere other than in my class."

Pausing for a second, he continued, "I asked what was the main thing you learned in this class."

"Uh, I learned a lot, Mr. Hinson. You're a great teacher, by the way."

The other boys in the class started snickering, and from the back of the room somebody called out, "Suck up." That comment brought even more laughter, and Odell felt the heat in his face increase another notch.

The teacher shook his head and started walking down the aisle toward Odell. The teenager was beyond mortified, as he could never remember a moment like this. Mr. Hinson stopped beside Odell's desk and looked down through glasses that made his eyes appear larger than they were.

"No, really," croaked Odell. "I mean, learning about cellular structure, heredity and genetics, evolution, and ecosystems was interesting. I didn't really know much about any of that stuff before you taught us," he continued in a clearer voice while trying to force a smile.

Mr. Hinson gave a slight nod at the response and then looked around the room as if searching for another target. His eyes settled on a kid on the back row who was slumped in his seat. Bartholomew Durden was an infamous figure in junior high, and Odell wondered if he was going to the tenth grade next year since Bart never seemed interested in anything relating to the class.

"How about it, Mr. Durden? Did you learn anything this year?"

The kid's smirk indicated he was thinking of a smartass reply. Odell was glad the teacher's attention was on someone else, but silently worried what Bart might say or do.

Odell remembered the first time he'd met Bart a couple of years ago. They had shared the same supervision and first period English class in the eighth grade. Bart had peed in the corner of the room when the teacher wouldn't let him go to the bathroom. The very proper older lady was writing something on the blackboard while he got up from his seat to whip it out. The wide-eyed rest of the class couldn't believe the brazen behavior.

He later carved a profanity on the teacher's prized lectern after she put him in detention. Odell thought it probable that budding juvenile delinquent Bart would be permanently expelled sometime in the future.

"Yes sir, I learned all about reproduction. Before your class, I didn't know much about intercourse," Bart said through a toothy grin. "Now I understand why those two dogs I saw were stuck together. I'm not sure how that works butt to butt, though," he finished.

The class erupted into spontaneous laughter. Odell tried to swallow his snickering, which only partially succeeded. The tears forming in his eyes burned as they ran down his face. To make things worse, Mr. Hinson turned around and looked down on him again.

There was nothing more difficult for Odell than trying to suppress laughter. His closest friends had often taken advantage of Odell's inability to do that, much to his embarrassment. All Odell could do now was to duck his head so that he could bite into the sleeve of his shirt.

As the laughter subsided and Odell struggled to contain his, the wizened teacher turned his attention back to Bart. Mr. Hinson took a few steps away from Odell's desk and cleared his throat causing the class to immediately quiet down. It was a sign of irritation recognized by all of them.

"Biology is science, Mr. Durden, and reproduction is a vital part of that. Since you mention that part of the course study from this past year, I sincerely hope you'll remember going forward that some members of their species shouldn't take part in those efforts," said Mr. Hinson with a slight smirk showing on his face.

There were a couple of oohs from the class as the teacher's retort had effectively silenced the class clown. Bart's grin turned downward as it appeared he was contemplating some further response.

The bell rang at that precise moment and the commotion caused by students closing books, getting out of their seats and multiple conversations at once ended any chance of further dialogue between Bart and Mr. Hinson. Bart then broke into another smile and flashed his middle finger towards the adult before joining others as they left the room. Odell couldn't leave because of the teacher's presence blocking his exit.

As the room cleared, a few teens lingered talking amongst themselves, and a couple of others came by the location of Odell's desk and spoke to their teacher before exiting. These were guys Odell thought of as fellow classmates who cared about learning as opposed to those who didn't care much about the high school course of study. They, like Odell, were members of the Jr. Beta Club.

After a long couple of minutes, the older man stepped away from Odell's desk allowing the teen a chance to gather his things and free himself from the wood and metal contraption. He stood across from Mr. Hinson and noticed the guy was about his same height and weight and suddenly realized that had not been true at the beginning of the past school year. Odell switched everything in his possession to his left side and held out a tentative right hand.

For the first time, Odell could see the teacher's wrinkles had deepened and the hazel eyes behind his glasses had softened. It was almost as if the man had aged before the student's gaze.

"Uh, Mr. Hinson, I just wanted to thank you for teaching me this year. I-I really enjoyed it, no kidding," stammered Odell.

The teacher smiled without showing any teeth and nodded in slight response. His demeanor relaxed and he gripped Odell's hand firmly and shook.

"Thanks, Mr. Sterling. It was a pleasure having you as a student. If you stay focused, I see a great future for you."

Odell took a moment for the compliment to sink in. He couldn't remember hearing Mr. Hinson say that kind of thing before, at least not to him directly.

"I'll sure try. Stay focused, that is. It can be hard sometimes," Odell replied as the handshake ended.

The older man nodded again and said, "I understand. Believe it or not, I remember being your age. Back then I didn't think very much about what I might be doing now. I sure didn't see myself teaching, or I guess I should say trying, to teach teenagers biology. After doing this for a while I can get a sense when a student shows promise. You've got that potential, and I think you'll figure it out."

The room had cleared, and Odell was in a hurry to join up with his friends outside, but he was blown away by Mr. Hinson's words and wanted to say something that would show his appreciation. He just couldn't think of anything that sounded right.

"Thank you, sir. I've got to catch my ride. Have a good summer."

With that Odell made a bee line out the door with only a side glance toward his now former teacher. It never occurred to him it would be the last time since the man wouldn't come back next year. The summer of 1967 was now Odell's main priority.

CHAPTER 2

Odell stood in a small circle of friends near the street connecting the junior high facility and the senior campus of Willingham. The two buildings were on the same side of the road separated by a football field and dirt track. The structure nearest Odell was new having only been built the year before and didn't match the older one in the distance. On the opposite side of the road up an embankment stood the McEvoy campus where all the girls attended.

There were a couple of yellow buses parked within hollering distance in the process of loading students. Odell took it for granted that they had been manufactured in nearby Fort Valley because of the Bluebird emblems shown on the vehicles.

He had been transported in one of the behemoths many times starting in grammar school. He now considered himself fortunate, however, because one of his friends from the neighborhood had a driver's license and allowed Odell the luxury of avoiding the noisy and bumpy rides.

"Well, if it ain't Slow-dell Four-eyes. You looking for a hitch, buddy?"

Walking like a rooster strutting around his granddaddy's chicken coop came Ricky Lee Smith. He was considered a friend although Odell thought him to be on the arrogant side.

Their relationship had developed over the last few years of playing organized baseball against one another until last summer when they were on the same sandlot team. The team name had been *The Crazy Nine,* and they had come in second in the fifteen and under city recreation league. Odell had thought the name appropriate mainly because of his pal.

"No, I'm waiting on Johnny White. He should be here in a few minutes," responded Odell while pushing up his horn-rims with his middle finger. It was a bad habit but sometimes useful in shooting a bird at somebody who was obnoxious.

Ricky Lee, often called by both first and middle names, grinned like the Cheshire Cat. His smile reflected white and perfectly straight teeth, and for some reason made Odell uneasy.

"Oh, I see you forgot to shave this morning," Ricky Lee said.

Before Odell had time to realize his friend's intent, Ricky Lee grabbed the two whiskers growing out of a mole on his chin and yanked them out. The act caused Odell's eyes to water and more pain than he expected.

"Damn it, Ricky Lee!"

The taller teen danced away as Odell swatted at him. After missing the mark, Odell dabbed at the stinging spot on his face half-expecting to find blood. Finding none on his finger, he glared at his still hooting friend holding the hairs up like some trophy.

"You're a dick, Ricky Lee! I'll get you back for that. When you least expect it."

"I'm so scared, O-dell," replied Ricky Lee through his big grin. He finished by flicking away the whiskers, then grabbing his crotch and shaking it toward Odell.

"See you on the ballfield, hairy, or should I say, hairless?" Ricky Lee was laughing as he jogged toward one of the waiting buses.

Odell extended a middle finger wave toward his retreating friend and continued to self-consciously feel the mole with his other hand. It was only about the size of a pencil point and barely noticeable, but it was yet another source of embarrassment along with the occasional bumps on his face.

Ricky Lee had only reminded him of the experienced shame and insecurity when whiskers started coming through the raised dark spot a couple of years earlier. He must've forgotten to clip them the last couple of days. Since his beard was spotty and sparse, Odell didn't shave every day which had led to the recent plucking.

The area where Odell stood began clearing as the buses departed and older kids driving from the other campus picked up other younger students. He was left with his younger brother, Kenny, who had walked up as Ricky Lee ran away, and Ken, who was the same age as Odell and the younger brother of Johnny White.

Both boys shared the same first name of Kenneth, but neither was called that way unless a parent used it to get their attention.

Otherwise, everyone living in their Bloomfield neighborhood knew them as Ken and Kenny.

"That guy's a butthole," said Ken with a frown before continuing, "I don't know if I'd want him as a friend."

"Aw, he's alright. If you don't know, he's a hell-of-a good baseball player. I was on his team last year in the city rec league. I could play with him again this summer, but I've been thinking we should get our own team," replied Odell.

"Would I have to catch?" asked Kenny.

Odell studied his younger brother before responding. Kenny was the best catcher by far in their circle of friends and knew Odell's pitches due to their many throwing sessions over the last few years. However, Odell knew that Kenny wanted to play some other position from past discussions at home.

"Let's see who we can line up to play, and then we'll decide," Odell said.

Ken shifted from foot to foot and added, "I'll play if we can get enough guys. I don't think there are enough of us to compete in the fifteen-year-old league."

"I'm sure we can get enough to play, but we might not have very many our age," said Odell.

A lull in the conversation caused Odell to mentally count the guys in the neighborhood who could man a position and how old they were. Of course, he would pitch. Other fifteen-year-olds included Ken who was a decent fielder, and Dewey who was slow and neither good in the field or at bat. Every other kid he could think of was between the ages of twelve and fourteen with varying degrees of talent. He could come up with a team, but it would be young.

"Mitch Fuller can catch," broke the brief silence.

Odell laughed at his brother's obvious return to the subject of who would be the catcher for the unset team. Mitch was a decent alternative behind the plate though, he thought.

"Okay, maybe so," Odell replied to his brother.

From down the street, an older model Chevrolet sedan sporting big fins and patches of Bondo showing in several places on the fenders and doors sputtered into view. It was a classic car, but in obvious need of a paint job and engine repair. When it pulled up beside the boys, it rocked a little indicating the shocks probably needed changing, too.

Johnny White grinned at them and said, "White's taxi service. Where to, gentlemen?"

"Bloomfield, squire," said Odell as he climbed in the back seat following his brother.

"Yeah, home," said Ken as he got in the front seat next to Johnny.

Johnny shifted the gears to first on the steering column and let out the well-worn clutch. The old vehicle lurched toward Williamson Road and launched a celebratory mood of another school year ending.

Odell rolled down the window on the backseat passenger side and yelled to some guys still waiting for rides, "Woo-hoo, school's out for summer!"

"Hell yeah," called out Ken from the front.

As the car stopped and then turned onto the road toward home, Johnny popped the clutch, floorboarded the gas petal, and the rear tires spun out a squeal that caused all the boys inside to laugh and yell some more.

The drive was a few miles down a stretch that was heavily wooded on both sides and undeveloped because of rather swampy ground. It was not particularly scenic, and sometimes could produce air that caused the boys to suck in and hold their breath. But today, because of the pending summer vacation, the funky smells be damned, and it didn't even matter that the early June day was over ninety degrees in the shade.

Odell smiled to himself and looked out the window. He got lost in the moment, and it seemed the other guys did, too. They all got quiet as Johnny controlled the steering wheel by draping his left wrist over the large-ribbed circle.

Part of him knew these days were fleeting. His parents had told him many times that working hard for what you wanted in life was the only way to success. Odell believed them. Being fifteen restricted his ability to earn some money during the next few months, so the other part of him said this would be the last summer to play. He promised to make the most of it as an idea sprang into his mind.

Looking back to the driver, Odell asked, "Johnny, how would you like to coach our sandlot team this summer? You're too old to play in the league, but you could help get us to the games and keep our heads in play."

A smile came to the older boy's lips that Odell detected in the rearview mirror. He was a pretty smart teenager and had a sense of organization that could be helpful to the neighborhood team.

"I could do that," was all Johnny said.

"Great! We should start practicing tomorrow. I'm pretty sure we need to register by the end of next week, and we need to figure out everybody's position and other stuff," said Odell while feeling the excitement growing.

Johnny turned onto the road leading to their neighborhood and passed by a brick house on a hill with a big yard needing a cut, thought Odell. It was one belonging to the widow Mrs. Taylor that he had mowed for the last couple of years. It usually took him a couple of hours using his dad's push mower, but she paid him a few bucks he wouldn't otherwise have. He'd need to get with her in the next couple of days to make sure she was ready to have it done.

Cutting grass was one of the ways Odell could earn money for stuff that his parents wouldn't otherwise buy him such as a new Louisville Slugger bat or Rawlings glove. That was okay, because he had both although well-used and broken in like a good pair of Levi's jeans.

No, what he had in mind for his next purchase was some men's cologne. He was sure it would help him with the girls at the skating rink. Hai Karate was a favorite among some of his friends, but Odell knew he would never ask Mom or Dad to buy him a bottle. Daddy would tell him he could just use some of his Old Spice, and while he had tried it once or twice, it never had worked for him.

As he dreamed of smelling better, Odell saw a lone figure walking along the side of the road ahead. It appeared to be the new girl who lived up the road from him. He really didn't know her and had only seen her a few times since she moved into the drab house about a half-mile from where they lived.

"Hey, Johnny. You want to stop and ask the girl if she wants a ride home?" Odell blurted before thinking.

Johnny didn't reply but slowed down to a creep. Odell's window was already down because of the steamy Macon air in June, and he partially stuck his windblown head out to address the female.

He could see her thin but shapely legs purposefully striding along the grassy area adjacent to the road. Dressed in a blue shift and flat shoes, she had a slight sway to her walk, and it accentuated her behind in a way that was pleasing to Odell. He desperately tried to remember her name as the car approached where she walked.

Just as the carload of boys got next to her, she turned her head with shoulder length wavy brown hair toward them, and Odell saw a cute, rounded face with blue eyes and pink lips regarding him.

She had an uneven smirk with a slight dimple noticeable, but then gave a full smile revealing white teeth. Odell found himself speechless and smitten with the girl and wondered why he hadn't spoken to her before.

"Hey," he croaked as the car came to a standstill in the lane. "I'm Odell Sterling. Live up the road a bit. Would you like a ride home?"

"Better not," she replied. "Daddy would get mad at me for getting in a car with a bunch of boys."

"Yeah, I guess that's right. Do you mind if I walk with you?" Odell asked.

Somebody in the car let out a softened "Oo-wee," and Odell hoped the girl didn't hear it. He could feel his face start to blush, and he surely didn't want to sound like a jerk.

She seemed to ponder a response and then asked in return, "Do you even know my name? If you do, I'll consider it."

As his brain raced, he heard his brother whisper, "Kathy. They call her Kat."

"Uh, I know we haven't been introduced, but I've heard it's Kathy."

Her grin became broader and she shook her head up and down. "Okay, Odell. I'm probably about a half-mile from home. Let's go."

Odell grabbed his spiral notebook and jumped out the creaking door of the old Chevrolet. The other guys were mumbling, and he didn't know if it was due to jealousy, displeasure or happiness for Odell. At that moment, he just didn't care a whit.

"See you guys later," Odell said with a wave of his hand as the car pulled from the scene.

***

Odell stood facing Kathy for an awkward few seconds as she brushed the hair from the side of her face. It was a moment that he thought he would always remember because she did it without reservation, and he felt some connection when she smiled at him. There was a natural sense of her being real, and he wanted to be the same with this girl. It was a new feeling he'd never experienced.

His throat felt like it was closing and for a moment Odell wondered what to say next. This girl made him nervous and excited. He didn't want to blow the opportunity to impress her.

"You're cute," he said without knowing how it came out of his mouth or where it came from.

Her smile was genuine, and the gleam of her eyes made him want to melt into the hot Georgia asphalt. "That's a sweet thing to say," she replied.

She had a similar notebook clutched in her right hand and a small purse strapped across her shoulder on the same side. He didn't know the brand name, but he had seen several girls carry that style of pocketbook. It was brown and tan leather and looked to be new.

"I'd be happy to carry your book if you'd like me to," Odell said after a quick study.

"Okay, that would be nice. Nobody has ever done that for me," she said still smiling as she handed over her blue binder.

They started walking along a path worn beside the road that led past Odell's house. They both turned their heads toward the modest brick structure as they strolled by, and Odell was somewhat surprised that his mother's car was not in the driveway. She usually got home from her job before he and his brothers got there after school. He knew Daddy would be later in the evening because his shift wouldn't be over until five at the earliest.

"You've got a neat place to live," said Kathy.

Odell looked at the trimmed shrubbery, grass-carpeted lawn with a big magnolia in the center of the yard and had to agree. The house was fairly small but was immaculately kept. His parents saw to that and kept the kids doing chores throughout the year to ensure the place stayed that way.

"Yeah, I guess so," he replied.

"Ours doesn't look nearly as good as yours," she said with a touch of sadness in her voice.

"Uh, I think it's fine," Odell answered and hoped he sounded sincere.

He had heard disparaging remarks from his parents and others in the neighborhood about the dingy house that sat on a rise a few houses from theirs. It had been vacant for a while before Kathy's family moved in less than a year ago. As far as he could tell, little had been done to improve its condition during that time.

As they neared her home, Odell changed the subject hoping he could see her again sooner than later. He studied her profile and wondered again why he hadn't talked to this girl before today.

"Are you in junior high?" he asked.

"Not after today. I'll be in tenth grade in the fall."

Odell had been fishing and was pleased to find out she was his age. For some reason, he had thought she might be a year or two younger.

"Uh, I guess I should give your book back now," he said as they got to her driveway. He silently berated himself for continuing to say "Uh" as he handed it back.

She smiled again causing Odell to feel tongue-tied and unsure what the next move should be. As he gazed into her gleaming eyes, there was a momentary unrecognized connection. A lump had formed in his throat as he finally rasped a question.

"Do you like to skate? If you do, maybe I could meet you at Durr's Saturday night."

"Are you asking for a date?" she said coyly.

Odell felt the rising blush again but managed, "Uh, maybe."

Before the conversation ended the front door to Kathy's house opened and a slender woman stepped out onto the small stoop. She wore an apron that she used to wipe her hands.

"Kat, you need to get inside. Your dad will be home in a little bit and I need your help with supper. Hurry up."

"Sorry, I gotta go. Thanks for walking with me," she said turning from him abruptly.

As she hurried away, Odell thought he heard her say in a lower voice, "I'll check about Saturday."

He couldn't hear the conversation between Kathy and her mother as they went inside, but Odell got the impression it was not particularly happy and might even be about him. Nevertheless, he headed home hopeful the summer in front of him would be memorable.

CHAPTER 3

Odell scrubbed the green and white tiled floor in the hall bathroom with a string mop. It was a ritual on a typical Saturday morning after breakfast and had to be completed before he could head outside to do whatever he wanted. He dunked its wet end and then squeezed the excess water into a silver galvanized bucket. It left the pungent odor of pine cleaner on his hands as well as in the small room.

While he worked his mop magic, Odell could hear the deep whine of the vacuum cleaner his brother Kenny was using on the carpet in their bedroom. Sometimes they swapped jobs, but more often Odell stuck to the soapy concoction because inspection by their mother afterwards was likely to be favorable when they stuck to the chores they were busy doing. If she didn't approve of their efforts, they would have to do them all over again, and neither of them wanted that outcome.

Although he didn't know where his other two younger brothers might currently be located, they had chores to complete as well. They were probably dusting, taking out garbage or doing the breakfast dishes before plopping in front of the television to watch their favorite cartoons. It all made for a busy and somewhat noisy household.

After rinsing out the mop and bucket, Odell put them away and grabbed his prized Rawlings glove containing a well-worn baseball strapped in its pocket. He paid passing attention to the trophies on the shelf where the oiled leather item had been as he slipped it on his left hand and gripped the ball across the seams with his right.

The trophies brought back memories of games and represented accomplishments. There was one for being an all-star, one for winning a championship and one that recognized him for being the Most Valuable Player on his grammar school team. They brought a smile to his face, and he wondered if he could bring one more to the shelf this summer.

Baseball had been his number one summer priority since he was nine years old. A kid in his class had introduced him to the game on the playground at school and soon Odell was consumed with throwing, catching and hitting that hard-round ball.

B-Team Little League was soon to follow, but he saw a lot of the bench that first year as he learned more of the basics of the game. A lot of his teammates were better than he was which only made him want to practice more to be as good as them, if not better. That was the goal he set for himself and used every opportunity to play at school, at home or anywhere else there was a game he could get to.

By the time he was a year older, Odell's skills had dramatically improved, and at the next spring try-outs, there was much more attention paid to him on the field. His arm strength was particularly good, and he threw hard with accuracy. For that reason, he could field any of the positions, and his coach that year started training him to pitch.

His initial windup that resembled throwing from the stretch was changed to facing the batter and releasing the ball from a more three-quarters position rather than directly overhanded. Odell was taught to load his weight on the right foot and push off the pitching rubber.

Because he was only ten and the focus was on hurling strikes, Odell's delivery was allowed to progress the way he wanted as long as he could maintain control of the pitches. What developed was a somewhat deceptive and exaggerated motion that was pretty much the same the pitcher still used five years later which helped to hide the breaking pitches that were now a part of his arsenal.

Odell went out the back door of the house into a large yard bounded by aluminum wire fences on both sides and Log Cabin Drive at the rear of the property. Virtually all the neighborhood kids had been playing in this area since the Sterlings moved into their house a few years before. With a standing invitation to anyone interested, the yard had become a baseball field, football stadium, basketball court and a battlefield for games of capture the flag or dodgeball.

Until a couple of years ago, the place had seemed huge and capable of hosting the games everybody played. Since Odell had grown bigger, however, the yard was too small for him to swing his bat out of fear of hitting a car like he had done before.

He smiled to himself as he remembered belting a baseball into a passing police vehicle when he was thirteen. Most of the kids had run away as the cop pulled into the yard, but the guy didn't arrest anyone or even tell Odell's parents. The bemused officer simply informed the remaining kids they should flip the field so they would be batting toward the house.

"Yes, sir. I'm really sorry I hit your car," Odell recalled his words to the officer.

As soon as the vehicle left, everybody's consensus was they sure as hell couldn't hit toward the house, so they would have to find another place to play ball games. A couple of other fields were found located near local church grounds, but the backyard was still perfect for pitching and other fundamental practices.

Odell looked around the familiar surroundings and knew things were changing for him. He had mixed emotions because on the one hand he longed for everything to stay the same. On the other hand, the teen wanted to experience new stuff. A perfect example was provided as he thought again about Kat. She had been on his mind since walking her home yesterday.

He wondered if she would go to Durr's this evening. If she did, he would ask her to skate with him during "couples only" and maybe even make a date to go see a movie. Not having a driver's license would present a problem to that plan, but he would figure out something.

"Hey, O. Are we playing a game today?"

Interrupting thoughts of romance, Odell turned to find Sandy, a short kid from across the street. He was young, the same age as

Odell's brother Wayne. Wearing his usual toothy grin and carrying a glove that looked way too big for his hand caused the older boy to smile.

"Is a four-pound robin fat?" replied Odell.

Before any further conversation could be had, the boys who lived up the road appeared from around the side of the house. The White brothers were accompanied by the Smith teenagers. They all carried gloves and Dewey, the older of the Smiths, had a large barreled bat on his shoulder. As usual, he was arguing over something trivial with the younger Billy.

"You need to shut your stupid face," said Dewey.

"Screw you, fatty," Billy sneered.

Dewey whipped the bat inches from his brother's nose and Odell thought another epic fight was about to occur. The two Smiths had fought several times over the last few years and didn't seem to mind making each other bleed. They were both hot-headed and often not pleasant to be around.

"Y'all shut up before Daddy hears you and makes y'all go home," Odell hissed through clenched teeth. "Do you want to play ball or get on Daddy's bad side?"

Odell's father was in the house, and he knew his dad wouldn't put up with another fight. He had stopped the brothers from fighting in the past, once when they both were swinging Coke bottles. Everybody respected him and was a little scared of him, too. They all had seen him unfasten and whip his belt out of the pant loops, wrap it around his fist and commence to flail butts for violations of his rules. Such an exhibition was almost as bad to watch as it was to be on the receiving end.

Dewey and Billy calmed down momentarily and nodded in Odell's direction. As did most of the boys who played the various games in the Sterlings' yard, they tended to follow Odell's lead. The respect had been earned, and Odell used it when necessary to keep the peace.

On cue, other boys began showing up in the backyard carrying their equipment. Mitchell had a big grin on his face as he juked in between the guys standing around. He was by far the quickest of the bunch as he had demonstrated on the football field playing running back.

"Danger, danger, Will Robinson," he mimicked as Dewey swatted at him darting through the crowd. The kid loved *Lost in Space.*

As his brothers Kenny and Wayne joined the group, Odell looked around them and wondered if they could field a team in the recreation league set to start in two weeks. There were only two of them his age of fifteen years, and the rest ranged from twelve to fourteen. He was sure most of the teams they would face were comprised of mainly the max age he shared. He wanted to, no matter what the odds, as he had decided it would be the last chance to do something like this.

Odell cleared his throat and spoke in what he hoped was going to be inspired words. "Before we start a game, I want to ask everybody how y'all would feel about playing in the city rec league. I've already mentioned the idea to a few and they're willing. The thing is, we'd be playing in the fifteen and under division and we'd be at a disadvantage since we only have a few guys that old."

"Hell, yeah," exclaimed Dewey which caused Odell to glance around looking for his dad. Odell then grimaced toward Dewey who lowered his head.

Ken White, usually the quietest of the bunch, said, "Hey, with O pitching, I like our chances. My vote is yes, too."

In quick succession the remaining boys joined the first two affirmative votes. Johnny, who had been quiet, added, "Odell has asked me to be the coach since I'm too old to play."

Odell noticed that Dewey frowned at that message and was afraid another outburst would come from his downturned mouth. The two boys had fought in the past over who would wear catcher's equipment. Odell knew another dispute this early could jeopardize the plans for a team.

"Yeah, Johnny will be the coach and he'll drive some of us to the games. We need him," Odell interjected while looking intently at Dewey.

As he glanced around the group, Odell continued, "Of course, we'll need a little help from some parents, but I don't think that'll be a problem. I've decided not to play Colt League this summer, so I'm sure I can handle pitching at least a game a week. I'm pretty sure that's all the schedule will be."

Excited discussion followed concerning what positions everyone would play on the team. None of the kids other than Odell had ever played in the recreation league before, which led to questions about opponents. Billy wanted to know about their name and the uniforms.

"I've been thinking about our team name, and I like The Renegades. We could probably get some tee shirts and caps printed pretty cheap. That's about all the uniforms we can afford," replied Odell.

"Ain't a renegade a bad thing? I like being a badass," said Dewey with a half-grin.

"I think of the term kinda like us going against the rules. I had thought about calling us The Misfits, but Renegades sound a little more dangerous. Since we'll probably have the youngest team on the field, I want the other teams to at least think we're a little scary," answered Odell.

Odell knew the rest would go along with whatever he decided, so the name was set. They practiced and played for the rest of the morning until being called in for lunch. The Renegades had been born.

CHAPTER 4

The two older Sterling brothers, Odell and Kenny, stood outside the skating rink waiting for it to open. They each had their own black-booted skates which were tied together by the laces and slung over slender shoulders.

There was a line of adolescents and young teenagers talking excitedly in front of them, and a few older kids milling around a giant oak tree to the side of the big barn structure that would soon fill with skaters going around in circles. Most of those older than him wore jeans and tee shirts while smoking cigarettes and only paid side glances to the younger group standing in line.

Odell didn't really know any of the ones blowing smoke, but he had seen a lot of them in the past. They could be a little rough on the hardwood surface throwing an elbow or tripping those who got in their way. They otherwise didn't seem that interested in skating and were more attentive to the cutest girls who showed up on a Saturday night.

Those guys were mature enough to drive, and Odell saw their cars parked near the tree. A couple of the vehicles were beat up and didn't appear safe. Another two or three had to be their parents' autos. There was also a Chevy muscle car with an elevated rear end.

What stood out in Odell's view though was a shiny new Mustang. Since he would be turning sixteen after the first of the year, all Odell could dream about was having something like that to drive. Jealous thoughts flooded his brain.

For a minute he got lost thinking about tooling around in his own *'Stang* while spinning the tires and revving the engine at all the hangouts on his side of town. He'd have a good-looking girl in the passenger seat and all of his friends would be envious just like he was of the kid over there.

Odell snapped out of the pleasant thoughts when reality hit him that he could never afford such, and the front door of the establishment opened to let the crowd inside. He shuffled his sneaker-clad feet feeling temporary melancholy over the prospects of not having such a ride anytime soon. *Maybe one day,* he thought.

The brothers paid their entry fees and walked to the area containing benches where they sat changing into their skates. After lacing them securely, they found a spot to store their shoes and were among the first few skaters on the floor. Arms swinging in rhythm with feet sliding inside to out, they were soon circling the familiar hardwood and grinning with the gathering speed. Once others got on the surface, it would be trickier to go that fast.

Music began as they were into the third lap and the familiar sounds of the Beach Boys blared throughout the structure. Odell loved the group and had several of their albums and a few of their 45's as well. He swayed to the beat and felt energized.

By the time of the next record, another rocking tune by The Beatles, the floor was full of kids laughing and singing along. Kenny had spotted one of his friends and had left his brother's side to join him. Odell was content to let the song seep inside as he scanned the large room looking for anybody he knew.

The next ten or fifteen minutes were spent in the same fashion as the owner kept spinning a collection of recent and some older pop hits that kept the crowd on the floor in tune with the records. Odell kept watching the crowd and weaved in and out between the slower skaters.

There were a few he recognized, but no one he really wanted to talk with. He spoke to a couple of guys from school and nodded to a pretty girl who was not his type because she was maybe an inch taller than he.

That brief encounter started self-reflection on females in general and what attracted him in particular. He realized how little he knew on the subject, primarily because he had so little experience with girls.

I'm a little over seven months from being sixteen, and I've only kissed two girls, he thought.

Both had been at a party he'd gone to last year during a game of spin the bottle. It seemed like a lifetime ago now, but he remembered how nervous he had been yet excited when it happened. Neither of the girls known to him since grammar school had any interest in Odell that he was aware of, and he actually felt the same about them.

His limited encounters were seemingly so much less than other guys who bragged about making out and even feeling up their girlfriends. Odell didn't know whether he should believe some of the exploits he'd heard about, but if and when such happened in his life, he resolved not to talk about it with others. Those kinds of memories should be private and not shared in some locker room.

Just as he was getting depressed, someone tugged on Odell's shirttail and he turned to see Kat skating slightly behind him on his right side. She smiled at the surprise he was sure that reflected on his face.

"Hey, Odell. Happy to see me?"

He swallowed and then nodded. The flush rising from his neck felt like it was creeping into the bangs on his forehead.

"You sure? I saw you skating alone with your thoughts, so I thought I'd speak before you got involved with somebody else," she said while continuing to show her pleasant smile.

"Uh, I'm not involved with anybody," he replied and immediately thought how desperate his response sounded.

Kat's laugh was contagious, and Odell joined in the fun as he found himself at ease with this girl. He realized how unusual it was to feel comfortable with someone he found attractive and showing some attention to him. Their joint laughter continued as the record ended and an announcement that couples only were allowed on the floor.

The lights were dimmed and a good portion of people who had been skating left the floor. A slower-paced song started, and Kat took Odell's hand. Her grip was firm yet soft in his slightly larger fingers. He hadn't skated with a female in a few months, but this moment instantly felt natural.

Other couples appeared on the rink, some holding hands like they were and a few with the guy wrapping an arm around his partner's waist. Odell knew he could do that as he and a former girlfriend from elementary school had skated that way in the past. He was, however, afraid it was too soon to try that move right then. For sure didn't want to risk the embarrassment of a trip and fall.

"You're a good skater, Odell."

"Thanks, you are, too. I don't remember ever seeing you here before, though."

"I have, but probably at different times than you. Most of the time I've gone to Bibb Skate Arena, though," she replied.

Odell shook his head up and down. The place Kat was referring to was on the opposite side of town. He had been there a few times and even had his thirteenth birthday party at that location. That had been his one and only birthday party.

"The floor is smaller than this one, but I like it over there," he said.

"A lot more convenient to come here," she said with a smile before continuing, "Besides, I like the company better."

Odell felt a blush coming on again. She was actually flirting with him, he thought.

"Yeah, me too. I mean, I really like you," he blurted.

"Well, you haven't gotten to know me, yet," Kat almost whispered as she brought her face closer to his.

He could smell peppermint on her breath and for a second Odell wanted to kiss her. The loudspeaker interrupted the thought as "All skate" rang out, and the lights became bright again.

They continued to skate as a couple, and Odell found himself telling Kat about his plans for the summer. They talked about baseball, books and other things each liked to do. It seemed they had quite a bit in common. Occasionally, someone would speed past them and make comments, but neither cared nor little attention was paid to them.

Song after song played as they skated, and they agreed which records they favored and the ones they didn't. Odell couldn't believe he'd found this girl who lived so close to him. She was the proverbial "girl next door."

When the next announcement called for "Ladies choice," Kat asked coyly with batted eyes, "Would you like to skate with me?"

Odell grinned and dropped her hand that he had been holding for the last twenty minutes. She looked momentarily hurt, but then surprise showed on her face as he slipped his right hand around her petite waist and took her left hand with the free one. The fit was perfect and soon they were gliding in unison.

The smell of her shampoo was pleasant to his nose, and for the first time he caught a whiff of a light floral scent he suspected came from her neck below the ear. Odell held her slightly tighter as he reached over to take in the fragrance never smelled before.

"God, you smell so good," he whispered inside her left ear.

Before he knew what was going on, she guided him to the rear corner of the rink where the already dimmed lights were practically non-existent. They stopped in the darkness and she leaned against the handrails, and then kissed him daintily on his lips. This was followed by another that was firmer, and he responded to with equal pressure. The third exchange caused him to feel pressure in his jeans as she darted her tongue into his mouth.

When they finished the last kiss, Odell could hear the song winding down on the record player. He had always liked the Dave Clark Five's "Because." Now he knew he would always associate the song with this amazing girl. He was smitten and wondered if the moment could last longer.

CHAPTER 5

Almost a week had passed since the fateful night at Durr's, and Odell couldn't get it off his mind. He had walked past Kat's house every day hoping to get a glance of her and a chance to talk with her again. So far, he'd failed miserably.

He kept reliving the moment in the rink's corner. After they had finished that time together, he had bought her a Coke and they sat on a bench continuing their previous conversation. She was a dream come true. With Kat he did not have his normal difficulty of talking to girls. Odell found himself losing his inhibitions as she made him laugh uncontrollably over and over again.

She had shared some of her dreams of the future. Some were similar to his, like going to college. Neither of them had any relatives who had gone through higher education, so they only knew what they had read about the experience. They both were goal-oriented individuals wanting the most out of life, and while there was nothing wrong with working in blue-collar jobs, their visions were loftier.

They had promised to see each other again soon, but Kat couldn't say when. Her dad was very strict and didn't want her dating until she was at least sixteen. Her mom was protective as well, although from what Kat said, she was more understanding. Odell gathered that she and her mother were both scared of her father. He understood because Odell felt the same about his own dad.

Dating wouldn't be easy under the current situation anyway because of their ages and that fact only led to more frustration in Odell's mind. He had asked for Kat's phone number, but she had declined to give it to him on account of her dad. It seemed like everything was working against him at the moment.

It was a hot day in early June, and Odell knew the weather was only going to get steamier as the summer continued. The Renegades had practiced in the coolest part of the morning for a couple of hours, and the guys had retreated to their homes to pursue other activities. Odell felt pretty good about their chances with the team set to play their first game next Wednesday. Now his brain, however, just wouldn't let up on figuring out some way to see Kat sooner rather than later.

An idea came to him in a flash, and he got off the couch and headed outside. He was dressed in a pair of grey sweat shorts, white tee shirt and the red and white cap he had worn since last season when he played for the Ambucs pony league team. The scarlet A was smudged with dirt, and the sneakers on his feet were pretty nasty looking, too. If Odell had thought about how he might look to Kat or possibly her parents, he would've taken time to clean up some or at least change his cap to something else. He had plenty of hats to choose from stacked on a shelf in his closet.

Odell went to the small outbuilding that Daddy had built last year containing his tools, and various other items important to him. The space was his and generally Odell and his brothers didn't go inside without some specific need.

The lawn mower was kept in one corner along with a metal gas can. The mower had been bought from Sears a few years before and still looked new because it was cleaned after every use. His father insisted on it. He claimed it would keep the machine working properly. Odell always followed those instructions so he would be allowed to use it, and he had earned money over the last few years by cutting yards around the neighborhood.

Odell filled the mower's gas tank from the can. As he pulled the mower from the framed house, he tried not to jostle the contraption. It was a little unwieldy because of the angles involved, and he had to pick up the base before placing it on the ground.

Once outside, Odell started pushing the mower out of the yard and headed toward the road in front. He was on a mission now.

Striding up the road toward Kat's house, he kept rehearsing what he'd say when he got there. He'd done variations of the pitch before when seeking new business. He had to show he wanted to help.

When he finally got to Kat's house, Odell started to doubt himself. *Damn it, what was I thinking.*

It only lasted a few seconds until he pushed the mower up the driveway. He couldn't quit now.

Odell stopped near the front door of the modest house. His palms were sweating, and he looked at what he was wearing for the first time. He was full of self-doubts and hoped they wouldn't show.

No time to stop now.

He stood on the front stoop and knocked. There was a rustling inside and a small dog started barking.

Gradually, the front door opened. A screen door kept a little dog from coming outside but didn't keep it from snarling at Odell. Its front canines were demonstrated prominently.

The lady standing there stood facing Odell and didn't seem very happy with his appearance. Immediately, he saw an obvious displeasure, but she definitely was her daughter's mother. Attractive without makeup. Frowning, but couldn't hide a pretty smile somewhere.

"Hello, Mrs. Norman. I'm Odell Sterling from down the road," he said while dipping his head and touching the brim of his nasty cap.

"I know who you are. Saw you with my daughter last week. She told me where you live. Why are you here now?"

"Uh, I thought you might would like your grass cut. I brought my dad's mower just in case. You probably don't know that I cut a few yards in the neighborhood. The first one is usually for free, so potential customers can see the quality of my work," Odell said using a pitch that had been successful in the past.

The lady looked past him at the lawn mower and then surveyed the yard. There were tall shoots of Bahia grass prominent in patches around the area, with weeds clumped in other spots.

"I guess the yard could use a haircut," she replied after a moment. A hint of a smile appeared on her lips for the first time, and it caused Odell to return the gesture.

"Yes, ma'am. I'll do my best to please you."

"Okay then. Show me what you can do," she said with a nod.

The door was unceremoniously shut with Odell disappointed that he had not at least caught a glimpse of Kat. *Crap, I don't even know if she's at home,* he thought.

He mapped out a plan in his head of how to mow the yard, and then pulled the cord to start the engine. It fired up on the first pull, a credit to his daddy who always kept the spark plug in good shape, and then began pushing the mower around the farthest edge. For the first thirty minutes, Odell continued around the grassy area in a concentric circle.

Because there had been little rain for the last couple of weeks, the ground was hard and made his trips around easier than they would have been otherwise. It also helped that the blade had been sharpened recently.

With the most noticeable part of the job completed, Odell kept the mower going and headed to the left side of the house. There were a few shrubs that he had to negotiate around, and Odell made a mental note that they could use a trim also.

There were two windows partially hidden by the shrubbery. The first showed closed blinds preventing any view inside, but when he got to the second one, there stood Kat watching him through a clean and unobstructed view as he worked.

She was dressed in tight cut-off jean shorts that revealed her toned and shapely legs. A baggy top fell past her waist. Her hair had been pulled back with a clip that kept it off her forehead. Odell saw that she held a can of furniture polish spray in one hand and a dust rag in the other. She waved it at him in a gesture that made him think of a damsel in distress.

He stood near the window gazing at her image. Odell didn't think he'd ever known a prettier girl. The sweat he felt dripping down his face and in his armpits was real, and he wasn't sure if it was due to the heat, strenuous activity, or the vision before him. Whatever was causing all the perspiration, this made the effort worthwhile.

Odell realized he wasn't moving, and the sounds of his machine would probably cause Kat's mom to be curious and want to see the cause of the pause. He grinned, waved at her, and then backed the mower up so he could continue the job.

The total time to complete the yard was a little over an hour. He adjusted the lever on the handle to cut off the motor and rolled the mower back to where he had started. He wished for the first time he had thought to bring a towel so he could have wiped off his face.

Before Odell started to the front door, it opened, and Kat walked outside the front entrance. She held two glasses of beverage in her hands as she sauntered toward him.

She nodded her head at a large oak tree where a swing was attached by chains to a low-hanging branch and said, "Take a break with me and have a glass of lemonade."

He was in heaven as he followed like a puppy and sat down beside her on the squeaky seat. Kat handed him the cold glass, her fingers brushing his during the exchange. It was a small but intentional gesture that didn't go unnoticed by Odell.

After a big gulp of the tart, yet sweet liquid, Odell said, "God, that's good. Thanks."

"I made it myself," she replied. "My mom taught me her recipe when I was just a little girl. In fact, it's the first thing I ever learned to make."

"I'm impressed. Hard to beat fresh lemons and lots of sugar," he responded.

They sat quiet for a few minutes sipping their drinks. At some point Odell glanced at the front door to see Kat's mother eyeing them. He doubted she could hear their conversation from where she stood, but he wanted to talk to her more privately.

"I had a really good time with you at Durr's last week. Are you going to be there again tomorrow night?"

She frowned and shook her head before saying, "I doubt it. Nancy, the friend I came with last week is out of town. That was how I got there. I don't think my parents will take me there without someone to go with."

"Maybe you could go with me and my brother. I'm fairly sure my mom wouldn't mind giving you a ride."

"I don't know. I'm a little afraid to ask Daddy. I didn't tell him and Mom that you were there last Saturday. For sure, I didn't let them know we spent time together. If I had, I don't think they would've let me go with Nancy. They're very protective."

He took another sip of the lemonade trying to make it last. *It sucks to be this age,* he thought.

"I wish I was old enough to drive. I've got another eight months to go, but when I am, I'll get a part-time job and a car. I hate having to depend on others for a ride, especially having to go places with my parents," Odell said.

Kat's knee bumped his, and once again Odell thought the slight touch was on purpose. She didn't say anything as it occurred but gave an affirmative nod to his statement.

"I'll try and find another friend that I might can go with. I can't promise, but I'll call Cheryl to see if she wants to. She likes to skate, but she's clingy. If I can, I will, but she'll probably want to hang with me a lot closer than Nancy. I'd told her I liked you, so she gave me a lot more freedom than Cheryl will. I really want to get in that dark corner again," she said with a side glance.

Odell heard the front screen door open, and Kat's mom walked in their direction with a glass pitcher of lemonade. He hoped she was going to offer him some more.

"Well, young man. I must say you've done a nice job on the yard," she said as she got close to the swing, and then continued, "I see you're empty. Would you like some more?"

"Yes, ma'am. Thank you."

She filled his glass and added some to Kat's as well. In the light of the sun, Odell thought her mother was even more attractive than he had first thought. She was a little taller than Kat although they had many of the same features. It reminded him that a gym teacher had told the guys in class one time that if they wanted to see what a girl would look like when she grew up, they should look at her mother.

With her free hand, Mrs. Norman pulled two dollars from a pocket of the apron she wore. She held it out to Odell and said, "I hope this will cover your work today."

"That's very generous of you, ma'am, but I was happy to do it for y'all. Like I said earlier, I've done other jobs for free the first time. If you like, maybe I can start doing the yard whenever you want."

He was sincere and hoped it showed. Odell thought it would give him an opportunity to see Kat on a regular basis, and maybe her parents would get to know him better. Hopefully, that could give him and Kat a chance to possibly have a relationship. Getting paid wasn't really Odell's current motivation.

Kat's mother seemed to contemplate what he said, and then put the money back into her pocket. "I appreciate that, Odell."

Hearing Mrs. Norman call him by name for the first time caused him to grin. Odell took a big swallow of lemonade and replied, "Thanks, and you're welcome."

"I'll talk it over with Mr. Norman and let you know. I think he'll go along with the idea since we don't have a working lawn mower right now. I'll leave you and Kat alone, but she'll need to come back inside soon to finish her chores."

After her mother returned to the house, Kat looked over at Odell and whistled softly. "This was absolutely brilliant, young man," emphasizing what her mother had called him.

"Thanks," he said pleased with the realization that his hatched plan had worked, at least so far.

They flirted some more and talked for another ten minutes until Kat said she needed to get back inside. Odell watched her walk away and wished he had a better voice because she made him want to sing.

Afterwards, Odell hummed the Dave Clark song as he pushed the mower to his house. He found himself doing it the rest of the day as it stuck in his mind.

CHAPTER 6

The Renegades were gathered in the dugout along the third baseline just a few minutes before their first game was to begin. They had gotten to Macon Memorial Park an hour ahead of their scheduled start and watched a game between two other future rivals that was already underway. When that game finished and those teams left the mostly hard clay field, Odell and the rest practiced a few minutes with Johnny hitting some grounders to the infielders and a few flies to the outfield.

Their rivals for the day had hooted and hollered at them as they went through the short pre-game preparations. Most of their team looked to be older and larger boys, and now a few of the Renegades were exhibiting nerves while sitting on the wooden bench enclosed with what could pass as chicken coop wire.

"Odie," said Wayne, using a nickname for his older brother, "All of those guys are at least your size, and I see a couple of them taller. How do we know they ain't sixteen?" he asked.

"Yeah. We look like punks compared to them," said Sandy, who like Wayne was only twelve years old.

Odell had already scoped out the other team and knew most of the players. That was not unusual since he'd been playing organized baseball since he was nine years old and you got to know just about everybody else who also participated in such activity.

They called themselves The Hot Rods, but Odell didn't believe that name fit at all. There were two guys Odell recognized as decent hitters and true enough, all of the guys across the field were good-sized. However, Odell felt confident that he could strike out most of them without too much trouble. He wasn't that concerned with them hitting, but if any of them did, most of the Renegades could at least field the ball fairly well, he thought.

"Y'all worry too much. I know all of them. Just play your positions like we've practiced, and we'll be fine," replied Odell.

The portly umpire who looked as if he'd lost his razor in the last few days called the captains to home plate. He held a facemask in one gnarly hand and had a well-worn chest protector strapped across his torso. His grizzled appearance matched his gruff voice. He had a gangly teenager standing close by who didn't look much older than Odell as an assistant umpire.

"Listen up, fellows," he began, "I won't put up with any cussin' or other foul language. If I hear any, that player will be thrown out of the game. My calls are final. If I miss one, I might change my mind, but I doubt it. Just suck it up and keep on playing."

Odell and the captain of The Hot Rods shook their heads up and down in unison as the ump looked at them directly. The other team's leader, Donnie, had snickered during the instructions. The older man added further instructions directed to him, "And I ain't trying to be funny, either."

"Yes, sir," Donnie said.

Odell had known Donnie Sherrell and his younger brother, Pete, for several years and thought they were okay guys. Along with Randy Nixon, Odell felt striking them out at the plate would be the key to winning the game today. Donnie had always been a little bit of a cut-up and didn't take playing ball as that important, so Odell was counting on that tidbit of information as well.

"Alright then. Renegades are home team, so y'all are in the field first. Hot Rods are batting. Shake hands, and let's play ball."

Odell and Donnie did as instructed and retreated to their respective dugouts. Odell felt that competitive spirit come over him as it always did at the beginning of a game.

"Gather up, Renegades," he said to the rest of the team.

The boys stuck their gloved hands together as Odell continued, "First game, first win. One, two, three. Win!"

They shouted the command together and ran to the field. Odell trotted to the mound and waited until the umpire threw him the game ball. He loved the feel of a brand-new baseball in his fingers. After gripping it across the seams, he threw only a few warm-up pitches to Mitch behind the plate since he'd already thrown to him earlier and was ready to play.

Before the first batter stepped to the plate, Odell looked behind him to make sure everybody was in position. Ken was ready at third; his brother, Kenny was stationed at shortstop; another brother, Wayne, was hunkered at second; Dewey who always seemed out of place wherever he played was located at first as was his brother, Billy, behind him in right field; Bruce Williams was in center and his cousin, Sandy, was playing left.

The Hot Rods' lead-off hitter was in the batter's box with an open stance. Somewhere in the past, Odell had pitched against him, and he remembered instantly that the kid couldn't hit any pitch on the outside of the plate. To his credit, Mitch had set up there.

Odell proceeded to fire the first two pitches into Mitch's mitt on the corner without the batter swinging his bat. Odell followed up with a curve ball off the plate with him making a weak swing for an opening strikeout.

The next batter crowded home plate initially until Odell threw a fastball up and in. From that point, it proved easy to strike him out, too.

The third hitter, who was one of the players known by Odell as a key to getting out, would prove to be more difficult. He appeared unfazed by Odell's speed and fouled the first pitch straight back indicating to Odell that timing was not a problem. Odell then threw a hard slider and was rewarded with a grounder right back to him that he fielded and threw to Dewey for the last out.

They ran off the field to the dugout where the guys were clapping and cheering excitedly. Odell received several slaps on the back. Mitch, who was busy removing the catcher's equipment since he was leadoff batter, was grinning and exposing his dimples.

"Man, you are on fire, Odie," he almost screamed.

"Thanks, now get us started and let's score some runs," Odell replied.

Johnny had taken his position as coach seriously but had consulted with Odell about the Renegades' batting order. They both had agreed to get their best speed at the top and then hopefully have somebody on base for Odell, Kenny or Bruce to knock them in, as they were the best hitters on the team. Since Mitch was the fastest runner and an adequate batter to put the ball in play, he was elected as the leadoff man.

Mitch crouched in the batter's box and gave the appearance of a cat about to pounce on some unsuspecting rodent. Donnie's first two pitches were high, and Mitch kept the grin pasted on his face. The third throw was across the inside part of the plate. Before anybody on the opposite team could react, Mitch laid down a perfect bunt down the left side of the infield, and he easily reached first base.

Kenny followed with a soft liner over short that prevented Mitch from going to third, but now they had two runners on with no outs. Johnny coaching at the third base line was clapping sweaty hands.

Donnie showed nervousness by then walking the only left-handing hitter on the team, Bruce. Odell confidently stood in the box as the cleanup batter ready to hit the ball hard somewhere. He knew Donnie's pitches as well as the pitcher did. He swung his bat slowly toward the mound in anticipation of what would be thrown his way.

Odell had become a better hitter a few years before when his then-Coach Hooks had put a larger barrel bat with a skinny handle in his hands at practice one day. Odell learned how to whip through the strike zone so well that he had bought his own like it that he now held in his hands. He'd hit a few homeruns with the stick but wasn't thinking of that now. *Just make good contact,* he told himself.

The first two pitches were outside, and Odell thought Donnie would try to come inside next. He adjusted his stance slightly and was ready when he saw it coming. The liner that came off his bat skipped past their third baseman before he could react, and Odell's teammates were heading home. All three on base scored while he ended up with an easy double.

After that hit, the game was really over. While the Renegades didn't score again, the Hot Rods only got one run on one hit and two errors by Dewey. He dropped a perfect throw to first that would've been the final out and then compounded the mistake by over-throwing to Mitch at home that allowed their run.

They were now 1-0 and the younger boys on the team were hooting because of beating older kids. Summer still had a way to go, but optimism ruled.

CHAPTER 7

Kat was stretched on her bed staring at the cracked, dingy ceiling. Her record player had a 45 playing softly. Daddy wouldn't let her play it as loudly as she wanted. Otis Redding was crooning, and she was feeling his soul while thinking about the boy down the road.

She had felt a connection to him from the start. Of course, she couldn't let him know that at first. For several reasons.

Odell was a sweet and considerate boy. No guy had ever walked her home or offered to carry her books. Maybe it had been a little on the corny side, but she had found the gesture endearing.

He wasn't the cutest guy she'd ever known, but certainly not butt ugly for sure. She liked his smile and loved hearing his laugh when he got tickled about something. His smarts and manners were attractive features in her mind. Besides, behind those glasses, he had blue eyes which was her favorite color.

He wasn't too tall, and the two of them fit well together. He was athletic with nice legs, also. When they skated that first time, it was natural, and she felt safe somehow when he held her. She'd never felt that way about somebody else.

There were a couple of pimples, and he was self-conscious about that and the small mole on his chin, but everybody had some bumps at their age. Unless they were perfect. She didn't like perfect anyway.

She let out a sigh as she thought about that first kiss. It had not been planned, but when it happened, she was the instigator. Why she had done it, she wasn't sure. It had been the first time in her life she had wanted to do that, and it had left her tingling in parts of her body which had never felt quite like that before. She didn't have regrets about her actions and couldn't wait for another opportunity to do it again. Maybe being a tad aggressive with Odell would open him up a little more, and she was starting to feel that might prove to be a good thing for both of them.

The past weekend had proven frustrating. After Odell had been so clever to come to her house and cut their grass, she had to come up with a plan so she could see him at Durr's again. That necessitated her calling Cheryl to set it up. She was okay as a friend, but when they got to the rink, Cheryl stayed in her business the whole night.

Kat and Odell were able to skate together a couple of times that night, and they were able to talk privately during those times. There was no making out in the corner, however, because Kat was scared that Cheryl would be nosy. The look on his face made her sadder than she already felt when she told him they couldn't.

She'd only had one other boyfriend. His name was Phillip and was the son of one of her dad's friends. That was the only reason her dad had let them go out. Kat had been vague when she told her parents they had broken up after only a few dates.

He was a year older and much bigger and stronger than she. A nice-looking guy, but very pushy. He had tried to grope her more than once after she was alone with him in his car. When he even took it a step further and forced his hand into her panties one night, she slapped him as hard as she could to make him stop. He had called her a bitch and took her home. Kat had not seen him since.

No matter, Phillip was long gone in her mind. Odell occupied that space now.

God, will I ever get out of this hell.

Kat dreamed of being on her own. She loved her parents, but they smothered her. Her mom told Kat that she didn't want her daughter to end up like her. Kat wasn't sure exactly what was meant by that statement. She supposed it had something to do with her father's controlling behaviors which sometimes had an undercurrent of violence attached. He had only spanked her once a few years ago, for being disrespectful he said, but she still remembered it.

Dad always had the final say on any topic in the household. If Kat's mom tried to resist, her dad would only have to give that squinted look conveying growing displeasure to cause no further discussion. Mom always gave in to him.

The record had finished and the next single stacked on the spindle dropped on the turntable. *Groovin'* always lifted her spirits, but it only made her daydream about Odell even more. They had discussed The Young Rascals' music and agreed the group was one of their favorites.

Kat kept listening to her records until finally getting sleepy. She could hear her father's snoring from the parents' bedroom across the hallway. She let out a long sigh as her head sunk into one of the pillows on her bed. Kat hugged the other one and pretended it was her boyfriend. She realized that's how she thought of Odell now.

Somehow, some way, she thought. *We'll get back together.*

CHAPTER 8

It had been a busy day for Odell. He had cut grass in a couple of yards and made a few bucks earlier. The money had been stored in an old cardboard cigar box where he kept his earned cash and unused allowance. A quick count confirmed what he already knew. There was fifty-eight dollars and seventy-four cents, and he'd need to make a deposit to his savings account at the bank located within the Westgate Mall. Since his parents had opened the account for him two years before, the teen had already accumulated almost two hundred dollars, an impressive amount, he thought.

Thinking about Westgate gave him an idea. Maybe he and Kat could figure out a way to catch a movie at the theater located there. *To Sir, With Love* was currently playing and Odell had heard it was a good flick, but his main motivation was to have some alone time with Kat.

Although it wasn't official yet, Odell had a good feeling about his growing relationship with Kat. He had decided the very next time he had the opportunity; he would ask her to be his girlfriend.

Since Odell had little experience with such matters, he needed some advice. As much as he hated to admit his deficiency, he knew his mother would be honest with him.

Odell went into the kitchen where his mother had started preparing supper for the family. She was an accomplished southern cook, and he loved everything she made. He often watched and helped when she allowed. Odell had already learned many of her techniques and would fix a few meals on his own including her signature spaghetti and meat sauce.

With the heavy black cast iron frying pan on the stovetop and two packs of fresh pork chops on the counter, it was obvious they'd be having fried meat for the evening meal. Anything cooked in that pan whether cubed steak, crispy chicken, hamburgers and French fries, was always delicious.

She had a big bag of Russet potatoes on a separate countertop near the sink, so it was easy to figure out that mashed 'taters were on the menu. There was also a paper sack of fresh green beans awaiting to be washed, snapped, and put into a pot, too.

"Need some help, Mama?"

"I could use a little," she replied while offering a pleasant smile.

Peeling potatoes had been one of the first jobs Odell had been taught. He grabbed a paring knife out of a nearby drawer and pulled the garbage can by the sink. Odell used skill not to cut anything other than the dusty peels off the white spuds. You didn't want to waste food or slice your fingers.

As he finished each potato, Odell placed it in the sink to be washed. It took a little while to do because the family consumed a few pounds of spuds each time they were served.

"I could use a little advice," he began the conversation tentatively.

His mother was diligently dredging the chops in flour and then dropping them in hot grease causing sizzles and pops. She glanced at him after a moment and said, "About what?"

"I've met a girl, and I really like her a lot."

She turned completely away from the stove and said, "Really?"

Mama almost sounded pleased, thought Odell. "Yes, ma'am. Her name is Kathy, but everybody calls her Kat. She lives up the road."

"Hmm, is that the Norman girl? Part of the family that moved into the vacant house a few months ago?" she asked.

"Uh, huh. I think you'd like her, Mama. She's smart and cute, too. I'd like to take her to the movies, if she can go. I'm not sure she'd want to go with me or even if her parents would let her. So, I need your advice," Odell said in a hurry.

A loud pop coming from the pan caused his mother to turn back to the stove. She flipped the meat over which caused more searing noise, and Odell could now smell the food. His mouth watered involuntarily like Pavlov's dog. When the meat quieted again, she turned around to him.

"Probably the best approach is to just ask her if she would like to go with you. If she says yes, then you can find out if her folks will let her. I don't know why they wouldn't. You're a good boy, Odell. Nobody should mind," she finally replied.

Mother and son continued their private conversation as they worked to prepare the meal. Odell could talk to her about such things a lot easier than he could with his dad. They discussed other issues interspersed with the original topic, and by the time the potatoes and beans were boiling, Odell felt better about everything that had been bothering him.

CHAPTER 9

Summertime in middle Georgia was always hot and most of the time also muggy. The weather could make it hard to sleep under those sauna-like conditions.

The box fan located in the window next to Odell's bed only moved the stale air around, it for sure didn't cool it like the air conditioner unit in his parents' bedroom. For most people he knew, that kind of thing was considered a luxury although they were becoming more popular and even a necessity in the south. Daddy had said that by next year the family would get a central heating and air system, and Odell was excited by that prospect. For now, he'd have to keep sweating and trying in vain to keep his brain from racing.

It was still way too early to get out of the bed he shared with Kenny, but Odell was anxious to start the day. The guys had planned to practice a little around mid-morning, and he thought it might be a good time to take the mower to Kat's house before then. That way, not only would it be cooler to cut the grass, but he'd also hopefully ask her if she would, and could, go with him to the movies.

This time in his young life had to be the worst, he thought. Too old for some things, too young for other stuff. It was confusing, and frustrating as well. He was smart enough to realize these feelings should pass eventually, but right now time was moving too slowly to suit his restless self.

The droning a/c noise from the next room, the whooshing of the fan and the otherwise stillness of the house was just too much to contend with. He got out of bed, put on his glasses and grabbed his guitar off the stand from the corner of the room. Odell took it with him to the den at the front of the home. Even though it was dark, his eyes had adjusted to the lack of light since he had been awake for at least thirty minutes. He switched on a lamp to further illuminate the sofa where he sat down.

He started idly strumming chords on his prized instrument. Very little sound could be heard from his playing since the white Fender Mustang with a red pick guard was electric and not plugged into the amplifier left in his bedroom. It was not unusual for him to play this way so as not to disturb others.

Odell hadn't been spending much time with it lately as he felt he didn't have enough talent to perform. He and Kenny had each gotten identical guitars the previous Christmas and had taken lessons for a few months afterward. It was fun for a while, and they had even played at a friend's birthday party. There were a lot of guys who were much more accomplished, and he just didn't want to put in the amount of practice it took to play better. Now, he thought of the activity as more of an occasional hobby.

After a few minutes, he heard the shrill alarm clock from his parents' room over the hum of the air conditioner. His mother would be coming through to the kitchen very soon. She worked the day shift at Keebler and had to be there at 7:00 a.m. His father rotated shifts at Inland Container and was currently on the day rotation, too. His workday didn't start until 8:00, so he'd probably be cooking breakfast for the boys this morning, but his mom usually made each of them a pan of biscuits before she left for work. Odell admired their work ethic and liked to think he had a little of that trait as well.

"You're up mighty early," his mother said when she came by.

"Yeah, couldn't sleep. I've been thinking about what we talked about yesterday. Thanks for your advice. I'm going to try and follow it today."

She gave a nod and went into the kitchen. Odell followed and watched her get out a bag of flour and a can of shortening from one of the overhead cabinets. Next, she retrieved her rounded wooden bread bowl from a cabinet underneath the Formica countertop. The final ingredient she needed to make her famous biscuits was a gallon of milk that came from the fridge.

Odell had watched this ritual countless times over the course of his lifetime. She made it look so easy, but he never could do it like she could no matter how often he tried.

Mom had on her work uniform consisting of a cotton tan dress with a pointed collar and a hair net covering her brown hair. She never wore makeup but had put on some lipstick.

For as long as he could remember, he'd never heard her complain about having to work. She had said the family needed the money to help them have their house and plenty of food to eat.

"You can help me by getting the pans," she said as she began preparing the dough.

Odell got out five aluminum pans of equal size and then quickly washed his hands in the sink. He then dipped out a small amount of Crisco from the can and lightly greased each pan with the lard. A second washing of the used hand followed.

Mom patted out the biscuits placing at least three in a pan and lined them on the counter as she completed each one. It was amazing that she prepared all four boys and their father separate servings, but they each liked theirs baked to varying degrees of doneness and some might be eaten earlier than others.

She put away everything, cleaned herself up and gave Odell a little hug as she hurried out of the kitchen and exited through the back door. "Bye, sugar. Stay sweet and everything will work out fine today."

***

Odell had eaten his breakfast, used the bathroom and dressed in a clean tee shirt and shorts. He put on a cap that wasn't so dirty and then headed up the road to Kat's house.

His father had left for work just a few minutes before and told him to watch out for his brothers during the day. It was a responsibility Odell didn't take lightly and made him almost feel like the man of the house. Although the younger boys were pretty responsible and followed household rules fairly well most of the time, Odell had to pull rank on occasion. For that reason, he wanted to get his job done quickly and get back home before any potential crisis could arise. His two youngest brothers, Wayne and Lynn, could get sideways with each other, and Odell might need to stop any major conflict that might develop between them.

When Odell arrived, he was a little surprised to see what he recognized as Kat's dad's truck sitting in the driveway of their house. Kat had mentioned he worked long hours and often left before sunup and not getting home until after sundown. Odell had never met him and had only seen him from a distance.

Odell was conflicted as to whether he should start mowing because they could still be sleeping. It wouldn't be good to wake up the girl's parents when he wanted to ask for permission to take her to a movie. Also, he couldn't be gone from his house for very long either since he was ultimately accountable for everything there during the day.

Dang it, why does everything have to be so complicated, he thought.

After standing frozen in the position for a few minutes, Odell decided it would be the safest alternative to go back home. Maybe he could slip back again after lunch. Just as he turned around to leave, the front door opened, and Mr. Norman came outside.

"Where you going?" he asked in not the friendliest of voices.

"Uh, home, sir. I didn't want to take any chances of waking anybody," replied Odell.

"Everybody's awake. Come here and let me talk to you a minute."

Odell swallowed, then turned the mower back up the driveway. His knees felt weak and wobbly, and his mouth was suddenly dry. He wanted not to appear as nervous as he was.

"Uh, Good morning, Mr. Norman. I'm Odell Sterling," he said and held out his hand.

After an uncomfortable few seconds, Kat's dad gripped Odell's hand with his own well-calloused one. It reminded Odell of his father's strong hands. In fact, the more he looked at the man, he could see other similarities.

Both men were around two inches taller than Odell's five-feet, ten-inch frame. They were built equally wiry with dark hair and would be considered handsome. However, there was something about his penetrating eyes that made Odell feel even more uncomfortable than his own dad.

The man gave an extra squeeze and let go. He looked Odell up and down and then said, "You did a decent job on the yard last week. I guess you're expecting to do it again, huh?"

"Yes, sir. I was planning on it. I don't mean to take it for granted, though. I would've called first to make sure, but I didn't know your number."

Kat's father didn't change his tone dramatically although his appearance did seem to relax some. He pooched his lips as he contemplated.

After another pause, Mr. Norman replied, "I'll tell you what. I've got to work out of town for the next few weeks, and I do need somebody to cut my grass while I'm gone. I don't even have a mower right now. I might as well get you to do it. You can collect from my wife after completing the job to her satisfaction."

Odell let out a sigh and felt like he could breathe again. Enough tension had left his body that he now experienced a sudden newfound boldness.

"Thank you, Mr. Norman. I promise to do my best. I really like your daughter, by the way. She's very nice. I was hoping that you and Mrs. Norman would let me take her to see a movie sometime. I mean, if it's okay with her, too, of course."

Now the man's eyes closed almost to a Clint Eastwood squint, and Odell was afraid he'd gone too far. The stare he got made him swallow hard again.

"You old enough to drive, yet?"

"Uh, no, sir. But, my mom would take us and pick us up afterwards. I asked her last night when I thought about checking with y'all this morning," said Odell, immediately thinking he sounded lame.

Surprising Odell with his reply, Mr. Norman said, "You need to know Kat is my only baby. I won't put up with any foolishness, understand? With that in mind, you've got my permission, if she wants to go see a movie with you."

Odell broke into a wide grin and was on top of the world. Mama had been right.

CHAPTER 10

The last two days had been a whirlwind for Odell. After his initial conversation with Kat's dad, he had cut the grass in their yard while he floated on a cloud. By the time he'd finished the job, Odell had practiced in his mind the next steps. He then went by that script and landed himself a movie date with Kat for the following afternoon.

Odell got up early on the morning of the planned rendezvous and did all the normal Saturday chores. He was more excited about the date than anything else currently imagined, maybe even more than pitching in the city championship game. Until he had met the girl, that goal had been his ultimate desire for this summer. Now Kat consumed the boy's yearnings so that baseball had become secondary.

He desperately wanted the date to be special. Since it was the first time Odell would experience such a moment, his quest for perfection seemed endless. His mother had warned him not to overthink and just enjoy the time. Odell was really glad she had agreed to take them to the show and pick them up after it was over.

The plans had been set so that Odell would pick up Kat at 2:30 for the 3:00 matinee feature of *To Sir, with Love,* playing at the Westgate Theater located a few miles away. After the movie, they would walk across the parking lot to the nearby mall and enjoy an ice cream at Betty Ann's near the Colonial grocery store. Odell's mother would pick them up at the rear entrance of the shopping center at 5:30 and return Kat to her house in time for supper.

Odell had already told the guys he wouldn't be playing or practicing any ball that day because of his date, and there had been a lot of ribbing and kidding him. To Odell's knowledge, none of them had a girlfriend, so what did they know anyway. He had taken their good-natured teasing with a grain of salt, and it certainly didn't change his mind about taking the day off from baseball.

He had a few hours before seeing Kat and decided to call one of his closest friends, Mike Taylor. Although they were the same age and had been chums since the sixth grade, Odell thought of Mike as being much more experienced with girls. They had discussed the topic in the past, and his friend was free with the advice he imparted to Odell.

He took a seat on a barstool that sat beneath a counter separating the kitchen and the den area. Odell had eaten on that bar many times over the years, but the phone was also located on the wall at one end of it. He remembered most numbers he called often like Mike's and did not need to look it up as he removed the handset from its cradle and inserted his index finger into the dial.

"Hey, buddy. You got a minute?" asked Odell when Mike answered.

"Sure, man. I haven't heard from you since school let out. Been wondering what you're up to," replied his friend.

"Aw, the usual. Playing some ball, cutting some grass, pretty much staying at home," said Odell and paused before saying, "And I met a girl."

"Well, I'll just be damned. Tell me about her, you horny devil," exclaimed Mike.

Odell's face flushed at Mike's descriptive term. He searched around the room wondering if somebody else in the house was listening to the conversation. Maybe seeking his worldly friend's guidance wasn't such a great idea. Seeing nobody nearby, he continued the call.

"She lives up the road, believe it or not. I can't believe I really hadn't noticed until a couple of weeks ago. Do you know Kathy Norman? Everybody calls her Kat."

"Can't say that I do, but I like the name. Sounds sexy," said Mike and then made sounds like a cat. It started as a purr and ended in more of a growl. When he finished, Mike was laughing at himself.

He lowered his voice to almost a whisper, "You've got to be careful with pussies, don't you know? They can be soft and cuddly, but then they can scratch your eyes out if you're not careful."

More laughter was coming through into Odell's ear that was also turning crimson caused by Mike's crudeness. He was feeling more uneasy by the second.

"Come on, man. I'm calling for a little advice about a first date and maybe to ask a favor," Odell responded.

"Okay, O. Sorry about that, I just can't help myself sometimes. What 'ya need?"

"We're going to see a movie this afternoon, and I was wondering how I should handle the date. You know, I'm not sure if maybe I hold her hand or put my arm around her. And how about kissing?"

"Well, holding a girl's hand is a safe start, and an arm on her shoulder is not bad either. Otherwise, have you made out with her yet? You don't want to rush things because I know how shy you are, O," Mike spoke more seriously.

"We kissed a few times at Durr's a couple of weeks ago, the last one was the best," Odell said while checking around the room again.

"Then you're golden, my man. Hell yeah, wait until an intimate moment, or at least a quiet one in the flick, and then reach over and get those lips going. The only thing I'd say is to watch out for popcorn getting stuck in your teeth. That could get gross," Mike said and laughed again.

"Good idea. I hadn't thought about that. Okay, I've got one other favor to ask. I don't have any cologne, so could I use some of yours?"

"If you think she can handle that intoxication, come and get it, buddy."

The call ended and Odell asked if he could take his bike over to Mike's house for a little while. Thirty minutes later he was back home with a bottle of Hai Karate in his possession. The only other advice Mike had given him was to use it sparingly to prevent clawing.

***

The final preparations had been made. Odell shaved with his single-edged razor and managed not to cut himself with an item that had been dangerous in the past. He took special care to remove the whiskers around the mole on his chin. He was pleased to note that his face was relatively clear from any signs of the teenaged acne that often plagued his existence, probably due to his recent exposure to lots of sunshine.

Odell had taken Mike's advice to heart and only placed a dab of the cologne behind each of his ears after a long shower. Ironically, he didn't really like the smell. It was on the pungent side, he thought, and the stuff was limey. It was, however, supposed to be the rage nowadays, and he hoped Kat would appreciate his attempts to smell good for her.

He had dressed in his favorite black jeans. For some reason, the color had become one of his favorites a few years ago, and when he put on a starched red shirt to go with the dark Levi's, Odell admired himself in the mirror. His recently polished bebops for some reason didn't work with the outfit, so he changed to his black penny loafers and nodded approvingly.

Odell brushed his teeth fiercely and checked his gums for any signs of blood. He'd already put a pack of Juicy Fruit chewing gum in his right front pocket as a precaution against future bad breath.

His slim wallet was in his right rear pocket containing a whole ten dollars. It should be more than enough to take care of the movie tickets, snacks and ice cream after the show.

The final prep involved combing his hair multiple times in order to get the part straight and the swooped bangs in place. He even used a little of his mother's hairspray to keep them in position.

Looking for mom so they could leave the house, he found her in the kitchen. She had been baking and he saw three of her special egg custard pies lined up on the countertop. The meringue formed miniature waves on the tops of the goodies that made him want to pinch one off and eat it on the spot.

When he reached toward one, she stopped him with, "Don't you dare."

He did as was told and replied, "Okay, Mama. I'm ready to go. Do I look alright?"

She removed her apron and studied Odell from head to toe. She smiled at him and he knew she approved which made the Mama's boy happy.

"You look like my handsome young man," she said and paused. She took out a Rubbermaid container for one of the pies and placed it inside.

"When we pick up your date, you can give this to her mother."

The gesture was typical of his mom. She was often thoughtful like that and had baked cakes, pies and cookies as gifts for family, friends and her co-workers. Everybody loved her treats, and Odell was sure Mrs. Norman would, too.

CHAPTER 11

Odell and Kat sat toward the rear of the darkened theater in the last two seats on the row. Patrons were scattered in the building that was maybe half-occupied. Kat had declined his offer to buy her popcorn or candy, but she did accept sharing a Coke which was sipped intermittingly.

The movie was pretty good so far Odell thought, and Kat seemed to be enjoying it as well. He would periodically glance toward her, and she appeared relaxed while slowly chewing the gum Odell had given her at the start.

They had held hands for a while when the movie first started, but that had ended at a tense moment in the show. Odell had followed up by putting his arm around Kat's shoulder without resistance on her part. She had even slid closer in his direction. The arms between the seats prevented closer contact than Odell would've preferred, but it felt so good to be there with her.

The acting and the story held their attention as they watched intently. Odell found himself immersed by the themes since it dealt with some of the same issues of growing up. Odell especially liked the character portrayed by Sidney Poitier and the way that he gained respect of the students.

As the movie was coming to a close, Odell felt hopeful about the future. He glanced at Kat who had a tear in her eye. He reached over and gently removed it with his thumb, and then the moment required a tender kiss. Their lips met not with passion, but the connection went deep into Odell's soul.

Is this what love feels like? He wondered.

As the credits rolled and other customers started to leave the theater, the two of them remained in their seats and let them pass. They talked quietly about what they had just watched and agreed that it was a great movie.

After most of the other people had left, Odell told Kat they should get moving, too since they only had about forty-five minutes left before his mother would pick them up. They strolled across the parking lot holding hands and each glistened with sweat caused by the afternoon heat until they got inside the first air-conditioned mall in the state.

To Odell, it was a cool place, literally and figuratively. There was nothing like the shopping center and being so close to where he lived and even closer to the high school he attended, Odell thought it might provide a part-time job opportunity when he turned sixteen early next year.

They walked past several stores without entering but stopping long enough sometimes to look in display windows. The smells wafting from Hefner's Bakery were especially enticing, and Odell pledged they would come back to the establishment in the near future.

By the time they got to the end of the mall near the Colonial grocery store and Odell checked his Timex watch, it was a little after five o'clock. He bought them an ice cream cone at Betty Ann's Candies, and they sat down on a bench.

Between licks and bites they continued to review the movie. It was a deep discussion that involved racism, relationships and respect which were themes addressed in the film. Odell kept gaining admiration for Kat's intellect which made her even more attractive to him.

A bespectacled man approached from the grocery store toward where they sat. He appeared heading to the little shop where the cold treats had been purchased. Odell recognized him as the father of a former teammate from a few years ago.

"Hey, Mr. Kitchens," Odell said.

The tall thin man with a balding head was dressed in a tie, starched shirt and dress pants stopped and looked through rounded lenses at the couple. "Well, well. Odell Sterling, right? Haven't seen you since the year Keith played with you on your daddy's team. You've grown up," he replied.

Odell stood up and grinned while sticking out his right hand. "Yes, sir," he said noticing for the first time a name tag identifying him as Manager pinned to his shirt.

"What are you doing these days besides hanging out with a pretty girl?"

"Just enjoying my summer vacation. I didn't know you managed Colonial. Need any bagboys?" Odell asked hopefully.

Mr. Kitchens nodded, "We can always find a job for a hardworking young man. But, you're not sixteen, yet are you?"

"No, sir, but I will be in a few months," replied Odell feeling disappointed.

"Sorry, company policy won't let me hire you before then. I'll tell you what. As soon as you have your next birthday, come see me and I'll see what we can do."

"Thank you, Mr. Kitchens. I will," he said with rising excitement.

The manager then left them to get his own treat. Odell told Kat a little about how he knew the man and how great it would be to work there. He shared his dreams about making enough money so he could get a car.

"Then I'll be able to take you out on a real date," he said.

"Don't sell yourself short, Odell. This has been a real date to me. I'll never forget it," she responded and almost looked like she would cry again.

"Before Mama gets here," he said checking his watch, "I want to ask you a question. Will you be my steady girlfriend?"

She sat speechless for only a few seconds and then said with a smile, "I can't think of anything else I want as much." It was sealed with a smooch in public.

CHAPTER 12

The next two weeks of vacation sped by in a blur. As June ended, the Renegades had beaten two more division foes and were still undefeated.

They had a closer game than the score indicated as they beat Pine Forest by a 5-1 final total. Odell had been disappointed when Ricky Lee wasn't present for the game since he knew that was the team he was on this year. Odell had wanted the chance to pitch to him and maybe buzz a fastball by his ear as payback for pulling the whiskers out of his mole on the last day of school. Odell smashed another big hit that scored runs and his brother, Kenny, was also hot with the bat.

The third game had been a blowout when Odell's team won 12-0 against the South Macon Braves. The strategy had been to have some of the younger boys go to the plate and not swing their bats since the Braves' pitcher couldn't seem to throw a strike. All of them were able to get on base via walks and then knocked home by the better hitters. Even the slow-running Smith brothers had gotten to home during the rout. The umpire called the game after four innings under the "Mercy Rule."

Other summer stuff had happened quickly as well. Since their first date, Odell and Kat were able to see each other more often thanks to her mother's relaxed attitude toward him and maybe due to the fact that her father was working out of town. Mrs. Norman didn't seem to mind them sitting on the swing and talking as they had done several times.

Kat had been welcomed by the Sterling family right away after Odell let them know they were "going steady." Kat was able to ride with Odell and Kenny to the skating rink and had been a dinner guest on another occasion. She seemed at ease among his brothers and his parents, too.

It was as if the pie Odell's mom had given to the Normans contained some magical ingredient that allowed him access to his now acknowledged girlfriend. He thought he was the happiest he'd ever been in his young life.

Another weekend had arrived, and it promised to be the best of the summer. The Sterlings had possessed a ski boat since Odell was thirteen, and all the boys were good water skiers. The first couple of years after it had been purchased, the family had made good use of the fourteen-foot craft with a seventy-five horsepower Evinrude motor.

They would pack up enough groceries for a weekend, or even a week if their parents had a scheduled vacation, and head to Lake Sinclair. One of Odell's uncles owned a place they would use any time it was available.

The lake house was nothing special and consisted of an old, rusted trailer with a screened-in porch running the length on the front facing the water. There were two small bedrooms and a galley kitchen inside the mobile home and several cots that were used for sleeping inside the other part of the structure. Odell and his brothers enjoyed spending nights on the porch underneath large ceiling fans while listening to the sounds of frogs and crickets. It was their version of camping out.

There was a wooden boat dock on the property where the boat would stay tied when not in use. The boys would often dive off the end into the dark waters of the lake and splash and swim for hours. Sometimes they would fish for perch or catfish at night by the light that was fastened to the structure.

For some reason, everybody seemed to have lost interest in those activities this year until now. It had been decided the family would go to the lake early and spend the entire day skiing, fishing and having a cookout. What really made it exciting to Odell was that Kat had been invited, too.

**

"This is so much fun. Thanks for bringing me along," Kat almost screamed over the roar of the outboard engine.

The two of them had spent the day doing the usual lake activities with Odell's family. Kat had seemed to really enjoy her first time skiing and playing in the water with Odell and his brothers.

She sat in the passenger seat of the vessel while Odell piloted. It was the first time they had been alone together all day. That was okay, but Kat had hinted that she would like to spend at least a few minutes with her boyfriend.

The opportunity arose from the need for more gas to power the boat. Odell's dad gave him some money and told him that he and Kat could drive it to the marina a few miles away. Daddy's trust in his oldest boy was something that made Odell proud.

Odell had been allowed to operate the craft by himself since last summer and had driven it to Haslam's Marina several times. Initially, it had been under his father's tutelage, but Odell had shown responsibility by not cutting up when he was behind the wheel. He often pulled his brothers or his parents around the lake while they skidded across the water on skis or innertubes.

He slowed down after leaving the dock on his uncle's property so he could make the trip last longer. Odell slid in his seat as far as he could to make some room for Kat to sit beside him. It was smooth enough on the open water, and she was able to take the few steps easily even though they were in motion.

Kat had on a two-piece swimsuit that complimented her figure. She was beginning to turn pink above her breasts, on her belly, shoulders and legs, despite her putting on lotion after first getting outside.

"Uh, I think you need some more Coppertone," Odell said as she nestled beside his more tanned body.

He spotted a secluded bay that he had fished in before and steered toward it. When he reached the area, Odell placed the gear to neutral and the boat slowly rocked until the wake dissipated.

"Can you reach the sunscreen? There's a bottle in the storage bin," said Odell.

This was the first time so much of their exposed bodies were touching, and Odell found himself becoming aroused. The tight trunks he wore seemed to be getting even tighter. Kat appeared to have noticed when she glanced downward. Before standing up, she peered into his eyes and then kissed him as passionately as they had yet experienced.

While his mind reeled in the moment, Odell watched Kat as she had her back to him while looking for the lotion. He had never felt so turned on and didn't know how to handle it.

"I really like seeing you in that suit," he croaked.

Turning around with the bottle in hand she replied, "I can tell."

His embarrassment kept Odell from saying anything else as she sat back down on the edge of his seat with her back to him after giving him the plastic container.

Silently he began applying the creamy lotion first to her shoulders, and then upper and lower back. Her skin was electric to his fingertips.

"You can unfasten the top if you want to," said Kat in a husky voice.

After looking in every direction and not seeing anyone, Odell struggled to unhook the clasp with nervous fingers. He added some lotion to the whiter skin now exposed, and then both hands followed the line to the front of her body. He couldn't see them, but he gently felt the firm mounds of flesh and the erect nipples of her chest fitting perfectly in his palms.

Odell heard a soft moan and at first thought he had made the sound, but then realized Kat had emitted it. He slid closer in the seat so that his chest was almost touching her back as he continued to fondle her. She dropped her right hand slightly behind to his leg, and it caused him to shudder involuntarily.

From a distance another boat could be heard approaching their location which destroyed the couple's moment. Odell refastened the top much faster than he had while undoing it, and Kat returned to her seat on the opposite side.

It was unsettling and upsetting to Odell as he started again toward the marina. They gazed at each other without speaking until they got there.

As an employee filled the tank with gas, Odell stood on the dock fidgeting with unspent energy. He finally said, "I'm crazy about you, Kat."

Her smile was enigmatic as she replied, "I feel the same about you, Odell. I just don't know how to handle the feeling."

"We'll figure it out," said Odell.

CHAPTER 13

Odell and his father were in the family car for a driving lesson. Having his learner's license for the last few months, Odell took advantage of every occasion to learn and practice his skills. Since his dad was always busy, it was not often enough that he got the opportunity, Odell thought.

The father/son relationship was not ideal in the teen's way of thinking. His dad rarely ever showed outward expressions of affection. Odell knew that Daddy cared deeply for the family by providing the best life he could for them, hence the long hours of working two and three jobs. Both of his parents saw to their welfare and often gave him and his brothers stuff that other kids didn't get, like the guitars that Odell and Kenny owned. He had never heard his father say that he loved him, however.

To be in the car alone was good for having some personal time. As his father passed on information about operating the Ford sedan, Odell listened intently, but had other questions.

"Daddy, when did you first know what love was?"

Odell could tell his father was taken aback by the query because he didn't answer, but asked another question instead, "Why are you asking me that? I'm trying to teach you how to drive."

"And I appreciate that, really. It's just that I've got these feelings about Kat, and I don't know what they mean. I have no idea what love is, and I'm trying to figure it out."

"Keep your eyes on the damn road, Odell," he said as Odell drifted off the roadway causing the right side tires to bump several times.

"Yes, sir, I'm sorry," replied Odell as he concentrated to keep the car between the lines.

After what seemed an eternity, Odell's father said, "You're way too young to be thinking about stuff like love. You'll know it when it happens."

"Okay, but when you and Mama got married, she was only seventeen, right? I'm less than two years from being that old."

Odell's dad seemed uncomfortable as he stole a glance toward the passenger side. It was obvious that his father didn't like the topic of conversation.

"Look, son. Nobody ever talked to me like you're doing right now. I understand if you've got questions about growing up. It just seems to me it's too soon to be asking those kinds of questions."

"So, who do I ask if not you, or maybe Mama?"

"Yeah, talk to her. Y'all are a lot closer anyway. She'll answer your questions better than I can. I don't know what to say. Do you know about rubbers?"

The subject had been changed without prompting. His dad was obviously thinking about practical stuff like not getting pregnant, not the more esoteric worries. They had never had "the talk about the birds and the bees" that other friends had described to Odell.

"Daddy, I'm not thinking about sex so much as I am about having deep feelings for somebody I care about. I'm sorry, I didn't mean to upset you."

The drive continued without conversation for several minutes. It seemed that neither of them wanted to speak further. At the very least, the subject matter had become an uneasy one. As the car approached an empty parking lot, Odell's dad directed him to drive there and park.

Odell turned to face his father who had lit a cigarette. The front windows had already been rolled down because of the sweltering summer heat and most of the smoke escaped out the passenger side. Some did make it to Odell's nostrils, but he was used to it since the elder Sterling had smoked for as long as the son could remember. The habit wasn't anything that appealed to Odell, but he could handle the inconvenience of being in the enclosed space because of the long exposure.

"I know you're growing up fast," he said after taking another long drag and then blowing out through the open window.

His dad continued, "I just don't want you doing anything to screw up your future, that's all. You know, I never even made it to the tenth grade like you'll be starting soon. I started working full-time when I was sixteen. I never got to know how to really have fun."

Odell knew a little about his father's childhood already, but it had never been anything Daddy wanted to talk about in detail. He only knew minor details about how the man who married his mother met her.

"I had been working for several years when your mama and I got together. I had a car, but I was still living with your grandparents and giving them most of the money I made. I didn't have a clue about having a place of my own or having kids or much of anything at that point."

The ash on the cigarette looked as if it would fall off any moment before his dad flicked it out the window. He inhaled again and continued the talk as the acrid smoke came out his nose and mouth simultaneously.

"When I first saw your mama, I think I became a little crazy. I couldn't get her off my mind, and then the next thing I know she's missed her period, we're getting married and everything has changed. We had nothing when we started out. You came along followed soon by your brothers," he said before finishing the cigarette.

"So, when y'all got married, I was on the way," Odell said.

The teen had noticed in the family Bible that his birthdate was seven months after his parents' marriage date, but he'd always assumed that he was simply born early. What he just found out was a revelation and explained a lot about his father.

"You're smart, son. You can be the first Sterling to go to college and maybe become a professional. You could be a doctor or a lawyer or anything else you want to be. That won't happen if you're not careful. That's all I'm trying to say," he said.

Odell never wanted to disappoint either of his parents. What he heard only reinforced that resolve. However, it didn't help with the feelings he had for Kat that were growing by leaps and bounds.

CHAPTER 14

Odell stood on the pitching mound and received a sign from Mitch to throw a fastball on the outside corner. It was a good call he thought as the batter had his front foot "in the bucket" as that stance was known. Since it was the second time through the opposing team's batting order, Odell had a pretty good idea on how to pitch to them.

Odell slid his right foot to the end of the embedded piece of rubber that had been slightly dug out from previous thrown pitches. He often moved from one end to the other depending on the angle he wanted to deliver from and would use it to push off the mound with his rear foot. Toeing the mound was his thought process.

Odell wound up and fired the ball into Mitch's mitt as the batter swung and missed the pitch by a good two feet. It was the third out of the fourth inning of the Renegades fifth game.

The week before, the team, led by Odell's two-hit shutout of the YMCA, had won 3-0 to keep them undefeated. If they could maintain the current lead against The Crazy Nine, the Renegades would be guaranteed first place for another week with only two games left in the regular season. There were only eight teams in the fifteen and under league, and they had been scheduled to play the other seven once before the playoffs began.

Their current opponent consisted of some guys Odell played with last year in the same division. He and Ricky Lee had been on the team then and their defection had weakened the Crazy Nine's lineup. They had won two of their four games and were now losing by two runs, so their chances weren't looking good with Odell throwing fire against their hitters.

Odell stepped to the plate leading off the bottom of the inning and facing his old teammate, Jimmy. J.D., as he was called, was a decent pitcher, but Odell knew him well and had already hit a double against him earlier in the game. Odell expected not to be pitched to, and he'd already decided a walk would probably result.

Odell feigned nonchalance with the barrel of his bat resting on his shoulder as J.D. fooled him by tossing a strike across the middle of the plate. Whatever the reason, J.D. seemed to be pissed off. This was evidenced by the scowl on J.D.'s face and the tightness of the next pitch causing Odell to lose his balance and almost falling down when he ducked out of the way.

When he stepped back into the batter's box, Odell glared back toward the pitcher and pumped his bat deliberately in that direction. It was an unspoken dare for J.D. to try and throw another strike. His former teammate couldn't ignore the challenge.

The ball and bat met with the former sent sailing toward left field. The kid playing that position realized too late that he needed to backtrack as the baseball flew over his head. Since the field had no fence, the ball rolled forever, and Odell easily ran around the bases to score another run.

The rest of the Renegades were standing at home when Odell stomped on it emphatically. He was breathing hard from the race but enjoyed the attention that included cheers and slaps on the back. A glance back to the mound showed J.D.'s slumped shoulders turned away from the celebration.

The end of the game was uneventful as Odell finished with another shutout. The team was undefeated with only two games left in the regular season. Chances to add to his trophy collection were looking pretty good, thought Odell.

CHAPTER 15

Kat and Odell skated around the rink holding hands and talking about things that had happened in the last few days since they had seen one another. She and her mother had gone on a successful shopping trip to the mall, and now Kat wore one of the new outfits purchased at one of the smaller boutique stores.

The soft polyester pants and top fit her to a T, she thought. Kat wanted to look good to Odell, and the way he kept observing her made her think she had done so.

As usual, he talked a lot about baseball and that their team had won again earlier in the week. Kat wasn't a big fan of the game but thought it would be a good idea to see him play. Anything her boyfriend liked so much couldn't be all bad.

"We've only got two more games left before the playoffs," finished Odell after going on about the last contest for several minutes.

"Would you mind if I came to see you play?" asked Kat.

Odell grinned, "Really? You want to go to a game? No, I wouldn't mind at all."

They discussed the subject more, and Kat told him she would ask her mom if she could attend the next game scheduled against the Boys Club team. He seemed excited when she told him.

"I like your new clothes. You look great in them," Odell said.

She was pleased he had noticed and replied with a simple, "Thanks."

"Hey, I just read a new book I got from the Washington Library that you might like," Odell said changing the subject.

Both teenagers liked reading and had discussed other books they had enjoyed. Odell had told her that he favored non-fiction biographies, as well as classic novels such as *Huckleberry Finn.*

"Yeah, it's called *The Outsiders.* I read it in three days, so I don't have to turn it in to the library right away. I could bring it to you Monday when I come over to cut the grass."

"What's it about? It's not about baseball, is it?" she asked.

He laughed, "Naw, it's a coming-of-age kind of book. I think it's probably a little controversial. Deals with some of the same themes from the movie we saw."

"Hmm, yeah. I'll try it."

The lights dimmed for "Ladies' Choice," and Odell slipped his right hand around Kat's waist. It was a move that had been perfected over a few trips to Durr's since the two of them had started going steady. His touch was gentle, but it brought intimate thoughts. She immediately began to survey the rear corners of the rink to see if they were unoccupied. When she saw that one of the areas already had an embraced couple, Kat steered Odell to the other.

They wasted little time once the couple got to the darkened spot. Face to face, Kat's body tingled as Odell took her in his arms and pressed his chest to hers before their lips met. No longer awkward in this aspect of their courtship, kissing was welcomed whenever possible. She liked his soft lips on hers and the tentative slips of his tongue dancing with hers was exciting.

When their mouths parted, Kat breathed, "You've certainly gotten better at this over the past few weeks."

His hands slid down Kat's back until they rested just above her rear end. The electricity she felt at the close contact seemed to be at a higher voltage and much like their recent episode at the lake. It made her nervous yet thrilled about the future.

Odell placed his forehead against hers and let out a sigh. She didn't know what he was thinking but could see through the dimness a tortured look in his eyes.

"God, I know we're too young for what I'm thinking about," he said.

"Yeah, me too," she said softly.

They kissed again, but with tenderness this time. The slow song by local great Otis Redding ended and the lights were bright too soon. Kat knew they were noticeable to other patrons paying attention, and there always seemed to be nosy people scanning couples in the recesses of the rink.

He took her hand and they skated slowly toward the front of the building. When they were about halfway there, someone speeding by curled a skate around Odell's left foot tripping him. He fell hard on his butt unable to break the fall enough with his free left hand. Because his right hand was occupied with Kat's left, she lost her balance as well and landed on top of him. She heard the breath leave his body and his head bounce off the hardwood floor.

A maniacal sound of laughter erupted from somewhere nearby. Kat thought that it was familiar, but her thoughts were directed at Odell at that moment. She knew firsthand how violent the crash had been, and she was worried he could be badly hurt.

As several other skaters formed a circle around the fallen couple, Kat got disentangled and removed herself off Odell's torso. "Odell are you alright?" she asked.

After a moment, he coughed and then sat up with his legs extended in front of him. Odell rubbed the back of his head a few times before looking at his hand as if he were checking for blood. He seemed dazed and confused to Kat.

Odell shook his head back and forth and said, "What the hell?"

A younger kid in the crowd pointed to the front rail and said with bad grammar, "That guy in the yellow shirt tripped you. I seen him do it, and he was laughing after he done it."

Before Odell could get up on his own, Andy, the proprietor, arrived on the scene. He extended his hand and helped Odell to his feet. "You okay?" Andy asked.

"I guess so," Odell replied while checking himself out further.

Kat felt shock come over her as she observed in wide-eyed wonder the guy wearing the yellow shirt. It was her former boyfriend, Phillip. He smirked in her direction when she inadvertently placed her hand over her mouth. He didn't dawdle and left the rink out the front door without removing his skates.

CHAPTER 16

Kat lay in her bed lost in swirling thoughts. Seeing Phillip Jackson at the skating rink earlier in the evening had been bad enough. What was really terrible, though, was knowing that he had purposely tripped Odell. At least she thought so.

It was a miracle that her present boyfriend had not been injured to a greater extent than he had been. Odell had even laughed it off shortly after falling and attributed the extra padding of his butt and the hardness of his head as saving him additional pain. Kat wondered if Odell was being truthful when he told her and couldn't help believing that the bump on the back of his head had to hurt. Guys had to be so macho sometimes.

She didn't know what to do about Phillip. In particular, she didn't know what to say to Odell about her ex, if that indeed was what she should call him. The relationship between them had been short and hadn't ended well.

Kat had always thought that he was jealous, impulsive and unpredictable, but she couldn't remember ever seeing Phillip's more violent side. There was no doubt in her mind that Phillip had meant to cause harm to Odell, but would he try something else next time if there was further contact between them?

Odell is just so much sweeter, she thought.

Comparing the two boys triggered memories of Phillip and why they had stopped seeing one another. They had first met because Kat's and Phillip's fathers were friends. The two dads worked out of the same pipefitter's local and had been called out together to work on various jobs.

There had been a cookout at the Jackson house last fall and Kat's family was invited. After eating, the grownups stayed on an outside patio drinking beer. The two kids had been allowed to go inside to listen to records.

Kat had been instantly attracted to Phillip who was older and nice-looking. He was tall with blonde hair and blue eyes and favored drummer Dennis Wilson of The Beachboys.

Phillip had a rakish quality that came out in his personality. He used profanities when he talked and bragged about his car that he had shown her before the meal. She didn't understand all that he told her about the specifics of the engine and the four-barrel carburetor, but Kat listened and tried to appear interested.

At some point as they sat on the edge of his bed, when her guard was down, Phillip had lifted her chin toward him and kissed her forcefully on the mouth. Kat had not expected the move, but it wasn't entirely unpleasant either. She didn't have any experience because being an only child had heretofore kept her protected and isolated by her parents.

It was really the first time Kat made out with a boy as Phillip continued the activity for the next few minutes. She attributed her lack of resistance to her innocence. It didn't end until he started to grope her breast causing her to jump up from where she was sitting.

Phillip had been extremely remorseful and seemed sincere at the time. He promised not to do anything like that again. Kat had accepted the apology and then agreed to a date if her parents would allow it.

Kat was a little surprised when the parents came inside shortly after the incident and Phillip asked permission to take her out. She thought it put her dad in a tight spot in front of his friend, but he agreed after Mr. Jackson expressed that he thought it a great idea.

They only went out a few times before the fateful night when Phillip tried to go too far and had actually scared her. She had not seen him for over six months until tonight.

Was Phillip Jackson trying to get back in her life? Had he followed her? Should I tell Odell? I don't know what to do.

CHAPTER 17

The next day Odell and Kat were walking back from church services at Smyrna Baptist located not quite a mile from the rear yard of Odell's house. It was another hot one already, but the couple strolled slowly up the road dressed in their Sunday best so they could have a little private time to talk. Before starting toward home, they had turned down offers for the short ride back.

The heat caused him to remove his dark jacket and loosen the tie around his neck as they traveled. Odell thought Kat's modest black dress had to be warm, and he wondered just how uncomfortable her shiny, matching patent shoes were. She looked attractive dressed up, though, and he was glad she had accepted his invitation.

Odell had been a member of the congregation for a few years and went regularly on the sabbath for Sunday school and usually attended the sermon that followed. He went less often for training union in the evenings and even less for Wednesday night prayer meetings. Odell didn't think of himself as being very religious, but he currently thought going to church was something he was supposed to do. He just didn't care for all the talk of fire and brimstone that often was preached and much preferred lessons of Jesus's love and forgiveness.

Lately, he had discovered there were aspects of the lifestyle that bothered him on some level. Since he was only a teenager, he made every effort to respect what his elders were attempting to teach him, but Odell kept noticing hypocrisy and other things that just didn't make sense to his way of thinking. He especially didn't understand the literal reading of the Bible that most, if not everybody else, seemed to believe. To him, there was much more symbolism involved when he was reading the holy book.

When he questioned his parents about some of the thoughts he had, they would answer that he was smart enough to come to his own conclusions. Maybe that's why they didn't go as much as they used to, thought Odell. At any rate, his mother and father never pushed Odell's beliefs either way, and he kind of liked that approach. He favored coming to his own decisions, right or wrong.

"This heat is a killer. Maybe we should've accepted a ride home," said Odell as they got off the asphalt onto a well-worn path beside the road.

"It's okay. Not even fifteen minutes before we're back," replied Kat.

"I'm sure Mom wouldn't mind if you wanted to join us for lunch," Odell said while wiping sweat off his face with the sleeve of his starched white shirt.

"Can't today. Daddy's home and we're having his favorite pot roast. He's been out of town so much lately, so I need to go home."

Odell nodded his understanding. Without thinking too much about it, he rubbed the knot on the back of his head. Kat watched and then added her fingers to the same area.

"That's a big bump you've got. Does it hurt?"

"Nah, I'm tough," Odell said with a laugh, "Or maybe just hard-headed."

Kat was quiet for a moment, and Odell could tell she was bothered because her mouth had pursed downward. They were about halfway to his house when she said, "I need to tell you something."

"Sure, you can tell me anything. I just hope it's not that you want to break up with me," he replied looking into her saddened eyes.

A sweet smile came to her face, and she shook her head from side to side. Kat switched her Bible to her other hand and then took Odell's free one. She gave it a slight squeeze.

"I don't even want to think that could happen, Odell. I'm happier than I can ever remember. I like you a lot, you silly boy."

Odell grinned and responded, "And I feel the same way. So, what's wrong?"

"I'm pretty sure I know who tripped you last night. I didn't see him do it, but I saw the guy dressed in a yellow shirt after the kid pointed him out. I dated him a few times last year," she said maintaining eye contact.

The revelation took Odell by complete surprise. Kat had never told him about dating somebody else. They had shared so many conversations during the last few weeks with no mention of another guy. At that moment, Odell felt a sense of betrayal and insecurity that cut deep inside. He'd never experienced such a hurt, and it caused him to drop her hand.

"You dated a guy? You never told me that. Was he your boyfriend?"

"I didn't tell you about him because he wasn't important. Maybe I should have, I don't know. I only went out with him because my dad is friends with his dad. I found out he was a jerk, so I stopped dating him. He's the only other guy I've ever been out with other than you, Odell," she said with tears forming in the corners of her eyes.

Odell's pain was turning to another emotion that he didn't often experience. Was it jealousy, anger or a combination of both?

"What's his name?" he asked harshly.

"Phillip Jackson."

Odell didn't recognize the name but wondered if he'd seen him in the past at Durr's. Odell was pretty sure he'd at least know the name if Jackson lived on this side of town.

"Tell me about him and why you think he tripped me."

"He's a year older than us. I'm not sure, but I think he goes to the vocational school. Drives a souped-up car and works part-time at one of the Piggly Wiggly's. I'm not sure he caused us to fall but I know he was there. He had a weird look on his face and left right after I saw him. Maybe it was coincidental, but I've got a bad feeling about him being there. Please, Odell. Don't be mad with me. I'm really sorry for not telling you," Kat pleaded.

Odell softened at the earnestness of Kat's words. With tears and sweat now rolling down their faces, they continued the trip to their homes after an embrace by the roadside. They resumed holding hands, but there was little conversation as Odell's mind raced.

CHAPTER 18

The summer was fleeting with only about six weeks until school started up again, and Odell now had something else besides baseball and a new girlfriend in his brain taking up space. The relationship with Kat had become more complicated due to what Odell thought was a lack of honesty.

Before yesterday when she told him about Phillip Jackson, there were no trust issues between them. Now Odell was not so sure that was true. He would have to try and find out more about the guy.

Why didn't she tell me about him sooner? Did she still have feelings for him?

True, it was more like a sin of omission and not one of commission, for her not to say anything about the other guy. Odell knew he was young, and this was his first time dealing with these emotions eating at his soul, so maybe he was being unfair. Being fairly informed for his age, he had read about teenage angst, and maybe this qualified.

But I've been totally honest with Kat. We've had a lot of conversations about all kinds of things. She knows I've never really had a girlfriend like her. The closest I've ever come were grammar school crushes. I even told Kat I'd only kissed two girls in my whole life. And, she's not mentioned Phillip Jackson while I'm opening up completely about myself. Kat says that it was because he wasn't important. It just doesn't seem fair, he thought.

Odell's spinning thoughts made him sick to his stomach. He hurried from the bed to the hall bathroom and made it just in the nick of time as he sat on the toilet. It was if he needed to void the bad stuff that had built up in his body. When he finished and cleaned himself, Odell found that everything didn't seem quite as bad now.

Walking into the kitchen, he discovered that his dad had already perked a full pot of coffee. Odell had not realized Daddy was up and must've taken some to his and Mama's room. There were two things that his father always seemed to have in his possession when awake, a cigarette and a cup of coffee.

Odell didn't always drink the brew but decided to fix one now that his stomach seemed to be settled. It was still too early in the morning to be thinking about eating breakfast, and before his dad went to work, perhaps they could talk for a few minutes. Odell felt like he needed a little parental counseling.

He got out a ceramic cup that was chipped on the opposite side of where he would drink from and poured it three-quarters full of the steaming black beverage. His dad always used two teaspoons of granulated sugar and close to the same ratio of milk to coffee in the concoction that would be consumed all day long even in summertime. Odell only used a pinch of sugar and just a splash of milk.

Going back into the den, Odell sat on the plush sectional sofa at one end where a small table was located while setting the cup on a nearby coaster. He sipped his coffee while waiting on his father to come back through the home. The house was quiet except for the light snoring of his brothers, but Odell knew his parents had to be getting ready for their work shifts. He had noticed Mom had already fixed biscuits and they were in the fridge when he got the milk for his coffee.

Dressed in her work uniform, his mother hurried from the hallway into the den. After glancing at the wall clock, she turned toward Odell.

"Everything okay?" she asked.

"Yes, ma'am. My stomach was upset when I woke up but seems okay now."

"Good. I know y'all have a game today. Sorry I won't be able to make it, but Sandy's parents are going to help get y'all get to the field and back. Win it for me," she said smiling.

"We'll do our best," said Odell returning the smile.

As she left through the back door, Odell's father came into the den with a lit cigarette hanging from the corner of his mouth. He held a mug in one hand and a newspaper in the other. Sitting in his recliner across from where Odell sat, he blew smoke out of his nose and then stubbed out the remainder of the cigarette in a pedestal ashtray located next to the chair.

"Your mama said you've got a game today at 2:00. They any good?"

"Yes, sir, we're playing the Boys Club this afternoon. I'm not sure how good they are, but the standings I saw in yesterday's paper showed them in third place with two losses. I'm not too worried. I think I played with some of their guys in Little League or maybe in elementary school," replied Odell.

His dad opened the newspaper while slurping coffee. He had a way of making his favored drink sound like the best beverage on the planet. Odell didn't want to bother him before work and while he was relaxing but wasn't sure when he might get another chance.

"Uh, Daddy. Can I ask you something?"

The father dropped what he was reading which signaled he was listening. Odell really didn't know where to start the conversation.

"When you were my age, did you ever get into any fights?" Odell asked tentatively.

"Once or twice, nothing too serious, why?"

"I'm not certain, but I think somebody Kat knows may have tripped me at Durr's Saturday night on purpose. I need to find out why he did it, but I've got a feeling it's because she's my girlfriend. I'm thinking I might end up in a fight with him."

The elder Sterling took another gulp from his mug and frowned before speaking. Odell noted that his dad's eyes had narrowed a bit, which usually foreshadowed some amount of anger.

"I've told you before that getting into fights ain't a good idea. It's trouble you should avoid unless you need to defend yourself or maybe your brothers. Sounds to me like you want to start something with somebody you don't even know, over a reason you ain't even sure about."

"Yes, sir. I remember what you've told me. It's just Kat is really important, and if this guy meant to trip and hurt me, he also caused her to fall, too. Thankfully, Kat wasn't injured, but she could've been," Odell responded.

His father finished the coffee he was drinking and went silently into the adjoining kitchen. The sounds of pouring another cup, stirring in sugar, opening the refrigerator to add milk and then the spoon tinkling against the mug was familiar to Odell.

When his dad returned to the den and set down the drink, he had a furrowed brow. He sat down heavily causing the leather recliner to squeak. Pulling an opened pack of Phillip Morris Commanders from the pocket of his work shirt, he shook out one and then tapped it against his silver lighter. The ritual only heightened the tension Odell was already feeling before beginning the conversation.

"I know you like this girl a lot," his dad said and then paused. "I'm pretty sure from how much you've been hanging around her and how y'all act together, that she probably feels the same way about you. She's not family, so I'm not exactly sure if it's your responsibility to defend her, but I think I understand what could be going on in this situation," he said and hesitated again.

"Jealousy can be dangerous, Odell. I've seen it cause people to do bad things. Just because somebody might be feeling that way toward you doesn't mean you should necessarily be suspicious about them."

Odell pondered his father's words and had to agree. He still didn't know what to do, however.

"What if I find out the guy tripped me on purpose? What should I do if he confronts me?"

"Like I've told you before about any decisions you have, use your brain first. If you find yourself in a situation that makes it necessary, my advice is to fight to win. Make that first punch count and make it hurt enough that the other guy wants to quit. As far as I'm concerned, there's no such thing as a fair fight," said Odell's dad.

Finishing his cigarette and then slurping the last of his coffee, the man got out of his chair and went into the kitchen. Soon bacon was frying in the cast-iron skillet that was the most used cooking pan in the house. The smell that would shortly wake everybody else up began permeating throughout the house.

Before his brothers got up, Odell went into the kitchen with his dad. He watched as the lanky man flipped the sizzling meat with a fork and then placed it on a plate lined with paper towels so the grease could drain. His dad was an expert at getting the bacon just the right amount of crispy.

"Thanks for the advice, Daddy."

"Yeah, no problem. I know you'll do the right thing. Now, you want your eggs scrambled or fried?"

Odell knew by the tone; his father was through with their conversation. He smiled to himself since the man was occupied with getting breakfast ready for the rest of the family before he headed to his job. It was just another example of his parents' love for them that was expressed in ways others might not understand.

"I'm good with whatever you want this morning, Daddy," Odell replied.

"Alright, then. Over-easy for me and over-medium for you. Get the eggs out, and it won't take but a minute or two with this hot grease," his dad said without turning around.

Odell complied, as he always tried to do.

CHAPTER 19

After the morning meal was completed and the dishes were washed, dried and placed back in the cabinet, Odell dressed in his usual cap, shorts, tee shirt and tennis shoes that he wore when cutting grass. He got the library book to loan Kat and then checked the mower to make sure the gas tank was full before heading to her house.

He felt somewhat more clear-headed after talking with his father. Odell would trust his instincts in dealing with what he might face in the future. The main problem in his mind was so much that was going on this summer involved stuff that he had never dealt with before.

I've only dreamed about having a steady girlfriend before now. These emotions I'm feeling are new to me. I've got to be smart and not let them tear me up so much, he thought.

Mr. Norman's truck was in the driveway upon Odell's arrival and he assumed Kat's dad was at home. Odell walked up the steps to the front door and knocked lightly hoping they were awake. He didn't want to take any chances about starting up the mower if they were still in bed.

Kat opened both the wooden and screened doors and immediately the Normans' dog came running outside where Odell stood on the stoop. It was a small terrier mix that had warmed to Odell since he became a regular visitor, probably due to him bringing the pet treats on occasion.

"Hey, Madi. How 'ya doing this morning?" said Odell.

She sat on her haunches, raised her front paws and then began pumping them up and down. There was an eager look on her cute face indicating she wanted Odell to pick her up.

When he complied with her begging, the dog began licking his face. Odell couldn't help laughing at the shown affection. It was all he could do to keep from dropping the book in one hand while holding the squirming animal in his other arm.

"I think Madi loves you more than any of us," said Kat as she came outside to join them.

"Love's a strong word," replied Odell looking into Madi's eyes before Kat's.

Kat smiled and nodded. "Yeah, it is, but some show affection more than others," she said.

Odell put the pet down and reached into the right pocket of his shorts. He took out a half-piece of leftover bacon from breakfast that had been wrapped in a piece of paper towel. Immediately, a more desperate version of the dance Madi had performed moments before began again. Odell removed the meat and gave it to the dog.

She was gone in a flash through the still open front door of the house.

The two teens stood looking at one another for a moment without speaking. Odell handed the novel to Kat and said, "It's not due back until Friday, but I think you won't have any trouble finishing it by then."

"Thanks, I'll make sure it's not returned late."

"Are your parents up? I was going to cut the grass before it gets too hot, if it's okay."

"Daddy's not here. He hitched a ride with one of the other guys he works with. That's why his truck is in the driveway. Mom's awake, so it's fine to do the yard. Don't you have a game today?" Kat asked.

"Yeah, it's at two o'clock, so I've got enough time to get this done," he replied looking around the yard.

He then continued, "You had said you might want to come to a game. Think you could today?"

"As a matter of fact, Mom's already told me that we would if you wanted us to. Some of you could pile in the back of the truck if you need a way to get there."

"That's great. We're always scrambling for rides. Sometimes a couple of the smaller guys even have to sit in a lap," said Odell with a grin.

Odell tipped the brim of his cap toward Kat and hurried down the steps two at a time. In no time, he had started the task at hand. As the lawn mower growled and he circled the now familiar yard, Odell began feeling more confident about Kat's thoughts about him. *Why else would she want to see him play?* He thought. Excitement was building at the prospects of showing off his skills on the field in front of her.

After finishing the job in record time, Odell declined payment from Kat's mother citing her offer to drive some of the team later that day as more than sufficient. Mrs. Norman had appeared pleased with the teen's bargain, and they had agreed the Renegades that would be traveling with her should be at her house by 12:45 in order to make it to the park in plenty of time.

***

A total of six members of the team were in the bed of the turquoise and white Chevy pickup truck as they chugged to Macon Memorial Park. Odell sat in the corner directly behind the driver's seat so that he could look at Kat sitting in the passenger side of the vehicle. Periodically the two of them had their eyes lock in a gaze of unspoken emotions. He couldn't hear the conversation between Kat and her mother but could tell it must be funny since Kat laughed several times.

The mood of the guys in the back was jovial, too. The Smith brothers were used to riding there since their dad was an independent floor installer with a similar truck used in his business. The Sterling siblings had only ridden like this a couple of times and thought it was a treat as did Mitchell who had his usual chatterbox going while doing Red Skelton routines.

Clem Kadiddlehopper was his favorite Skelton character, and Mitch could always elicit laughs with his renditions. As laughter subsided, Dewey broke up

the mood when he punched Billy on his shoulder. They sat in the rear of the bed and had been picking at one another since the group decided who would be included as passengers.

"Yeah, the only one stupider than Clem is Billy," Dewey sneered.

"Stupider ain't even a word, dumbass," replied Billy and struck his brother in retaliation.

Dewey's freckled face turned red and a fight was near, Odell thought. At that moment some bad spot in the asphalt road caused the truck to bounce. The boys' butts did likewise which gave sensations not unlike a fair ride. It was exhilarating and a little scary at the same time.

"Whoa, mule!" exclaimed Mitch.

The teammates started laughing again, and the Smiths settled down their tensions as well. They were soon pulling into the park and climbing out of the vehicle. Dewey, Billy, Mitch, Kenny and Wayne all headed down an eroded slope carrying their gloves and other equipment. Odell lingered after removing himself from the corner where he sat so that he could speak to Kat.

"Sorry about that hard bump," said Mrs. Norman as she got outside.

"No problem, everybody's fine. You can tell how fast they left," replied Odell.

"Good, it's just why I worry sometimes about letting people ride in the back. I wouldn't be surprised for it to be illegal one day. You and Kat go ahead, I'll be down in a little while," she finished.

Odell and Kat took a similar path toward the field at a much slower pace. He wore his prized Mickey Mantle glove on his left hand and was a little surprised when Kat took his right hand as they walked.

"I'm glad you came. Hope I don't disappoint," said Odell.

"Happy to be here. I've been worried that you wouldn't want me to after yesterday," Kat replied.

He stopped walking and turned to face her. Odell thought about kissing her but knew this wasn't a good time or place to be seen doing that.

"I've been thinking a lot about what happened. I don't blame you at all. I was hurt that you hadn't told me about Phillip Jackson, but I think I'm starting to understand. I don't want to lose you. I think I lo…"

"Odell, hurry up," shouted Johnny.

Odell glanced to see their coach motioning him to the dugout. He then turned back to Kat. Before he could continue, she said, "I think I do, too."

She gave him a quick peck on the cheek. "Go win this game and we'll talk later."

As Odell ran to their side of the field, Johnny was pacing back and forth impatiently wringing his hands. He had a habit of squeezing them together when he was nervous that often sounded like squishy farts.

"Look at their pitcher," Johnny pointed to the guy warming up on the other side.

Odell turned to see a tall left-hander slinging balls side-armed causing audible pops as they landed into the catcher's mitt. Odell recognized him as a kid he had faced once before when they both played in the Macon Elementary school league.

"I've played against him before two or three years ago. He's definitely gotten taller since the last time I saw him. I think his name is Louie something," said Odell.

"We haven't faced a lefty, yet. He's big and fast. Looks menacing to me. I'm not sure we can hit him," fretted Johnny.

Odell studied the opposing pitcher's windup and delivery. While his control was not the best, he didn't seem to be overly wild and everything Odell witnessed seemed pretty straight. The two pitches that he tried to curve bounced in front of the catcher and by him.

"I don't think he'll be throwing too many breaking pitches. You're probably right that some of our guys will be scared of him, but really, it's just a matter of timing the speed since he's around the plate. We'll be okay, Johnny."

The rest of the Renegades were tossing practice balls back and forth as Odell found Mitch putting on catcher's equipment that actually belonged to Kenny. Mitch had turned into a decent player behind the plate, and it had allowed Odell's brother the opportunity to play shortstop in every game of the season. Given his choice, Odell would've preferred Kenny as his catcher, but it had worked out so far.

"Let me throw a few, Mitch. I don't think I'll need to warmup very much. I'm feeling pretty loose," said Odell.

He threw about a dozen pitches mixing up fastballs and curves to Mitch with his usual windup and three-quarter delivery. Then Odell told Mitch that he was going to try something he had been toying around with Kenny in the backyard. He tried the next few balls coming around his side, much like the Boys Club pitcher was doing on the other side of the field. Odell was pleased that his control seemed to be good with that delivery and it seemed his breaking pitches broke even more that way.

Odell walked with Mitch to their bench, placed his arm around the younger teen and spoke softly, "I may try the new pitches at some point in the game. If I do, watch for me giving you a sign that they're coming. I'll touch my left knee with my glove when I'm ready."

The same umpiring crew that the team had now seen several times were on the field again. The older overweight guy called for them to "play ball," and the Boys Club gang ran onto the hard clay while the Renegades gathered behind the wire of their dugout.

Odell made eye contact with everybody one by one. He saw apprehension in the youngest boys' faces and even on a few of the older teens. He needed to calm them down.

"Okay, listen up. Some of y'all are going to be nervous against their pitcher. I know left-handers can be scary, but we can score if you're smart. This is what we're going to do today, at least for the first time around in the batting order. Get as far back in the box as you can. Take a pitch or two so you can get used to the speed. If you think you can make contact, swing level. If you don't think you can hit him, bunt. Y'all have been practicing getting the ball down, and I don't believe they'll expect it. Even if you're not fast like Mitch or Sandy, you'll at least have a chance to get on base or move somebody else to another base. Let's go, Renegades!"

Mitch, as leadoff, followed the strategy to a tee. On the third pitch of the game, he laid one down the line and advanced all the way around to third on a wild throw from their third baseman. Sandy, who had been moved up to the second spot for this game, followed with another perfect bunt scoring Mitch and making it easily to first.

Their pitcher looked disgusted and didn't pay close attention to the runner on first. Sandy took off on the very first pitch to Kenny and stole second base without a throw by their catcher.

Kenny then chopped an infield hit to deep short that advanced Sandy to third. With runners on the corners and nobody out, Odell was up to bat. This was the kind of situation he longed for anytime he played baseball.

Before stepping in the batter's box, Odell looked behind the screened backstop and found Kat and her mother a few rows up in the covered seats. There were only a few spectators, and he could hear their cheers clearly. He tuned them out focusing on the pitcher instead. The guy was definitely not happy now evidenced by him talking to himself.

Taking his stance, he expected to see something on the outside part of the plate. If that happened and was over the plate, he was going to swing. It didn't occur on the first throw as the lefty attempted the curve Odell had seen before the game started. It got by the catcher enough that Kenny moved to second but not enough for Sandy to come home.

Odell thought that if he were in the position that his opponent found himself in, I'd walk me intentionally. The other pitcher must've been thinking about it because the next pitch was outside.

With the count now two balls and no strikes, Odell figured the next throw would be outside again probably in hope Odell would swing at a bad pitch. As the windup began, Odell shifted as close to the plate without standing on it as he could and was ready when the otherwise unhittable pitch was made. The sharp crack of the bat when it made contact sounded sweet to Odell's ears. The ball bulleted over the second baseman's head into the right-center gap and Odell had another homer as it kept rolling.

Now the cheering was much more indistinguishable as the rout was on when Odell crossed the plate. Of all the grins around him, though, Kat's from the stands was the one that meant the most.

CHAPTER 20

Odell and Kenny were in the cramped den along with his brother's friend, Craig, playing a few tunes. Craig had his drum kit set up in the middle of the room since that was the only spot where it would fit. The Sterling brothers shared a single amplifier where their identical Fender Mustang guitars were plugged into along with their only microphone. It was far from an ideal setup, but it was the only option available.

The three of them had played off and on together for the last year or so and could get through about fifteen songs with some degree of competence. Neither Odell nor Kenny thought of themselves as great musicians. Likewise, the two of them didn't like their voices very much, but somebody had to do it when they got together, so each would sing certain songs they played.

The activity brought lots of laughter to the three teens as they often butchered versions of songs made popular by groups like The Rolling Stones, Young Rascals, The Monkees and The Beatles. They tried to stick to music using simple chords that Odell felt comfortable playing rhythm on while Kenny was much better picking the lead parts in the chosen songs.

There were several good local bands in the area where they lived, and some of the most talented performers attended the same South Macon high school. Those groups would play at skating rink dances called "sock hops" because the participants were required to remove their shoes so as not to damage the floor. They would also play at other large venues catering to younger crowds.

Odell and Kenny knew that their skill levels were nowhere near those bands and held no illusions that they ever would, but it was fun to get together and play, or at least attempt. However, there was another reason they were practicing today. Odell's and Kenny's mother had told them that her hairdresser, Rowena, was having a birthday party the following Friday night, and she was willing to pay them five dollars each to play for an hour and a half. Since a birthday party didn't seem that big or threatening, the boys decided to accept.

"What do you know about this party?" asked Craig when they finished practicing *Twist and Shout.*

"Mama said this is the girl who cuts and styles her hair. She's turning twenty-one and throwing herself a party to celebrate. Her name is Rowena," replied Odell.

"Yeah, she was over here a few weeks ago and heard me and Odie practicing. She told us we sounded pretty good. Never thought anything else about it 'til Mama asked would be interested playing at the party," Kenny added.

"Strange name," said Craig pausing then added, "Sounds like Raw Weenie," and then struck the drums with a ba-dum-tss that ended with a strike of the cymbals.

They all howled with laughter at Craig's rimshot. Odell wished he could figure out a way to get it into the upcoming party, but quickly decided that wouldn't be something teenagers should do in front of adults.

"Or it could be what her boyfriend might have at the end of the night," said Craig followed by another rimshot with an even louder cymbal hit at the end of the punchline.

After they quit laughing, the three broke into another song that ended abruptly when feedback developed through the amp. "I hope that doesn't happen when we're playing at the gig," said Odell.

"Me, too. That would be embarrassing," Kenny added.

Their mother came into the room as the session broke down. She was always encouraging them, but Odell wondered what she really thought about her sons playing. He hoped she didn't hear Craig's comment about Rowena's boyfriend.

"You boys are sounding good. It's not Ricky Nelson, though," she said smiling.

Odell wondered why she loved the old television show star so much. Her tastes were totally different from his father's love of classic country music. Odell didn't care for either very much, but he preferred Mom's taste over Daddy's.

"Thanks, Mama. Maybe we'll try to learn one of his songs, but they're kinda old now. By chance, do you know how many people are invited to the party?" replied Odell.

"He's not that old, and I'd bet most of the guests would like to hear some of Ricky's music. Rowena, and that's the correct pronunciation," she paused and looked at Craig with a frown, "told me that it would just be about twenty or thirty people coming. They should be around the same age as she is."

"You know, Mama's got a point. Since the crowd will be a little older than us, they might like more stuff from a few years ago," said Kenny.

Odell thought about it a moment and realized his mother and brother were more than likely right. He had assumed everybody would just like their choice of music.

"I think y'all are right. How about this one we haven't played in a while?"

Odell started playing the intro to *Hi Heel Sneakers* and Kenny jumped in with his riff. Craig laid down a steady beat and they stretched the song for a few minutes with Odell singing the tune.

When they finished, all three shook their heads up and down in agreement. This would be their opening song at the party.

CHAPTER 21

Kat completed the list of chores her mother had given her that involved cleaning the whole house including the floors, changing and washing the sheets and sweeping off the front stoop. It had been a lot more than she usually was assigned to do because Mom had taken a part-time job and was not at home to help her. *Being an only kid has its pros and cons,* she thought.

She didn't mind being alone most of the time. Having a sister or a brother for company would've been alright with her and remembered one time when she was a lot younger asking her mother when one might come along. The memory of Mom telling her that would never happen caused a brief sadness. It had been the first time Kat had ever seen her mother cry and resulted in her never questioning the lack of a sibling in the family again.

She sat sideways with her shapely legs draped over an arm of the chair and her back resting against the other padded side. Kat preferred sitting in the overstuffed chair like that since it let the natural light of the room provide a clear view of the activity she was enjoying since finishing her work.

Kat was reading the book Odell had brought her earlier in the week. She thought he had been right about it and nearing the end, she was also liking the story. It was relatable on some levels to the current time in their lives. She thought her present age had to be the most difficult time of her young life so far, and she knew Odell felt the same way.

Madi was sleeping on an oval braided rug covering the hardwood floor near the open front door. Since the screen door was latched shut, she couldn't escape as she would've tried if it magically opened. It was a favorite spot for the spoiled pet who spent most of her time inside the house. She loved to go outside but had to be confined by a leash when she was allowed to do so.

A small oscillating fan swung slowly back and forth shifting the warm air inside the sunlit room. Even dressed in cutoffs and a cropped cotton top with bare feet dangling, it felt steamy inside the enclosed space. When the lone telephone rang, it reverberated around the small area and startled both Madi and Kat causing them to jump involuntarily. Kat stuck her bookmark inside, closed the novel and made it to the phone on the third ring.

"Hello," Kat answered pleasantly.

There was no response on the line. After a few seconds of silence, Kat's next hello was more of a question than a greeting.

"Hello?"

This time she heard some heavy breathing coming through into her ear. It sounded as if the caller was almost in some distress, and she became concerned.

"Is anyone there? Can I help you?" she asked after a few seconds.

There was a moan and then the phoneline went dead. Kat stood bewildered holding the handset. She guessed it must've been a wrong number before hanging up. Kat hoped the caller was alright.

Madi now stood below Kat with her head cocked to one side. The dog glanced at the front door and then immediately back to the teen giving the signal she wanted to go outside.

Kat laughed and said, "You want to go outside? Okay, get your leash."

Madi's paws skidded across the recently polished floor as she hurried to the door. Her leather leash hung from a mount close by, and she started panting with excitement when Kat hooked it to her collar. Kat slipped on her flip-flops that were also stored near the entrance of the house.

She pulled the door closed behind her as she went outside never thinking for a moment to lock it. Such was the practice of everybody she knew in the neighborhood. Kat didn't intend to go very far or be out for long.

Madi had a favorite spot of grass near the end of the driveway where she always tinkled, and that's where the pet led Kat. She tugged with persistence until reaching her "bathroom" where she squatted and did her business. Kat looked down the road toward the Sterling house and couldn't make out many details because of the distance. The summer heat was evident by a shimmering wave heading skyward from the asphalt road.

Almost as if the dog was sniffing out her boyfriend's whereabouts or was following Kat's gaze, Madi started in that direction at a brisk pace. Kat let her lead the way and figured she would soon tire and want to go back inside their house. It was surprising when the two of them ended up in front of Odell's home ten minutes later.

Kat could hear music coming from inside the residence and realized that Odell and his brother were the cause. He had talked about playing a guitar occasionally, but she had never heard him play. She stood listening for a minute as they finished the song. She thought it sounded a little rough, but not the worst she had ever heard.

Glancing down at Madi, she could see the pet was panting with her tongue hanging out. Kat reached down and picked her up.

"You need some water, girl. You've never walked this far," Kat said.

Walking around the side of the carport to the backyard of the house, Kat saw several younger boys playing outside. She recognized Odell's two youngest brothers, Wayne and Lynn, and another smaller kid who had played in the game she had watched earlier in the week. She thought his name was Sandy, but that's not what he was being called.

"Run, Poochie!" called out Wayne.

Sandy, or Poochie, was dodging and darting around a few of the others from the rear of the yard heading toward the back of the house. He held a nasty looking piece of cloth in one hand and sported a big grin as he stopped near where Kat stood watching.

"We win!" he exclaimed.

Madi growled in Kat's arms as the boy approached them. He waved the dirty material at the other kids in the yard in what Kat thought must be some victory dance.

"Will she bite? Can I pet it?" he asked in quick succession.

Kat responded, "Not usually, but be gentle."

The boy reached out tentatively as Madi watched warily. As he rubbed her back, the dog seemed to relax in Kat's arms, but the panting kept on going.

"She needs a little water. Can you get her some?"

As the rest of the kids started to gather around Kat, Sandy hurried to a spigot located midway of the house. There was a green rubber hose fastened there along with an old pewter pan laying on the ground nearby that he filled with water from the faucet. Hurrying back, he held out the container.

"Pooch, that's our water pot," said one of the other boys as Madi started lapping from it.

"I'll rinse it out later. Besides, everybody drinks from the hose anyway," Sandy replied.

Kat let Madi down still attached to the leash, and after a moment she was sniffing at the surrounding boys. She seemed to accept the attention much more than Kat would've thought since her pet often barked relentlessly when exposed to strangers.

The back door opened, and Mrs. Sterling said, "Kat, come in and let me get you something cold to drink. The boys can watch your dog."

Kat passed the leash to Sandy who seemed to have a new canine friend. She then went inside to the kitchen where Odell's mother was getting ice cubes from a tray which was then put into a tumbler.

"Sweet tea okay?" she asked.

"Yes, ma'am. Thank you."

The sounds of loud laughter coming from the den was followed by a voice Kat hadn't heard before. "I've got to get home, you guys. Dad will be here any minute to pick me up."

"Okay, we'll help get your stuff outside," Kat heard Odell say.

In a moment, Odell appeared in the doorway between the two rooms carrying a tom-tom. Surprise showed on his face when he saw Kat standing in the kitchen. Kenny stood directly behind him with a snare drum in one hand and cymbals in the other.

"Uh, hey. Didn't know you were here," he said.

Kat smiled and took a swallow of her drink. "I was in the neighborhood and just dropped by to see where the music was coming from."

Odell's face flushed, and Kat knew he probably felt embarrassed. She hadn't meant to cause such a reaction and quickly followed with, "Let me get the door for you."

The two oldest Sterling boys took their loads outside to a small concrete patio as the last of the band trio came into the kitchen carrying the bass drum. Stopping in his tracks and letting out a short whistle, he looked up and down at Kat.

"Hey there, cutie. I'm Craig."

Now it was Kat's turn to feel embarrassment. Before she could respond, Odell's mom interrupted.

"Craig, this is Kathy Norman from up the road. Everybody calls her Kat. Just so you know, she and Odell have been dating this summer, so be respectful," she said.

"Yes, Mrs. Cleaver. You look beautiful today, as well," Craig said imitating Eddie Haskell from *Leave it to Beaver.*

He snickered and went through the doorway. Kat looked at Mrs. Sterling who stood shaking her head back in forth with a frown on her face.

"I don't know about that boy. He always has something to say and tries to be funny. Don't let him bother you, Kat," she said.

Kat shrugged and replied, "It's okay. Thanks for letting him know about me and Odell. I really appreciate you. You're special."

The woman patted Kat's arm and smiled at her. An unspoken moment of affection passed between them that was interrupted by ringing of the telephone. Mrs. Sterling excused herself and went to answer. Kat could tell from what she could hear of the conversation that the call might last for a while.

Kat finished her tea and went outside to see Madi running around unconnected from the leash which caused momentary concern. A few of the boys were chasing her but unable to catch the quick little animal. It appeared that Madi was grinning at their inability until she finally stopped, and Sandy picked her up.

"I want her on my team when we play capture the flag again," he said.

A station wagon driven by Craig's dad pulled into the yard and the band loaded the equipment into the rear of the vehicle. As soon as the car left, Odell walked over to Kat. He petted Madi as she now rested in the crook of Kat's left arm.

"She looks like she could use a nap," he said.

"Yeah, I should get her home. She walked farther than I've ever seen to get here," replied Kat.

"I'll walk back with you."

Kat and Odell strolled to her house taking turns carrying Madi. On the return trip he and Kat talked about upcoming plans including the birthday party. It was so easy to talk to this boy. The deepening feelings she had for him made Kat want to spend more and more time with him.

She told Odell about hearing part of the last song they had played and that she would like to hear them some time. Kat had thought she might invite Odell inside when they got to her house for a make out session, but those plans were dashed when she found her mom had gotten home.

Oh well, I'll plan better next time, she thought.

CHAPTER 22

The blonde-haired teenager studied himself in the mirror as he got ready for work. He spit out toothpaste into the sink careful not to leave any residue. His mother would fuss and complain if he didn't cleanup after himself, and he sure didn't want any of that drama. Sometimes, resentment over some trivial complaint she made against him would build up to the point that he wanted to punch something. He'd even put his fist through a bedroom wall one time which caused him to come up with some outrageous lie to excuse his actions. Phillip hated being nagged, and it could bring out his anger.

He used a comb to get the part on his head lined up, and then finished getting his hair in place with a soft-bristled brush. The hairstyle was popular among guys these days and the bangs he sported were a little shorter than he would've preferred. The manager at the grocery store where he worked part-time, however, would raise hell if he let the golden locks get any longer on his forehead, and he needed the job to maintain the car he drove.

Being sixteen was not bad at all when you had a hot car like he had. Not many guys had a Chevelle SS 396, and he knew how lucky he was to have a dad helping him out. Dad always told him he wanted his son to have things he never could've, but Phillip had to earn money to help pay for it.

It kind of pissed him off to have to depend on Dad so much, though. He dreamed constantly of getting through the next two years of high school and getting a real job instead of one that required him to wear a stupid white shirt with a clip-on tie like he had on right now. The first thing he would do when he got that job would be to go and tell his manager to stick that piece of cloth right up his ass. Time was going by too slowly, and he hated working in that friggin' store.

Phillip didn't have a real plan for finding work when he graduated from Dudley Hughes Vocational School. He just knew there was no way he would go to college because of how much he hated school. To his way of thinking, anybody who was busy trying to get good grades so they could, had to be stupid. You could be making money for at least four years while those idiots were still going to school.

Maybe he would go into a trade like his dad. He was always telling Phillip that he could get him into the apprenticeship program when he graduated. The only problem with that idea was his father might be working with him side by side, and Phillip wanted separation from both parents as soon as possible. There were other available trades he could check out, or maybe one of the local factories that paid well, too.

I need my own place, he thought. *I'm tired of people telling me what to do, and I'm sick and damned tired of people who think they're better than me.*

He could feel that resentment rising inside him again. It could make him do stuff sometimes that he wished he hadn't done later on. But really, it was all their fault, not his.

Just like that bitch, Kat. She's a prick tease and thinks she's so much better than me. Probably that new boyfriend does, too. No matter, I can beat his goody-goody ass any time I want to.

Phillip remembered seeing them fall at the skating rink and laughed to himself again. He hadn't planned on doing that, but after seeing them there together, it seemed like something he ought to do to pay back the teasing little bitch. It had been easy to trip them.

Since that night, he'd found out the guy lived right down the road from Kat. Phillip wondered if Odell fantasized about her like he did.

Probably not. He looks like a candy ass.

CHAPTER 23

Odell and Kat were alone. He couldn't believe how it had worked out, but he was in her bed. Odell was so nervous and excited as their foreplay was heating up.

He had been dreaming about this moment almost since he had met this girl. Kat was cute for sure, but she had many other qualities that made her attractive.

Odell didn't think of himself as necessarily special. He knew that he was pretty smart, though. Kat was the same way and so easy to talk to. The many conversations they had shared over this summer showed him that.

Thoughts jumbled around his head in a disjointed fashion. One minute he knew this was crazy and wrong. The next, it felt so right. A kaleidoscope of emotions full of color circulated throughout his mind and body.

Their bodies moved in unison while all this took place. He had to stop soon, or it would be too late. There was no slowing down at this point, though.

When the release occurred a moment later, there was panic. What had he done?

That's when Odell woke up from the dream. He felt the stickiness in his underwear that was seeping into the gym shorts he slept in.

Oh, crap!

He slung the cotton sheet that covered his body off him afraid the mess in his britches would spread everywhere. It felt like the climax just experienced was still going on.

What a mess! I've got to clean up now, he thought.

Odell got off the bed and felt shaky. His knees wobbled as he headed to the bathroom. On the way, he grabbed clean underwear and another pair of shorts from the chest of drawers in his and Kenny's room. His brother didn't seem to notice as Odell left the room.

As he went into the short hallway to the bathroom, he passed Wayne and Lynn's bedroom and heard their soft snores. All he could hear from his parents' room was the hum of their air conditioner. He wasn't sure what time it was, but knew it had to be early.

Odell silently closed the door and turned on the light. Sliding off the garments, it seemed there had been an explosion in them. This had only happened once before, and he was embarrassed.

Running the water in the sink, he began to clean himself. He felt tears form in his eyes, and the guilt started.

Is this normal?

He had read something about what other guys called wet dreams. Odell had learned the term nocturnal emissions from one of Mike's men's magazines when he was at his house maybe a year ago. The close friend always seemed to know more than Odell did about such issues, so he had gone to Mike's house to find out what he knew on the subject.

Odell had told his friend about the first occurrence and had asked him the same question. Mike had told him that there was not anything abnormal about it, but Odell didn't know whether to believe what he said or not. Since he saw it in print, he thought maybe it was okay.

Odell had experienced self-pleasuring, but this was different. It was involuntary and not planned. He was just so confused about all that he had been going through the last year or two since reaching puberty. And he really didn't want to talk about it with anyone, not even Mike.

He changed into the fresh clothing and left the bathroom. He passed through the den glancing at the clock. Three o'clock on the nose. Silently as he could manage, he went out the back door and to the outside storage room where the washer and dryer were located.

Odell decided that he would go ahead and put the soiled clothing in the washer, and maybe in the morning add some other dirty stuff. He sometimes washed a load whenever his mom asked him, and this wouldn't seem weird if he cleaned some clothes.

Going back inside the house, he didn't feel sleepy, although he'd only been asleep for a few hours. The tv wasn't an option because the signal wouldn't come back on for a while. He currently didn't have a book to read, so he sat down on the couch to think.

You could always think better if not distracted. That's what came to mind. He decided there was a lot to contemplate based on the dreams he had just experienced.

He grabbed a small pillow and rested his head. Immediately his thoughts drifted to Kat.

Odell knew they were too young to be involved in what he'd dreamed about tonight. It didn't mean he didn't want to, as evidenced by the fantasy. It was just frustrating and added to the tension felt.

Were there options? Maybe, he thought.

CHAPTER 24

Saturday promised to be a fun day. Odell had come up with an idea to spend it with Kat after his personal disaster that happened the night before. It required parental consent from their respective mothers, but that had been getting easier to do after several dates they had been on together.

The plan was to catch a city bus at the stop located down the road near the Mini-Market and travel to either the Westgate Mall or to downtown. The route could take them either place, and then they would ride back after spending the day together. They could get lunch somewhere and maybe do some shopping or catch another movie. Maybe they could go to the Washington Library, too. Either choice was fine with Odell because he would be alone with Kat and they wouldn't have to depend on a parent driving them. Odell loved his parents but thought they might cramp his style in his attempt to be alone with his girlfriend.

His mother was obviously not keen on the idea at first for two stated reasons. First, she had said Odell didn't need to ride the bus because she was available to take them wherever the two wanted to go. That mode of transport was for people who didn't have other means and there were safety concerns, she had told him. Odell had thanked her for the offer but countered the argument by telling her that adventure was part of the date and many people used the system every day.

Second, she said that the date was too vague in the planning. He agreed and then tried to comply with that concern. After Odell checked to see what movies were playing, he ditched that idea as part of the date and thought more about what they could do to assuage those doubts. He settled on making the outing more of a lunch date at the Nu-Way on Cotton Avenue and then include window shopping at some stores downtown. Odell assured his mother they would be home by mid-afternoon, and she finally said he could go if Kat's mother allowed her.

Odell had followed up by calling Kat's house and speaking to Mrs. Norman. He told her of the plans and made the same promises. She somewhat surprisingly gave permission without resistance, and now Odell and Kat were awaiting the bus to pick them up.

"I've never ridden on a city bus before, have you?" Kat asked.

"No, and it didn't look like I would today either. I had to really convince Mom we would be safe. I just thought this could be an adventure for both of us without a chaperone," replied Odell.

"Yeah, I agree. You amaze me with how you come up with opportunities for us to get together, my smart boyfriend," she said while cupping her hand on his cheek.

The public show of affection caused Odell's face to flush. He liked her touch, but he was uncomfortable what others might think. He glanced around to see an older woman sitting on a nearby bench eyeing the couple. Odell recognized her as one of his customers and couldn't tell from her appearance whether she approved of the behavior.

"Uh, hey Mrs. Wilson. Are you waiting on the bus?" he asked.

"That's why I'm sitting on this hard-ass bench. Can't think of another reason I'd be here," she replied.

Odell laughed at her plain speech. He knew she didn't mince words based on previous encounters with her when he took care of her lawn. She had once told Odell that he should watch out for dog shit while doing the job because the neighbor down the street had a large canine that thought her yard was its personal commode.

"Sorry if I offended, Mrs. Wilson. Let me introduce my friend, Kathy Norman. She lives up the road. This is one of my customers who lives just over there, Mrs. Georgia Wilson," said Odell while pointing toward a house a few doors down and across the road.

"Nice to meet you, Mrs. Wilson. Please call me Kat, everybody else does," said Kat with a smile.

The older woman's wrinkled face cracked as Odell saw a grin appear for the first time since he had met her. It was an indication that she was someone other than the dour lady he had always thought of her as.

"I like your name, young 'un. And you're polite like the boy, too. Not all kids today are, you know. I heard what y'all were talking about, and I'll give you a few pointers about riding the city bus. Since you've been introduced as a friend, and you're a girl, I'm guessing you're Odell's girlfriend, right?"

Kat glanced at Odell and with some hesitation responded, "Yes, ma'am. We've been going steady for a couple of months now, since the first of the summer."

"Good for you both. Enjoy yourselves while you can because life can beat you down the older you get. Now, just a little bit about public transportation. Either one of you bothered by colored people?"

Odell thought for a moment and replied, "No, ma'am. They're people like us, just a different color, right? I had a few on my paper route last year, and they treated me nice."

"That kind of talk might cause you some trouble with a lot of folks, not with me though. The reason I asked is there's a good portion of the riders who'll be colored, or black, as they like to call themselves nowadays. Since I don't have a problem, I don't mind at all riding with them. I just wanted to make sure y'all don't," she said earnestly.

Kat who had stood listening without responding interjected, "I feel the same as Odell. I know plenty of others who hate simply based on skin color, but I'm not one of them."

Odell could see the bus approaching in the distance. Dark smoke billowed behind the lumbering vehicle.

Mrs. Wilson looked at the teen couple and had a twinkle in her eyes. As the bus pulled up, she said, "You young 'uns have made my day. For an old woman born in 1900, sixty-seven years ago, y'all give me hope for the future."

***

Odell and Kat wandered down Cherry Street holding hands and stopping to look in windows when something caught their attention. Westgate Mall had cut some into the businesses downtown so that it was not quite as crowded, but it was still fun to walk on the sidewalks and take in the sights. Mainly, Odell was enjoying the time alone with his girl.

The ride had been a new experience for them both. As all buses were to Odell, it was bumpy and loud, but it served their purpose well. They had sat near Mrs. Wilson who chatted the whole time until she got off at the mall so she could go to Newberry's, a retail store that carried a little bit of everything. Before she got off, Odell had promised he would be back to her house next week to take care of her yard.

Lunch had been at his favorite place, Nu-Way Weiners on Cotton Avenue. It was an iconic place with its misspelled name, soft drinks over shaved ice, and the best chili dogs imaginable. You could order them all the way served in soft buns, with slaw or even scrambled. There was no way you could eat just one, and their slogan was, *I'd go a long way for a Nu-Way.*

The two of them had sat and eaten their meal while listening to music on the jukebox that allowed you to pick songs while remaining in your booth. You could flip through the song choices and put coins in the machine to pay for them without getting up.

Odell and Kat had shared an order of crispy crinkle-cut fries with their dogs and took turns dunking them in ketchup squirted on the ceramic saucer on which they were served. Kat laughed at him when he got the dark red sauce on his chin, but he didn't care. It had been funny to him, too.

Afterwards, the two of them walked around town taking in the sights and sounds. As they went near the courthouse, Odell wondered how it would be to work there one day. It was like a brief premonition of things to come that he didn't comment on at that moment.

When, however, they passed by Thorpe's, a men's clothing store and Odell admired the well-dressed mannequins, he mentioned to Kat that maybe one day he would be wearing such a suit. He told her since his parents thought he might become a lawyer, such clothing would be needed. She agreed that could happen, because he seemed to be able to articulate arguments effectively and was able to get his point across to others. Odell had told her that he didn't have a clue what he might want to do, but he did like Perry Mason.

As the couple approached the corner of Cherry and Third streets where the Dempsey was located, Odell spotted an empty bench. They sat down on the metal structure and relaxed.

"This has been so much fun, Odell," Kat said.

"Yeah, I guess we need to head home in a little while. I don't want our parents worrying. They really have been great letting us go places together. I'll just be glad when I can drive so we will go on real dates. I think the first place we'll go is to a drive-in movie," replied Odell with his eyebrows moving up and down like Groucho Marx.

Kat laughed at the funny gesture and responded with seriousness in her voice. She looked directly into his eyes. "Don't get me wrong because I'd love being old enough to do that, too, but I count today a "real date."

She continued, "We've only got about a month before school starts and then we won't have time to do things like this. Something tells me this summer is going to always be special to us. I mean, it already has been for me. I've never felt like this before, and it's all because of you, Odell. Thanks for making this memory."

Kat then gently kissed Odell with her eyes shut. For some reason, he left his eyes open and watched the tender moment. He was convinced at that second that she was falling in love with him as he was with her.

CHAPTER 25

The four Sterling boys were home alone the following Monday morning slouching on the couch in the den. They had eaten their breakfast biscuits, and each had cleaned their own dishes.

The television had just been turned off after watching Captain Kangaroo. The older kids had endured the long-running show mainly because Lynn, the youngest brother, still liked it. Odell had to admit, however, he still laughed at some of the characters he'd followed since he was Lynn's age. It always tickled him when Mr. Green Jeans cracked up the title character.

Odell enjoyed these times with his brothers. Only six years separated the four of them, oldest to youngest, and Odell could identify with the issues of each age since it hadn't been that long ago, he'd passed through the same stages of life. Not only did he love these siblings, but he also liked them as well and felt a certain amount of responsibility for their well-being.

He thought it a little strange that they were all essentially different personalities although raised identically. Kenny was perhaps the sweetest and maybe the most introverted of the four although he had a lot of friends. Girls seemed to like him, and Odell had recently overhead Kenny playing his guitar over the telephone to one. Odell thought the gesture was indicative that the brother directly behind him in age was growing up.

Wayne, the next in line, was the clown of the family. He had a flair for the dramatic and would often perform for others. One of his favorite performances was to reenact their grandmother's visit to the house a couple of years prior when she slipped on a throw rug and fell hard on her behind. Fortunately, she hadn't been seriously hurt, and now Grandma was the butt of his joke as he would do a pratfall on the same rug while everyone hooted with laughter.

Their baby brother was probably the cutest, but the most volatile. Lynn had a trigger-temper that got him in trouble on a regular basis. He was fearless and would fight at the drop of a hat, many times with Wayne over some trivial matter. You had to be careful with him because he would have a tantrum if he felt you were not treating him right. You dare not say out loud that his out would not count when he was at bat, so there was an unspoken rule that whoever's team Lynn was on got an extra out when at bat.

All of Odell's brothers were much less interested in books, school and studying than he was, but they were much better using their hands like their dad than he. Odell already knew that he wanted to further his education beyond high school and likewise knew his brothers even at their young age would get out and go to work as soon as possible.

"Hey, Lynn and I have something to show y'all," said Wayne.

The two younger boys ran off to their bedroom. Odell and Kenny remained in their seats, and Odell wondered what was coming next.

When they entered the room a few minutes later, both had stripped down to their underwear. That wasn't all that unusual to see them dressed in their tighty-whiteys, but what was different were their headdresses. Lynn and Wayne had the same white cotton garments on their heads so that where their legs should have been now showed their eyes. They were in the weirdest masks Odell had ever seen, and he and Kenny laughed as tears ran down their faces.

"Introducing Mr. Wrestling Number One and Number Two in a fight to the finish," announced Wayne through the undergarments on his face.

Odell hoped the underwear on their faces were clean. Otherwise, they had to be breathing through stains.

"They're usually partners, but today they're mortal enemies," Wayne continued.

The two lined up across from one another and started histrionic moves. They imitated wild ones they had seen on television as well as those they had seen in person when their father had taken them to matches downtown at the auditorium.

They circled each other in the center of the den like they were in a wrestling ring. Arms flailed while they moved and then their hands turned into claws when they crouched as animals about to pounce.

They finally ran towards each other barely missing contact and then bounced off invisible ropes back in the same direction to the center. This went on for several tracks with choreographed precision. They swung at each other without hitting their opponent.

They finally grappled after several unsuccessful efforts with their wild punches. One second it would appear each had the upper hand in the match as they swapped moves. There was some commentary Wayne made as the match continued.

"Mr. Wrestling Number One lands a solid elbow to the neck of Number Two," he announced as he faked a blow to the younger Sterling brother forcing him to one knee.

Lynn countered with a simulated low blow to Wayne's crotch as he continued in a mimicked high voice, "Aww, a nut-cruncher!"

As Wayne now rolled on the floor holding his groin with both hands, Lynn strutted around the fake ring with both hands in the air flexing his arms like a body builder.

Odell and Kenny were laughing hysterically at the show. This was probably not a production for their parents although a lot of planning and practice must have been undertaken before now.

Odell briefly wondered if he should record a command performance on the family's eight-millimeter movie camera but decided he'd better not. This would just have to be a memory recorded in his brain, not on film.

CHAPTER 26

Kat lay in her bed staring at the ceiling as her mind wandered. Another Monday made her think of the song by The Mamas and Papas. She didn't feel like crying as the song said, but she felt a certain sadness that sometimes came when she had her period. She knew from previous experiences this feeling of the blues would last only a day or two, but it would probably stick around for today at least.

She remembered the first time it happened. Only a few days before Kat turned thirteen, she went to the bathroom and sat down. Horrified when she saw blood in her panties, Kat called for her mom. She was even more agitated when Mom didn't show up, but her father knocked on the door instead.

Kat was in tears as she begged him to get Mom. When she finally showed up after what seemed an eternity, Mom was understanding and told Kat her version of the facts of life. Kat already knew some of it, but it was good to hear from somebody other than classmates about what to expect.

Since then, learning about blooming sexuality had been a mixture of studying about anatomy in school and hushed private conversations with friends and acquaintances. The topics she found herself becoming more interested in weren't taught which led to anxiety and a lot of uncertainty. It was difficult to find practical solutions to the issues that she felt were so immediate right now.

Was thinking about losing her virginity normal behavior?

She had just recently started touching herself down there when in private while thinking about Odell. It was a new revelation and provided an exciting experience for her. Kat wondered if everyone experimented like that and concluded most people probably did.

Of course, she wasn't thinking of doing anything like that at this moment because during the heavy flow of her period she always felt dirty. Feeling herself would just be nasty right now.

All of these conflicting emotions made her feel melancholy. The sense of longing of more intimacy with Odell was not the only issue causing Kat some grief. There was something going on between her parents, too. Their relationship could get strained on occasion, and there must be a source of the recent tension Kat had noticed growing over the summer.

With her bedroom being so close in proximity to the parents' room, Kat could hear bits and pieces of them talking from time to time. Even when she couldn't detect all of the words passed, Kat could easily pick up on the tone of their conversations.

Over the years, Kat knew they had faced difficult periods of time. As she had grown older and better able to process those trying phases, Kat recognized that financial matters were often involved. This was due to times when Dad's work was spotty and also his general refusal to let her mother help by finding work. He was old-fashioned and had said many times that it was up to him to provide for the family. He felt strongly that Kat's mother should stay at home and take care of their daughter as well as the house. That's why it was a little strange that her mom had recently taken a part-time job.

Her father's attitude had led to the Normans never quite being able to own a home and led to them living in a string of rental houses for as long as Kat could remember. Their current residence was simply the latest, and Kat couldn't help but wonder if her dad would uproot the family again soon. She would be devastated if this led to a breakup with Odell. Right now, he was the most important part of her life.

A light knock on her door preceded her mom entering the room and interrupting Kat's thoughts. She was dressed in a pink floral print top and navy skirt, and Kat could instantly tell she was headed to her retail job.

"Good morning, sleepy-head. Are you feeling okay? You look a little washed out," her mother said as she walked over and felt Kat's forehead.

"I guess it's just that time of the month, Mom," replied Kat.

"You feel a little warm. Maybe you should just take it easy today. You can do your chores tomorrow and I'll help since I'm working today, Wednesday and Friday."

"Thanks. I'll get up in a little while. If I get to feeling better, I'll try to do some of the cleaning. I should at least be able to dust. Can I ask you something, Mom?"

"Of course."

"Why are you working now? We're not about to move again, are we?" Kat asked.

Her mother looked away momentarily as if she didn't want to answer. When she turned back concern for Kat could be seen in her eyes.

"Your daddy has been busting his butt trying to save enough money for a down payment on a house. That's why he's been working out of town and making a lot of over-time. I told him I could help, if he would let me. I had to convince him that you were old enough to stay by yourself if I got a job. We're both trying to do the best we can for you," she said earnestly.

"Y'all do, Mom, but that means we'll move from here, right? I like being in this neighborhood," Kat responded.

"I know you like Odell, Honey. I do, too. He's a sweet, respectful boy, but he's not the deciding factor in our plans for the future. Who knows when and where we might move to. I don't want you worrying about that, okay?"

At that moment, Kat thought she might start crying. She knew that her parents loved her, but she couldn't imagine being away from Odell. Equally concerning, however, was not upsetting her mother who was sacrificing so much for her.

"Alright, Mom. I'll try not to worry, but please let me know about any plans."

Kat's mother assured her that she would keep her informed. As soon as her mom left for work, the teen sobbed into her pillow over the uncertainty.

CHAPTER 27

The last game of the regular season had arrived, and it felt somewhat unimportant to Odell. The Renegades were undefeated and guaranteed a first-round bye in the championship tournament that would begin next week. That meant they wouldn't play again until the semi-finals week after next.

Odell had other stuff on his mind, and baseball had been relegated to a secondary role. He still wanted to win another trophy or maybe two. Besides the desire he had of winning his teammates a shiny statue, Odell now knew he had a real chance of receiving the leading hitter crown also. He had found out when he saw his name listed in Sunday's paper near the top of the batting averages for the fifteen and under league.

The primary focus of the summer had changed from the beginning of the season. There was hardly a moment that Odell wasn't thinking about Kat, and this distracted him from today's contest.

He was a little worried about Kat since talking briefly to her over the phone yesterday. She had assured him that everything was fine, but Kat hadn't seemed her usual bubbly self. When he told her that he could come over for a visit, Kat asked him not to because she was a little under the weather and just didn't feel like company. They had promised to get together on Wednesday since there was the game scheduled for today.

Odell absent-mindedly played catch with Mitch and paid no attention to the other team. That was unlike him since he always tried to study the opponents before a game. He often knew at least some of the other guys, or if he didn't, Odell could pick up on strengths and weaknesses of their game.

"Odie, don't you think you should throw a few pitches to the mitt before we take the field?" asked Mitch.

Odell snapped out of his mild funk and replied, "Yeah, I guess so."

Mitch crouched and Odell started pitching to his catcher. After making just a handful of throws, he nodded that he was ready. They walked back to the dugout, and for the first time Odell could ever remember, he didn't feel excitement about playing. It wasn't exactly a meaningless game, but it just wouldn't make any difference if they were to lose.

Oh, well. I still need to get a couple of hits if I want that leading hitter trophy, he thought.

The other Renegades were loose and chattering all around him. Finally looking over to the other side of the field, Odell saw several kids tossing balls to each other and a couple of others swinging bats. He knew they had only won one game, so they wouldn't be any real competition.

Let's just get this over with. I've got other things to do.

Play finally started with Odell striking out their first three hitters as his impatience kept growing. In their bottom of the inning, he stroked a double to left-center field that knocked in a run and then scored on a hit by Bruce.

With every passing frame, Odell found himself in an increasing hurry to finish the game as quickly as possible. He wasted no time on the mound and would fire a pitch as soon as the batter stepped in. He told Mitch in between the innings to set up and not bother too much with signs because fastballs were going to be the order of the day. Odell didn't think any of their batters could touch him today, and his philosophy proved to be correct.

The final score was 5-0 with Odell slinging a no-hitter. He also collected another hit and two more runs batted in.

Any other time, he would've been pumped up with his performance. Right now, all Odell cared about was getting home so he could call his girlfriend.

***

The telephone rang a few times before Kat could answer. Her mom had gone to the grocery store and left her finishing cleaning the bathrooms. Kat was scrubbing tile around the toilet and had to get off her knees to get to the phone. When she finally made it, all she heard was a dial tone. She wondered if it had been Odell calling to check on her and started to call his house, but decided she needed to finish her chores instead.

Kat figured his game might be over by now and knew he was concerned about her since the last conversation they had. She had cut it short and told him that she wasn't feeling well. That had been the truth between the cramps she had and what her mother had said. She felt some guilt for not telling Odell more at that time but decided it would be a better topic to discuss in person.

The possibility Kat could be moving in the near future had ripped at her heart. The more she thought about it, the sicker she felt deep in her stomach. She could only imagine what Odell would say when he heard because she thought the two of them were in synch.

Their burgeoning romance was something genuine despite the fact they were so young. As she thought about it, age was irrelevant.

Weren't Romeo and Juliet younger than them, and their love was real, right?

Kat was sure the grown-ups wouldn't understand. *Would they?* she thought.

She was confident these thoughts swirling around her brain wouldn't have even been possible just a couple of months before. Now Kat felt just as confident about her current feelings, or did she? That was the thing about love, it was often irrational.

Kat finished cleaning the floor and admired her work. She then rinsed out the pail of soapy water and the big sponge she had used and put them away as the telephone began ringing again. There almost seemed to be an urgency to the sound.

"Hello," Kat said as she picked up on the third ring.

"Hey, are you okay?" replied Odell.

"Yeah, I guess. Sorry I wasn't able to get to the phone earlier."

"This is the first time I've called. I just got back from our game. We won by the way," said Odell.

"Oh, good. I thought it was you, but whoever called will probably call back later. It's sweet of you to think of me. I really didn't feel very well yesterday when we were talking. Just a female thing, you know. I've been missing you today," she said.

"So glad you're better. Uh, I think I know what you mean about being a girl. I mean, I don't know what it's like being a female, but I think I get your drift. You've been on my mind, too," Odell blundered.

"If you're not too busy tomorrow, I was thinking you might come over tomorrow afternoon. Mom will be working and Daddy's still out of town. We could talk some, and maybe…," Kat replied leaving the sentence unfinished.

There was a long pause and Kat thought she could hear Odell swallow before he answered, "Uh, that sounds promising. I'll plan on being there after making sure my brothers get something to eat for lunch."

"Okay, I'll fix you something, so get here as soon as you can. It'll be good."

They hung up and Kat began to anticipate the lunch date. Her parents would be mortified if they knew what she was thinking.

CHAPTER 28

Odell hung up the phone with excitement and uncertainty coursing through his veins. Between what Kat had just said and what he thought were unspoken words, they might be on the road of taking their relationship to the next level. He needed advice and immediately thought of his friend, Mike.

Their friendship had endured since grammar school, and Odell knew he could trust Mike to give him the skinny on what the next step should be. He had been right about the date to the movies and had even loaned his cologne to Odell before that occasion. They had not spoken since Odell returned the bottle of Hai Karate the day after.

Before he could think anything out himself, Odell called Mike who told him to come on over. Neither of his parents were at home, and he assured Odell they could have a private conversation.

When Odell parked his bike and walked to the front door, Mike opened it and held a beer in his hand. He grinned from ear to ear as he asked Odell if he wanted one.

"Are you kidding me? What if your parents come home? I can smell it from here. My daddy would beat my ass if he even thought I was drinking," replied Odell.

"Aww, loosen up a little, O. That's one of your problems, you're always so uptight about everything. Come on in, and tell me what's going on," said Mike as he led the way.

The two friends sat down in the darkened den of the house. Mike flicked on a lamp beside an over-stuffed chair where he parked and then took a sip from the can he held.

"You sure you don't want one 'cause it's sho tasty," he said smacking his lips.

"No, man. I'm good. You must be pretty sure your parents aren't coming home anytime soon."

"Nah, they've actually gone out of town for a few days. They're on vacation in Savannah and said I could stay home with my sister if we didn't want to go. So, we were like, cool with that," said Mike grinning again.

"So, Pam's home, too?" asked Odell.

"Well, not at the minute. She's at a friend's house and won't be home until tomorrow. So, you can talk freely. I'm guessing you want to discuss that new girlfriend," Mike said with raised eyebrows.

"Yeah, you know me pretty well. I don't really have anybody to talk to except you. I know you'll be straight with me and maybe not laugh at me. Can I ask you something first? Have you gone all the way with a girl?"

Mike almost choked as he was drinking when Odell asked him the question. After coughing, he replied, "A gentleman never tells of his conquests. It's a good thing I'm not necessarily a gentleman, and you're a good friend."

"I agree, Mike, not talking like that about a girl you've been with. I really think that should be private and it pisses me off when I hear guys bragging in the locker room. I feel like most of that is just bullshit anyway. I just need advice concerning when it's right to go a little further and what steps I should take. I figured you'd know."

Mike eyed Odell for a moment without speaking. Odell thought he could see the cogs in his friend's brain grinding.

"Okay, I'll tell you what I've discovered, but you've got to understand something, O. I ain't no expert. Believe it. I don't know if guys ever become all that skilled because a lot of us are just too damned selfish. Most are more interested in satisfying themselves rather than who they're with. I try not to be like that, at least when I'm with a girl, and I think that's one thing the opposite sex has always liked about me. I think you've got some of those same traits and that's probably got a lot to do with you having your current girlfriend. You told me before that she goes by Kat, right?"

Odell was taking in what Mike said and simply nodded yes. Mike took a swig from the beer and licked his lips.

"You know, I'll be glad when I'm old enough to buy these for myself. We've still got over two years before we can, as you know. That's another thing, buddy, don't get in a hurry with Kat. I'd bet you dollars to doughnuts she's going through some of the same stuff you're feeling right now. Take it slow, and most important, be safe. We don't need any accidents happening, if you know what I mean."

"I'm trying to, Mike, but I can't get her off my mind. She's right here all the time," Odell replied while tapping a finger to his temple.

"Are you sure she's not there instead?" Mike pointed toward Odell's groin.

Odell laughed nervously, "Well, maybe both places. That's maybe just wishful thinking on my part. It's pretty embarrassing to me when I get hard being around her, and I'm sure she's noticed. I dream about doing it with her, and I don't know if that's normal or if it means I'm some kind of sex fiend. That's one of the main reasons I came over. I don't know what to do about it. What can you tell me, man?"

"Yeah, I can tell you're getting desperate, O. Alright, here's the deal. I don't think you should be thinking about the ultimate prize, yet. That being said, sounds like you two are ready for some heavy petting which can be pretty doggone satisfying," Mike said and then paused.

He then continued, "Just to satisfy your curiosity, you're about six months behind where I am now. My girlfriend is one class older than us. She's already got her driver's license which helps a lot. Yeah, she was a little more experienced than me, but mainly we learned together earlier this year what I'm about to tell you."

Odell listened intently. He had not known that Mike was going with a rising junior, and he was impressed.

"One thing Sue has taught me is that we can learn together what we like. Touching each other is important, O, but with respect and restraint. Don't grope, and don't be too rough."

"Okay, I think I can do that, but where should I touch?" replied Odell.

"The main thing is to be gentle, at least at first. Cup her breasts and feel the nipples between your fingertips. If they're erect, you're on the right track. You might even get to nibble with your teeth and suck on them softly. You'll feel like you're in heaven, if you get that far. Just remember, don't force anything. If you get to do that, you're real close to going to the next phase. You might be able to slip your hand into her panties. Here's where you go, if that happens. Your middle finger goes to the top of Virginia and rubs. If she responds, you're golden."

Odell could only imagine what Mike was saying. He spoke with experience, though, and he respected Mike's insights. "Virginia?" he asked.

Mike started laughing. Odell didn't know if his friend was tickled at what he'd asked or at his ignorance in general.

"Just Sue's name for her honey pot, vagina or whatever euphemism you call the female privates. Hey, come up with your own name for it. Since your girl's name is Kat, maybe you can call it Miss Kitty. Whatever, when you finally get inside, you'll never be the same, buddy. She'll love you, and you'll love her. All will be right with the world, and then maybe you'll be ready for another lesson."

"I don't know where this is headed, Mike, but I appreciate it. So, you haven't answered me yet. Have you gone all the way?"

Mike smiled enigmatically. "Let's just say, I'm ahead of you, O."

CHAPTER 29

Phillip was antsy. He'd tried to call the bitch earlier today, but she never answered. He hated that he couldn't get her off his mind. The thought of her made him horny and angry at the same time. He wanted to hear her voice when he rang her number, so he could get some release, but was frustrated when she didn't.

He drove his car to the neighborhood where she lived. He went up and down the road and all he could see was her front porch light on. It was the same at the punk's house she was seeing. He guessed everybody went to bed early in South Macon. Phillip wanted some kind of revenge for what she'd put him through. He'd thought about beating up their mailboxes before coming up with a better plan.

Earlier today he had put some out-of-date eggs in his car. They would be ammunition in the attack planned. It was a benefit of working in the grocery store.

Slowly, Phillip rode by the asshole's house. There were no other cars insight. He stopped in front with the car still running.

Grabbing a few of the eggs, he stepped out of the car. He slung them at the house and heard them make contact.

Next, he drove to Kat's house and did the same thing with the rest of them. He could hear the splats as the eggs hit the house. It made him feel powerful, and he had to fight the urge not to scream in triumph.

Phillip drove to his house and laughed all the way there. He wanted to hurt both of them, and this was all he could think of.

Screw 'em. They deserve it.

CHAPTER 30

Odell got up the next morning and felt a little out of sorts. He'd been dreaming again. There had been some combination of fantasy and reality that left him not knowing what was real, and what wasn't.

Nobody else was awake yet although he knew his parents would be getting up soon. He heard the tinkling of milk bottles underneath the carport which signaled the exchange of empties for fresh milk being delivered. Odell opened the door and walked outside to retrieve the cold containers as the milkman drove away.

He decided since he was already outside, he should walk to the front and get the newspaper out of the box. It would save his dad a trip, and Odell sometimes liked to at least look at the headlines before Daddy did.

Odell padded on bare feet against concrete to the end of the driveway. Morning was breaking and sunlight was dancing against the front of the house as he removed *The Macon Telegraph* from the circular tube attached to their mailbox.

For a moment, Odell thought the sun was playing tricks on his eyes as he noticed streaks of yellow beneath the window of his bedroom. He walked across the yard that was damp with morning dew until it became obvious what was the source of the color. There were bits of eggshells stuck to the brick and putrid smelling yolks ran down behind shrubs under the window.

Somebody egged our house, he realized.

Knowing he couldn't do anything about it right away, Odell went back inside carrying the paper and the four bottles of milk with him. He placed the newspaper in his dad's chair and then took the milk from the galvanized tray that held them and set the containers in the fridge. All the while he pondered who could've thrown the eggs and why.

The act had to be a prank by someone who knew him or another of his brothers. It was something an adolescent or maybe a teenager would do out of spite.

Dewey and Billy Smith came to mind because they were definitely pranksters capable of doing such, but Odell couldn't imagine why they would do it. None of the other kids living around them would have any reason either, he thought.

No, it couldn't be anybody living in the neighborhood. Anyone have a grudge against me?

Odell began thinking about possible guys that he had played against in the baseball league. The only one he could think of who was a big enough a-hole to egg a house was Ricky Lee. But Odell hadn't seen him since school was out. Besides, Ricky Lee despite being a prick, was considered a friend. A friend wouldn't do this to another friend.

The only possible enemy I have is Phillip Jackson, and I've never met him. Surely, he couldn't have done this. That doesn't make any sense.

***

It took over an hour to clean up the mess made by the thrown eggs. His parents had not been very happy when Odell told them what he'd found earlier in the morning. Before they left for work, his father had told him to "wash that shit" before it baked onto the house. He had questioned Odell about suspects, but Odell had told him that he couldn't think of anybody who would have a reason.

While his brothers ate sandwiches for lunch, Odell had taken a quick shower and shaved his sparse whiskers. Looking at himself in the mirror, it seemed as if he was filling out a little more than before the summer. He was definitely more tanned, and his skin was not nearly as broken out.

He donned cotton shorts and a pull-over shirt that he left unbuttoned. He was far from being considered dressed up, but he was not in his usual garb that was even more casual.

The anticipation of seeing Kat filled all his senses. He told his brothers that he was going to Kat's house for a little while and for them not to get into any trouble while he was gone.

Odell hopped on his bike and rode on the edge of the roadway to Kat's house. It only took a few minutes until he arrived, and then had his hopes of special moments with Kat dashed to smithereens.

Standing in front of their home were Kat and her mother. Both had large sponges in their hands and were scrubbing areas of the house. Right away, Odell knew they were victims of egging, too. What was also obvious was there wouldn't be any private time with Kat. Not today, anyway.

"Hello, ladies. Can I do anything to help?"

Kat and Mrs. Norman turned toward Odell as he dismounted from the bicycle. Kat's mother wore a frown that distracted from her pretty face and grubby clothes that were soiled from the cleanup efforts. Kat's tee shirt had become wet which clung to her form and caused Odell a silent curse for what could have been.

The damage to the front siding was more extensive than it had been at his house as it appeared that more eggs had found their mark. The odor produced was rotten and much worse than what Odell had cleaned a few hours before. The hot Georgia sun certainly had a role in the foul smell.

"We'd appreciate it, Odell. I can't imagine who'd do such a thing as this. It's vandalism pure and simple," Kat's mother said with disgust.

"More than likely just kids, our house got hit, too. I cleaned up ours this morning. It wasn't as bad as this, though," said Odell.

The three of them worked for the next hour or so scrubbing with brushes and sponges and then rinsing the beige-colored siding with water from a garden hose. Odell held his thumb over the end to make the water squirt out more forcefully. When they finished, the yellow stains weren't nearly as noticeable, but could be detected in one or two spots upon close inspection. The smell of bleach had replaced any lingering stench from the eggs.

Kat barely spoke during their toils, but her periodic side glances at Odell expressed anger and frustration. Odell looked at his Timex and saw he'd been gone for an hour and a half. He returned an agonized peek to Kat trying to convey his emotions before telling them he needed to go home to check on his brothers.

Irritation was building inside as he pumped his legs to gain speed and to burn up negative energy. He studied every house between Kat's and his without seeing any other evidence of damage. This had to be directed at him and Kat, and Odell could only think of one suspect.

Phillip Jackson.

CHAPTER 31

Odell, Kenny and Craig were setting up their equipment on a little stage inside the Bloomfield Community Clubhouse. It was a small open building that had once been someone's residence but had been converted for such events as Rowena's birthday party being held tonight.

The honoree was also the host, and she busied herself decorating the few tables located on the other end from the band. A streamer hung from the ceiling proclaiming HAPPY BIRTHDAY. On a counter near a small kitchen there were trays of finger foods along with a cake containing twenty-one candles.

She had told Odell they were welcome to any of the food and other displayed goodies as well as soft drinks in the refrigerator. When he looked inside the old appliance Odell noticed there were at least two cases of PBR beer stored inside as well as various brands of soda. Craig had noticed the cans of alcohol and had whispered maybe they could get one of those later. Odell had shushed and warned him what his daddy would do if he caught them drinking.

The sun hadn't quite gone down, and the party wasn't to begin until another twenty minutes. Rowena grinned ear to ear at the boys when she approached them. They had just completed a sound check and the noise died down as the young bleached-blonde woman stopped in front of the stage. Her newly coifed hairstyle was popular with women and had been swirled and puffed up to give the petite female several more inches of height and took probably a half-can of super-hold hairspray to hold it in place.

"You guys are going to blow the roof off tonight. Sounding good, y'all. I'm going to introduce the band before y'all start playing, so I need to know your name," she said gleefully.

"Uh, we've really not settled on one, so how does *The Sterlings Plus One,* sound?" asked Odell.

"I get it. Sure, that sounds fine to me. I'm looking forward to celebrating with y'all tonight. Here's the money I promised," she said taking out three five-dollar bills.

Odell gave the other two guys their money as he slipped his into the pocket of his pants. They were all dressed the same in black dress slacks, white long-sleeved button shirts covered by buttoned-up red vests.

She then placed an empty jar on the stage in front of them that she had labeled, Tips, and continued, "Just in case any of the guests want to add to your earnings."

"Thanks, Miss Rowena. We hope you have fun tonight. We're going to try to play the best we can for you. Happy birthday."

"Thanks, guys," she said as she hurried off to make more last-minute preparations.

"This dump is the fanciest place we've played," said Craig.

"Hey, it's not a dump. I think it's pretty neat," said Kenny.

"I just hope they'll get up and dance when we play," chimed Odell.

"Don't worry, O. Once they start drinking all that beer, they'll be hootin' and hollerin' and cuttin' a rug," said Craig with a grin.

"Dang, I'm kinda worried about a drinking party. My parents are really strict about alcohol. I've never seen them have a drink, maybe because there are a couple of alcoholics in the family, and they're afraid one of us might end up that way. I've only tasted a beer one time and I was scared to death Daddy would smell it on me. I think I brushed my teeth three times to hide it," said Odell.

"My parents drink all the time. It loosens people up, O. I bet you'll see that tonight. I still say we might can sneak us a beer during a break. I think this is going to be a night to remember," replied Craig.

"Yeah, you should've seen our mom's sister showing us how she danced one time when she was visiting. She's a big-time partier. Odell and I played a song and she started moving all over the living room. We called one of her moves "The Praying Mantis," because that's what she looked like when she was picking at the air with her hands. We were pretty sure she had been drinking a good bit that day," said Kenny.

Guests started arriving and Odell tried to size them up as they walked around the room greeting each other. Most of the men wore slacks, dress shirts and Sunday shoes, but there were a couple of guys who had on jeans, plaid shirts and boots. Just about all the women were outfitted in dresses or skirts cut at the knees although one or two had on shorter lengths. Most also wore their hair piled up like Rowena.

Some of them looked pretty red-necked to Odell. There were at least a couple of guys with slick-backed hair that looked scarlet-faced already like they had been either drinking heavily or out in the sun, or maybe both.

Rowena was having a good time, and the party really hadn't started. A few minutes later she walked up to the microphone with a big grin plastered on her face.

"Everybody, thanks for coming to my birthday party. I can't believe I'm twenty-one today. I'm glad you're here to help me celebrate. Let's have a good time. To help me tonight, we have The Sterlings Plus One," she announced.

Odell counted down, and they started with the song they had decided upon a few days ago. Almost immediately, there were a couple of the guys who started whooping and dragging women to the dance floor.

When they finished, the guys who had been dancing continued showing their pleasure. Odell wasn't sure that the song had been performed very well, but everyone seemed to enjoy it.

For the next forty-five minutes, the band continued to play their set list without a break. The attendees seemed to be enjoying themselves and there was a lot of dancing. The boys in the band were having almost as much fun as the guests.

When there was finally an opportunity to stop playing, Odell and the rest of the band grabbed a Coke and walked outside. They were stoked at the success of the set.

"These people are having a ball. We should be, too," said Craig.

"I'm having fun," said Odell.

"Me, too," said Kenny.

"Y'all are really way too straight," replied Craig, and then paused. "I'm going to get us a beer," he continued before walking back inside the center.

Odell looked at his younger brother. Kenny was a little wide-eyed but seemed excited.

"You okay?" asked Odell.

"Yeah, you?" Kenny replied.

"This is pretty fun. These people seem to really like us. I wish we knew some more songs. We've played everything we've practiced," said Odell.

"Let's just play 'em again," said Kenny, "I doubt they'll even notice."

Craig walked outside with three beers in his hands. He produced an opener and then cracked them. "Cheers," he said.

The three boys sipped the frothy brews. Odell thought they would need something to cut the smell before their father picked them up from the gig. He had Wrigley's Spearmint gum in his pocket and hoped it would work to kill the odor that would be on their breath.

It only took about half a can before Odell began to feel the effects. He was content, but things felt somewhat woozy. Inside, there was a lot of noise indicating the party was cranking up to new levels.

In just a moment, Rowena came outside to where the boys sat. She had a big grin on her face when they tried to hide the cans they were drinking from.

"You guys are great! Everybody's having a great time. Keep on doing what you've been doing. Don't worry about the beer 'cause I won't tell."

She went back inside, and Odell noticed she was a little unsteady on her feet. He realized that there were probably a lot of them that had been drinking more than they should have.

Craig turned up his can and drank down the remaining contents. Odell and Kenny looked at one another and realized they wouldn't finish theirs. They set the unfinished beverages down before entering.

"Alright, let's go back inside and replay what we've already done," said Odell.

The three went through the door to find a happening going on. Odell didn't necessarily know what a party should be, but this had to be pretty close to what he could imagine.

The Sterling brothers had never been around grownups when they were acting this way. It appeared all the guests were happy as loud laughter filled the room. All were drinking heavily, and beer cans were visible everywhere. Odell noticed a half-empty container of a clear liquid on the counter that he thought must be vodka. He began to worry what his father would say when he came to pick them up.

Smoke from cigarettes filled the poorly vented space as the band got back on stage. The air was heavy, and Odell was glad when he saw one of the men open a window in the back.

As Odell slipped the strap on his guitar over his shoulder, one of the guys with a bulging belly hanging over his jeans approached him. The man's face was beet-red, and his nose seemed to take up half of it. He held a couple of dollar bills that were dramatically placed in the band's tip jar.

"Doin' good thar fellers. Play that song again about puttin' on them sneakers and wantin' to fight," he said loudly over the noise of the party.

"Thank you, sir. We sure will," replied Odell.

Kenny turned on the amp and then jacked up the volume to the max. Craig did a drum roll and then Odell announced there had been a special request. They started up the song again, and the first one on the dance floor was the man who had just tipped them dragging a bleary-eyed redheaded woman with him. They were soon followed by other couples, some of whom still held drinks in their fists.

Half-way through the tune something sounded different as Odell glanced in Kenny's direction. One of the strings of his guitar had snapped and stood up from the neck of the instrument. He kept on playing but had to join in strumming rather than picking the lead.

When they finished to clapping and cheering their efforts, Odell walked over to his brother who was inspecting the broken string. "I'm not going to be able to play anymore," he said.

Rowena came to where they were standing. "Oh, no. I don't guess you've got another string with you. Can y'all still play?" she asked.

"I'm sorry, we don't have one with us and I don't think we've got another at home. We won't be able to play without one. I'm really sorry," said Odell.

"It's okay. Y'all have done well, and I appreciate it. Some of us are going to a club in a little while anyway. There's a phone in the kitchen if you want to call somebody to pick y'all up," she replied.

Kenny placed the guitar in a stand behind him and went to make a call to their parents as Rowena told the crowd that the live entertainment was unfortunately through. There were some groans, and somebody said "Shit" loud enough that everyone could hear.

When Kenny got back to the stage, he told Odell and Craig that Daddy was on the way. Odell was concerned about what their dad might say and told them they should get their equipment outside before he arrived. He retrieved the tip money, then passed a stick of gum to each of them. He furiously chewed his own piece as they took the guitars and drums out to the front of the building.

There could be no denying what their father saw and heard when he pulled up. Beer cans were visible and loud voices could be heard through the closed door. He was obviously unhappy as the boys loaded everything into the deep trunk of the car.

"This kind of shit will get you boys in trouble," their dad said while kicking an empty beer can near the driveway. "If I find out y'all been drinkin', I can still whip your asses. You ain't grown, yet," he finished angrily.

Odell almost swallowed his tongue when his father approached the three of them as they closed the trunk. Craig quickly jumped into the back seat without cracking his usual jokes.

The two brothers stood still as their dad stood menacingly close to them. They knew not to say anything that might set off his trigger temper. Odell hoped Daddy couldn't smell any alcohol on them and figured he must not have when he said, "Let's get the hell out of here."

On the way home, he muttered the whole trip while the boys kept their collective mouths shut. The last thing Odell heard him say was, "I told your mama there would be a lot of damn drunks at that party."

All Odell could think about was how he had just dodged a whipping. It had been more than two years since his last one, but he hadn't forgotten the pain or the humiliation. He resolved not to put himself in that position again because contrary to what Daddy might think, Odell was starting to believe he was more grown than not.

CHAPTER 32

Most of the neighborhood boys had gathered in the Sterling's backyard the next morning. With school approaching in just a few weeks, the mood was generally gloomy over that expectation. The members of the Renegades present had their baseball equipment with them for a planned practice in advance of their semi-final game next week, but nobody seemed anxious to take part in such activity.

Odell and Kenny were still getting over their party experiences from the night before. Their glimpse into adult life had been weirdly invigorating, and Odell's love of baseball was waning more by the day. All he could think about was seeing Kat tonight when they would go to Durr's again. He planned to tell her all about how it went. He was also hopeful that they could plan a more intimate time together.

He was sprawled on the ground with his head on his glove underneath a large oak tree providing needed shade from the August sun. The tree was on the Sterling side of a chain link fence separating their yard from their neighbors. A chain still hung from one of the lower branches that his dad had used last year to remove the motor from an old truck which triggered other memories of his dad.

Daddy was a skilled mechanic who seemingly could repair any machinery. He loved tinkering with cars and had single-handedly replaced the blown engine in a 50's model Ford pickup that he would sometimes drive to work, but it currently sat like a rusted-out dinosaur in an unused part of the backyard.

His latest project was a 1957 Ford Fairlane that he had bought for next to nothing from one of Odell's uncles. It had been painted some off shade of blue and had once been considered a fancy car. The odometer had long ago turned over a hundred thousand miles and it ran rough. Daddy had told Odell that when he replaced the brakes, muffler, plugs and points, it would run like a top and that Odell could drive it to school next year when he turned sixteen. Odell had shuddered at that thought, but at least he would have his own ride until he could find something better. That was going to require him finding a job so he could pay for it himself.

Odell could imagine taking Kat to the drive-in and having her close to him on the long bench seat in the old '57. They would practice their night moves together, and the older and more experienced they became, who knows where it would lead.

Of course, the huge steering wheel might be a hindrance. The car didn't have power steering and brakes like his mom's vehicle and might be more difficult to drive as a result, but it was spacious inside which appealed to Odell's sense of adventure when he and Kat could go parking. Besides, there wasn't a steering wheel in the back seat, he thought.

As he lay dreaming about spending evenings with Kat at the outdoor movies, an older sedan pulled into the back entrance of the yard and proceeded to the location where the boys were gathered. Odell recognized two older guys he hadn't seen in a while, but who lived nearby. PJ and Bobby were best friends and had just graduated from high school a couple of months before. They would come by the Sterling house on occasion to play a little touch football.

Bobby got out of the vehicle first, and Odell noticed right away his shaved head. He looked fitter than Odell remembered and was wearing a uniform.

"Hey, Bobby. What's with the hair cut?" one of the younger kids asked.

He rubbed the blonde bristle with one hand and said, "Just got through basic training at Paris Island. Ain't I purdy?" he said with a grin.

By that time, PJ had gotten out of the car and joined the group. "I guess you might be to somebody who likes a jarhead," he said.

"Watch out, buddy. Only another marine can call me that. Not some civilian pussy," he said laughing.

All the younger boys crowded around the two older ones. These two guys held almost legendary status in their eyes.

Lynn, being the youngest, was tentative looking up at the tall marine. He seemed in awe as he said, "Shazam! Do you know Gomer Pyle?"

Laughter erupted in the group. Mitch, the television aficionado of the neighborhood, said, "Lynn, you do know that Gomer ain't real, right? He's just a character on a tv show."

"I know that, Mitchell. I was just making a joke, stupid," the youngest Sterling said.

Sandy chimed in with another Gomer reference saying, "G-o-l-l-y," dragging it out as the star always did.

Odell had gotten up off the ground and reached over to shake Bobby's hand. Bobby had a strong grip and said, "Odell, I do believe you've grown some since I last saw you. You're taller and filled out some, too."

"Yeah, I guess so. You're looking like you're in great shape. I bet that training camp was tough," replied Odell.

"It was hell, but the sarge said it had to be to get us ready for Nam. I'll be in the jungle in a couple of weeks, so I was hoping we might could throw a football around for a while. I'm only home for the weekend."

"I'll go get it, private," said Lynn as he ran inside the house.

Odell and Bobby talked a little about the pending tour of duty, and Odell told him they were all proud of his accomplishments and would be thinking of him while overseas. Odell knew that a cousin who served in the Army last year had said the experience he went through in Viet Nam had changed him, and he didn't want to talk about it. Odell just hoped Bobby would be alright.

When Lynn came back in a few minutes, he tossed the ball to Bobby who gripped it on the seams. PJ took off running and held his left arm in the air. Bobby flung the pigskin and it dropped into his friend's hands for a perfect pass and catch. The grin on Bobby's face caused Odell to realize that the man throwing the ball was still a boy at heart.

Soon thereafter, the boys split up into teams and a football game was played in the hot summer sun for the next thirty minutes. PFC Bobby Morris seemed to be having as much fun as any of them that day and provided memories to the others that would always be cherished.

CHAPTER 33

Odell and Kat skated around the crowded rink holding hands and chatting about recent events. He had noticed a mood of sadness surrounding his girlfriend before arriving at Durr's as they rode in the back seat of his mom's car. That air of sorrow had now passed, and Kat seemed back to her normal self.

They had only been there less than twenty minutes when Odell spotted his friend Mike with a girl who he suspected was his girlfriend. Odell remembered Mike had told him her name was Sue, and she was old enough to drive. Mike motioned him to come over to the railing where the couple stood watching the skaters.

Mike wore a big grin on his slightly freckled face as he presented himself to Kat and then made introductions to Sue. Odell could see right away why Mike liked this girl as she was cute with a healthy bosom. She was also very friendly.

"Yeah, I told Sue that I bet you two would be here tonight and that we ought to ride by to check and see. We've got an idea y'all might like. How about we go to the Dairy Queen and get a milkshake or something?" said Mike.

Odell and Kat looked at each other with uncertainty. Odell knew his parents wouldn't want him to do anything like that without talking to them first, and he was pretty sure Kat's parents would think likewise.

"Dang, Mike. We'd really like that, but I'm not sure we should. I'm sure both of us would be knee-deep in crap if we got caught leaving here," replied Odell.

"Come on, O. Y'all have another two and a half hours before somebody will come and pick you up. We'll have y'all back in plenty of time. Your parents don't have to know. Besides, Sue's a careful driver, ain't that right, Baby?" Mike said glancing at Sue.

"I sure am, Sweet Cheeks," she said back to a blushing Mike.

Sue then faced Odell and Kat. She pursed her lips and then addressed them in a more serious tone.

"Look, I get it. I definitely remember feeling exactly like I bet y'all are going through right now. It sucks when you have to depend on anyone, especially your parents, to take you somewhere. No pressure, if you don't want to go, that's fine. We just thought you might want to have like a double-date," Sue said.

Kat spoke up, "I think it sounds like a lot of fun. Let's go, Odell."

Odell was surprised at Kat's response, and before he could think too much about potential dangers responded, "Okay. Let's get off these skates."

The couple changed into their shoes and took their skates with them as they followed Mike and Sue out the door. Odell was a little nervous that the owner might take note of him leaving, but he was nowhere to be found as they walked into the humid evening air. It had not turned dark yet, but it wouldn't be much longer before the sun set.

Sue led them across the crowded parking lot to a newer model Chevy Nova. After she unlocked the car, Kat crawled into the back seat with Odell close behind. Storing their skates in the floorboard catty-cornered from them, they got comfortable sitting side-by-side, as Mike and Sue got in the front with her behind the wheel.

Odell was suddenly excited over being this close to Kat. He checked his watch underneath the overhead light just before Sue closed her door. He thought they would need to be back at least thirty minutes before closing time to make sure which ever parent was picking them up didn't catch them sneaking out. That should give them nearly two hours to enjoy.

Kat squeezed Odell just above his knee with her left hand as Sue drove onto the roadway. He responded by placing his arm around her shoulders and whispered into her ear, "I think this will be more fun than skating."

While he was so near her, she then turned and kissed him on the mouth with her tongue darting inside for just a moment. He laid his head back against the seat as she nestled her head against him. Odell felt as content as he could at the moment, but knew they needed to talk privately about some things that were not appropriate topics right then.

"Alright now, y'all behave back there," said Sue looking into the rearview mirror at them.

Mike turned in his seat to look at them and grinned at Odell. Although it was nearing dark, Odell saw the exaggerated wink his friend gave him.

As they rode over to the south Macon area, the two couples talked, and the girls seemed to get along well together. The conversation focused on the upcoming school year. They compared information about subjects, teachers and other events that would come up soon like football games in the fall and prom in the spring.

"Well, here we are," said Sue as she pulled into the DQ on Pio Nono Avenue.

The ice cream parlor and grill was a destination point for all Maconites but especially those who lived on the southside of town. Odell had always thought it a treat to go there as a kid and get a chocolate malted shake, butterscotch dipped cone or a Dilly Bar that was his dad's favorite treat from the Dairy Queen.

The establishment was doing a brisk trade. Odell looked from his window around the parking lot more than a little paranoid that he'd see somebody he knew from the neighborhood. Thankfully, he didn't see anyone and breathed a sigh of relief.

"What do you guys want?" asked Mike.

"Ummm, soft-serve vanilla cone for me, Sweet Cheeks," said Sue while licking her lips rather seductively.

Mike blushed again as he had done earlier when called that name but didn't seem to mind very much as he replied, "You got it."

"Hmm, I wouldn't mind a hot fudge sundae," said Kat. "I haven't had one of those in forever."

"I'll get it for you and a shake for me," said Odell.

The two boys got out of the car and headed to the window to place their orders while the girls stayed inside the car. Odell couldn't help but continue to study the other patrons as they got in line.

"You seem a little shaky, O. Loosen up," said Mike.

"Hey, if somebody saw me here, I'd be in a world of trouble."

"You worry too much," Mike said shrugging his shoulders.

"Maybe so, Mike. I'll just be glad when I'm old enough that I don't have to sneak around. I do appreciate you and Sue letting us tag along. It was a real surprise when I saw y'all at the rink."

The guys ordered and stood at the counter waiting for the treats. They kept their backs to other customers behind them. Right before the order arrived, a loud voice could be heard from their rear.

"If these Willingham turds would get out of the way, we could get us an ice cream," the voice said.

Odell didn't recognize it as being from anybody he knew. Mike looked over at him and mouthed silently, "Redneck asshole."

They got their stuff and started back toward the car. While passing by, Odell saw three guys standing in line not far from where Mike and he had just left. One was taller than the other two, but all three were sneering in Odell's direction. He had no idea who they were, but the lanky one showed his middle finger to Odell.

Odell knew he couldn't afford to confront the guy for several reasons and kept walking. Mike said something under his breath, but kept walking, too.

They got back to the car and neither Mike nor Odell told the girls about the uncomfortable event that had just occurred. Everyone consumed their goodies and had a nice time getting to know each other.

After finishing the sweets, Sue drove to Shoney's located on the same road, and they circled through their drive-in waving at some young people known by them. There was a parade of other cars doing the same before Odell noticed the time was getting late and asked Sue to get them back to Durr's.

On the ride back, Odell and Kat made out in the back seat. The circumstances didn't allow for more than that. Any private conversation would have to wait as would possible further intimate physical contact.

They got back to the skating rink about twenty minutes before closing time and after telling Mike and Sue goodbyes, chose to wait out front rather than going back inside. Odell knew how close they had been to disaster when his mother drove up only five minutes later. Still, it had been quite a night, and he didn't notice the muscle car nearby that had followed them during the evening.

CHAPTER 34

Kat was stretched across her favorite chair wearing loose-fitting shorts and an even baggier shirt. Madi was ensconced in her lap, and Kat rubbed her soft fur from head to tail much to the dog's satisfaction. Kat's mother was in her bedroom getting ready for work. She had told Kat that she would be working all week, so Kat would be alone during the day for most of the time.

The weekend was now just another memory from a summer nearly over. It had been a memorable season for many reasons, and they all revolved around the boy living down the street. She couldn't believe how it had all worked out this way.

Kat had never thought about leaving the skating rink with Odell and the others on Saturday night until the offer had been unexpectedly made. It had been Kat's quick acquiescence that led to the young couple going along. Thinking back on it, she and Odell could have gotten into a lot of trouble had they been caught.

She had a really good time with Mike and his girlfriend, and Sue had promised they would get together again soon. Sue seemed to be a really affable girl even though she was a year older. They had bonded when alone in her car at the DQ, and Kat thought they could possibly become best friends. Kat's current cadre of friends didn't have the level of easy openness that Sue projected. If given the chance, Kat could envision the older girl providing much needed advice especially on the subject of boyfriends.

What would've happened if Sue had car trouble that night, or if we had a wreck, or if somebody saw us and told our parents?

Any of those things would have been devastating to her and Odell. Maybe the uncertainty of what could've occurred made the night even more exciting. She just knew that it had been fun, and it was leading her to believe taking chances might be in her future choices.

There had been a negative portion of the evening concerning her desire to tell Odell about her fears of moving. She had intended to relay those anxieties while they were at the rink that night, but never really had the chance because of the surprise double-date and the fact she dreaded the conversation, too.

Just yesterday, Kat's father had told the family over dinner that he had been offered a supervisor's position in Brunswick. The news had only intensified Kat's insecurity over the possibility of losing Odell, and she had lost control over her bubbling emotions. Halfway through the meal, she had excused herself from the table and gone into her bathroom where she cried into a towel in order to keep the sounds of grief muffled.

Later in the day, Kat's mom had tried to console her with hugs and assurances that no final decisions had been made about moving to South Georgia. It was an opportunity that would be hard to turn down, however. The salary raise would be substantial, and the Normans would be able to buy a nice home.

Her mother had also used a little psychology and said how nice it would be closer to beaches. Kat was aware how much Mom loved that environment and felt selfish to keep her away from those dreams. Mom deserved happiness and had always sacrificed her own for Kat. These conflicting thoughts only made Kat more anxious about the uncertain future.

A horn blowing in the driveway snapped Kat out of her thoughts. Her mother came through the room in a hurry stopping only for a quick kiss to Kat's forehead.

"Have a good day, Sweetie. I'll be home around dinner time. I've left some ground beef thawing, and I thought maybe meatloaf would be good tonight," her mom said.

Kat nodded absent-mindedly and watched her go out the door without saying anything in response. The hurt and desperation she felt over what seemed to be a situation over which she had no control was almost too much to bear. She could feel tears welling in her eyes again and just couldn't stop the floodgate when it opened just moments later.

In the fifteen and half years she had lived, Kat didn't think she had ever cried as much as she had over the weekend. Madi sensed her anguish and showed love in her dark eyes as she whimpered along with Kat before nuzzling against her again.

After several more minutes of feeling sorry for herself, Kat got out of the chair and went into her room. She went to her small desk and pulled out a sheet of stationary that had been a gift from her grandmother the previous Christmas. Until now, Kat had only used the special paper to write Granny periodically, but now wanted to tell Odell what she couldn't seem to find a way to say to him otherwise.

For the next thirty minutes Kat wrote from her heart and then sealed the letter in a matching envelope addressed to Odell. She then hid the envelope underneath other papers inside the desk vowing to herself not to send it or give to him unless they became separated. She could only hope that never happened.

CHAPTER 35

Poochie's, or as everyone called Sandy's, dad had a nickname for the neighborhood kids, "The Odie Boys." Odell wasn't sure how or why the name had developed, but he guessed it was because so much of the time everybody would congregate at his house and they were all guys. The few girls in the area rarely came to the yard, and the gathering of boys in the back today was pretty much standard.

Odell had become more or less the leader of the bunch, partly because he was one of the older kids in this section of Bloomfield, and maybe to some extent due to his sense of responsibility. He didn't mind being seen as such, and he realized those traits had spilled over into similar roles at school as he had served as Junior Beta Club president last year and planned to run for student council when the new year started. Leadership roles didn't scare him at all, and he'd rather be in that position instead of being simply a follower.

As everybody milled around the backyard this morning, it suddenly hit him again that he probably wouldn't be doing this next summer. He'd be working somewhere so he could get a car and take Kat out on real dates. The boys would have to find someone else to take his place and be in charge. It would be sad in a way to see the end of "The Odie Boys." Odell, however, was ready to move on to another chapter in his life that included more grownup activities.

He announced they would practice some fundamentals for a while in preparation of the semi-final tournament game scheduled for tomorrow. First, he hit ground balls to the infielders and had them throw to Dewey at first base. It was a pretty rough drill to complete successfully on the uneven yard, but the boys did fairly well. It became even more difficult when Odell told them to try to turn imaginary double-plays, and there were several missed balls and wild throws to Dewey who often had a hard time catching the most routine throws.

Realizing that the conditions were not the best for this practice, Odell finally had the infielders rest and told the outfielders to line up at the far end of the yard. He then took turns hitting fly balls to each of them. Sandy and Bruce were good at circling under the flies and catching them. Odell instructed them to throw the caught balls to Mitch the catcher with Bruce being much better as he had the stronger arm. Billy, the right fielder, didn't catch anything hit to him and every throw he made was completely off target.

Odell wasn't too worried about anything he'd seen at this point. They had played every game during the regular season without very many problems mainly because he had pitched around any errors. Besides, he knew they had beaten Pine Forest

Baptist already without problems, and they would do it again tomorrow.

"Do y'all want any batting practice?" asked Odell when he called them together as a group.

The August heat was quickly rising, and it seemed nobody had much interest. Odell looked at the kids sitting around him underneath the big oak tree. Most had sweat stains on their tee shirts, and Odell could feel the wetness under his arms, as well. Dewey's face was flushed to a bright red. Billy's tongue was actually hanging out of his mouth.

"Okay, let's call it a day. Everybody be ready tomorrow," Odell said.

He walked back to the house and went inside. Since he was sweaty already, he thought about going down to Kat's and cutting their grass. He got a pitcher of tea out of the refrigerator and poured a tall glass full not bothering to get out any ice.

Taking a big gulp, he went through the entrance to the den and over to the telephone. Odell didn't think much about it as he dialed Kat's number.

"Hello," said Kat.

"Hey. It's me. I've been practicing with the guys and pretty sweaty. Since I am, I thought I'd come to your house and cut the grass. Is that okay?"

She paused for a second and then replied, "Yeah. I'm at home by myself, so I don't have the money to pay you."

Odell thought Kat sounded a little strange. Her voice was shaky, and didn't she know he didn't care about money.

"Well, that sounds partly tempting. Too bad I'm probably more than a tad bit stinky right now," he replied.

There was another delay before Kat responded, "Sorry. Not feeling very well. I'll try to be better when you get here. Don't worry about how you smell."

"Okay, see you in a little while," said Odell.

There was something going on. Odell could feel it in his bones. He briefly wondered if he should take a shower before going to Kat's and then thought how stupid that idea was. He was going to cut the grass in ninety-plus temperatures. Odell loved showers, but he should wait until he was through with the work ahead.

He went outside and got the lawnmower. After filling the gas tank, he started pushing it up the road to Kat's house. Along the way, his mind raced.

I think I'm in love. I know I'm too young, but Kat is special. I don't think I'll ever meet anyone like her. I can't think about anything else. That's got to be love, right?

In less than three weeks, Odell would be a high school sophomore. Less than five months after that, he would be sixteen and could drive by himself. When he graduated from Willingham, he'd go to college and if he listened to his parents, maybe to law school afterwards.

Where did Kat fit in those plans? Everywhere. That's what he hoped for anyway.

He wanted somebody who believed in his dreams like he did. It was an idealistic view of the world that consumed him.

Odell got to the house, and he didn't go to the front door. Instead, he immediately cranked up the machine and started to cut the grass. He worked as fast as he could with clippings and dust flying around him.

It took him a good hour to finish. When he cut off the engine, Odell swiped his face with the shoulder of his tee shirt and headed toward the front stoop. He only intended to tell Kat he'd finished and maybe they'd have some time to get together later in the week.

Kat was at the front door as he stepped up the last step. Her face showed something new. They stood there for what seemed like an hour staring into each other's eyes. She appeared happy and sad at the same time. She slung herself into his arms and kissed him fiercely.

The next thing he knew, the two of them were inside the house. He had never held anybody as close as she was now to him. His chest was next to her breasts, and his groin was getting intimate with that corresponding part of her, albeit protected by the shorts they wore. He felt himself growing as their mouths consumed each other. With little knowledge and zero experience of the feelings or the acts, they found themselves on her couch grinding and writhing against one another while still clothed in sweaty attire.

It was an out of body occurrence for Odell as he broke away from kissing Kat and got lost in her eyes as they gazed at each other. Without warning and no words spoken, she lifted her tee shirt to almost under her chin so that both nipples were staring him in the face. Odell had only seen pictures of the feminine anatomy before, so this was a new breathtaking experience.

There was something about the contrasts of color that only led to a sense of intoxication in Odell's brain. The tanned skin of her flat belly ended where the roundness of her breasts began to form into perfectly shaped orbs punctuated on top by pinkish-red tips that were currently at attention. Speechless, but salivating, Odell lowered his lips down and tasted the left one while feeling the other with his right hand.

Kat moaned into his ear as he tried to be gentle like Mike had told him to be. Part of his brain was still telling Odell that he needed to stop, but he wasn't sure that was possible.

Oh, God! I love this girl.

"What did you say?" she whispered.

He snapped out of the moment and raised himself from the top of her body. He briefly stood up and then sat on the couch next to where Kat was still laying. She slid her shirt back over her bare breasts with him watching intently before she sat up and slid closer to him. He was totally mesmerized by her beauty at that moment.

"I'm crazy about you, Kat. You've got me thinking about things that make me excited and scared at the same time," Odell said with some exasperation.

"Yeah, I feel the same way," Kat sighed.

"I hope you know that I want to, you know…," he trailed off.

"Me, too," she breathed out.

"I'm just worried about so many things. Getting caught, not knowing what to do when we go that far, afraid of hurting you, and getting you pregnant are some of them," Odell said without looking at Kat.

She reached over and took his hand into hers. They sat for the next several minutes without talking. The cogs of his brain were churning hard as Odell wondered what to say next.

"Life's too short for us not to live it. Let's think about it a few days and get back together Thursday or Friday and see where it goes. Maybe we can be better prepared then," she said with a crooked smile.

She must be thinking the same thing I am, his brain told him.

"Okay, sounds like a plan to me," Odell replied and got up to go home.

He gave Kat one more kiss, and then as he was leaving, Odell looked back to see Madi come into the room and jump in Kat's lap. Right now, he wished that he could swap positions with that dog in that very spot.

CHAPTER 36

Odell had another fitful night with dreams of Kat filling every fantasy imaginable. He awoke feeling drained emotionally and had an ache inside that wouldn't leave him. He lay in the bed with thoughts of her swirling throughout his being. It took a while for the erection to subside leaving him feeling unfulfilled and more than a little guilty.

He had never felt so frustrated. Odell had always thought of himself as being fairly smart, but he didn't have an idea what to do about Kat. She obviously was experiencing growing pains as he was. Yesterday, he had felt as close to paradise as he'd ever come. He and Kat could've easily gone too far, and he knew it. In fact, he didn't know how he'd stopped before it did.

How would it end? he thought.

Odell didn't want it to end. There were a lot of good times ahead. The two of them would share them. They just had to.

He got out of the bed with Kenny lightly snoring on his side and went to the bathroom. The piss ran out of his body into the commode, and it caused a momentary lapse of anxiety. Odell thought he was flushing those feelings when he pushed the lever downward.

Odell glanced at the hallway clock as he passed into the kitchen. Just a few minutes before five a.m. He wondered if it would be alright to start his dad's percolator and decided maybe he should wait a while longer. It was pretty loud when it got going, and he didn't want to disturb anyone who could sleep longer than he seemed to be capable of.

He looked inside the refrigerator and got out a half-full bottle of milk that was wet with condensation. He swigged a goodly portion out of the container and then replaced it on the shelf. The heavy coldness sliding down his dry throat had a calming quality. It wasn't coffee, but it would have to do until Daddy got up.

After standing still in the center of the room for a few moments feeling a little disassociated, Odell padded into the den and flopped on the sofa. His thoughts, as they had for the last couple of months, drifted back to Kat.

They had time on their side, at least that's what he thought. There was no need to get in a rush with their feelings. He thought it inevitable that they would become more intimate, but they had plenty of time.

He had to figure out something in the next couple of days because Kat had hinted quite strongly there would be more intimacy than already experienced. What had happened had been significant already, and anything else might very well lead to the ultimate prize.

As he contemplated his future with Kat, his father walked through the den. He paused a few steps from Odell with a cigarette drooping from his lips.

"Up early again, I see. Everything okay? Y'all have a game today, right?"

"Yes, sir. Just fell awake. Not too worried about the team we're playing."

"Want some coffee?"

"I'd love a cup. I've gotten where I look forward to one every morning," Odell said following his father into the kitchen.

The coffee maker was turned on and it started slowly. The gurgling sounds built into a burping crescendo before calming down signaling it was done.

His father prepared his usual sugary concoction and then Odell did his own version of the black nectar. Both Sterlings seemed somewhat out of sorts with no conversation taking place during the preparation.

Odell wished he could talk to his dad about the jumbled feelings going through his head. The last attempt to have a discussion about Kat hadn't gone all that well. It was an awkward subject to bring up under the best of conditions; besides, Daddy seemed preoccupied with something, too.

Usually, his father would've gone out to get the morning paper or at least ask Odell or one of his brothers to make the trip to the box for him. This morning he just sat in his chair smoking and drinking from his mug while staring blankly ahead.

"Anything wrong, Daddy?" asked Odell after a few minutes of silence.

Turning to face Odell, he took a long drag from the cigarette and then slowly exhaled letting the plume of smoke drift around the dimly lit room. He did a little head shake showing that maybe what was on his mind shouldn't be discussed with a teenaged son.

"Probably shouldn't tell you, but you're smart and got a good head on your shoulders. My boss at the plant offered me a supervisor's job about a week ago. I don't know whether I should take it or not. Supposed to let him know by today," he said.

"That's great, Daddy. Why wouldn't you take it? You'd be getting a raise and a position carrying respect, right?"

The elder Sterling took another drag and then rubbed his other calloused hand over the left side of his face. Odell could hear the scratch of the overnight stubble from where he sat.

"You know I only went through the ninth grade. I ain't stupid, but that's all the schooling I got. A supervisor needs to be able to read and write good. You've got to do weekly reports and have meetings with really educated people. I don't think I could do that stuff," he said with a slight hint of dejection.

Odell studied the man's face and thought about how those bottled-up feelings might lead to a defeatist attitude. He'd always thought about the strength of his father and the basic goodness of him despite his roughness around the edges. His work ethic was admirable and equaled only by his mother's. Besides, he was a lot smarter than he probably realized. Book knowledge he might not have, but experience and hard work more than made up for that in Odell's mind.

"Daddy, I believe you can do whatever you need to in order to do that job. You read the paper every day from front to back. I bet not everybody does that, so I know you can read well enough. Your writing skills aren't bad either. You'd be looking over people doing the same job you've been doing for twenty years, so that would be easy for you. You should go for it. Maybe you won't have to work quite as hard as you do now and have more money, too," Odell said sincerely.

"I've thought about all that before. You don't know this, but they offered me the same job a few years ago, and I turned it down. I got worried about the same things bothering me now. Management ended up giving the position to somebody else who ain't worth a shit. He's lazy as hell and can't write any better than I can," his father said with a little anger in his voice.

"You'd never be called lazy, Daddy. You and Mama work harder than anybody I know. I really think you ought to take the job. If you want me to, maybe I could even help you write up a report. You can tell me what kind of info needs to go in it," replied Odell.

His father's face relaxed and he stubbed out the cigarette. "You're a good boy," he said huskily as he walked back toward his bedroom.

CHAPTER 37

Odell's mother had already gone to work, and his father was about to leave for his job, too. The last thing he'd done was to fry a pound of bacon now sitting on a paper towel lined platter, and to fix a big pot of grits that still sat on an eye of the stove cut down to low heat. He drained most of the bacon grease from the cast iron pan into a silver metal dripping container leaving just a little residue in the pan.

"You'll have to get your brothers up in a little while. All you'll need to do is cook them some eggs. I left the grits a little runny, but they'll thicken up. Your mama was running late this morning and didn't get any biscuits ready, so you might do some toast, too, if y'all want some. Sorry, we won't be able to see y'all play today," he said.

"No problem, Daddy. Sandy's mama and John are going to take us to the field. I'll get everybody up in a few minutes and take care of them. Did you decide about the supervisor's position?" Odell inquired.

The corners of his father's lips turned up slightly and he gave one quick nod, "Yeah, guess I'm going for it. I appreciate what you said this morning. Alright, got to go," he said leaving in a hurry carrying his worn tin lunch box.

As he went out to the old 57 Ford and cranked it up, Odell saw his father look through the windshield at him standing at the back door window. Odell couldn't quite tell due to the distance, but he thought Daddy wiped away a tear before driving out the back driveway. Odell had never seen his dad cry, so he wasn't sure.

Odell, being a fairly new convert to the beverage, rarely drank more than a cup of coffee but had gotten almost another half cup out of the pot before his father left. He now took it into the den and sat down in the chair where his dad had been earlier. The ashtray next to it was almost over-flowing, and Odell wished he had emptied the thing before sitting there. It had an odor that he was used to but was far from pleasant.

Odell sipped his drink and thought about the day ahead. The game was an important one since it was a single elimination tournament. They had to win in order to play for the championship scheduled for next week.

For some reason, and only he really knew why, the game didn't seem all that important. As he thought about it, he had played in other contests over the years with varying amounts of importance attached to them, and most had turned out well because of the concentration he generated before and during the game. The difference now was Kat-related for sure, and he just couldn't focus on baseball like it had once dominated his being.

We beat those guys last time. I'm not worried about them. I wonder what Kat's doing today, he thought.

The thoughts were typical at this point. Thinking about anything other than the girl down the road became clouded almost immediately. He considered calling her and then remembered it was still early in the morning.

He sighed and shifted his mind back to the Pine Forest Baptist team. It was the only church to sponsor a team in their league and being a large congregation should have a lot of boys on the team.

Ricky Lee hadn't played with them last time. If he did this time, Odell would definitely have to be careful with him. Not only was Ricky Lee a good player, but Odell had also struggled to find a way to get him out when they opposed each other in the past. They had a history as former teammates and adversaries.

Odell remembered a game in little league when Ricky Lee had gone three for three against him and had almost hit one out of the park. It was a source of pride that Odell had never given up a homerun to anyone, and his nemesis had come dangerously close that day when he blasted one off the left-center field wall.

Yeah, if he plays today, I'll need to watch how I pitch to him.

His youngest brother came into the room wiping sleep from his eyes. Odell loved the kid like he did all his brothers. Being the baby, Lynn could be a pain in the butt, though. He turned on the television and started watching without saying anything to Odell. Wayne, only a couple of years older, came through a few minutes later and plopped down near Lynn, followed last by Kenny.

Odell guessed that they were all used to getting up early because of their parents' work schedules. It didn't matter too much whether school was in session or it was summer vacation.

"No biscuits this morning. Y'all want toast with grits and eggs?" Odell asked.

"Yeah, but I want extra butter on mine," replied Wayne.

"Me, too," said Lynn.

Kenny, the most laidback of the three simply nodded his assent. He then asked, "What time do we play, two o'clock?"

"Yeah, John's coming by at one and picking up some of us. The rest can ride with Sandy. It might be a little crowded, but it'll work out. Y'all want fried or scrambled?"

After getting orders from the three, Odell was just about to get up and start frying eggs when Lynn addressed him again. He made a request that came around less often than when they all were a little younger, but it tickled Odell to hear it again. He laughed when Lynn asked that he tell a story.

The oldest of the four had once made-up tales to entertain them when they were all bored. The stories often came as a result of crazy or whimsical dreams that Odell had, but as he thought about it, most of those recent ones couldn't be repeated now because they would be X-rated.

"Alright, a short one because I need to get breakfast done. Once upon a time, there were four brothers living across from a forest that had the biggest trees in all of Georgia. I mean, these things were huge and stretched so far up in the sky that you couldn't see the tops of them in some places," he said pausing.

"The oldest one was named Odell, and he was brave. He owned a .22 caliber rifle with a scope. His brother, Kenny, had a

.410-gauge shotgun. Wayne had a pump-up pellet rifle and Lynn had a BB gun."

Odell proceeded to tell a short yarn of the brothers going into the woods to explore. At some point they got lost and then discovered another world hidden within the forest that was inhabited by dinosaurs and other creatures unknown in their world. They had to use their collective wits to save each other until they finally found the secret way out of the enchanted land.

When Odell finished the fanciful story by telling them he needed someone to help with the toast, they all volunteered. It remained the subject of conversation as they ate, and no one even mentioned the upcoming game.

CHAPTER 38

The boys unloaded themselves and their equipment from the two cars that had transported them to the ballfield. Sandy's mom, a small woman with a smoker's voice, was the only adult in the bunch and followed them down the hill to where the game was to be played. Odell thought she didn't seem very interested in the event, but he appreciated her help in getting the team to the destination.

As some of the Renegades started tossing balls back and forth, Odell strolled with Johnny to their dugout. They sat down on the bench and started discussing the upcoming game. As usual, the older boy was visibly nervous about their opponents.

"This is going to be a tough game, O. Look at them over there. They don't have little kids on their team like we do," Johnny said wringing his hands.

"So, what else is new? That's been true every game we've played this year, Johnny. You know, they don't look like they have enough guys to even play, at least not so far. I don't see Ricky Lee either," replied Odell.

Odell counted the other team and came up with only seven players. He scanned all of them and recognized several from the last time they played earlier in the summer. Although his interest in playing was still clouded by thoughts of Kat, Odell hoped to win the contest outright and not by forfeit of the opposing team for not having enough players. He hated the idea of winning that way and figured that some of their teammates were simply running late and would be there any minute.

There were still about twenty minutes before the game was scheduled to begin, so he grabbed Mitchell and started warming up. With just a few throws, Odell felt the competitive juices start to flow. He felt healthy, strong and confident of his abilities. As his pre-game routine continued, Odell didn't notice Ricky Lee's arrival along with another of his friends.

"Well, well, if it ain't Slow-dell. I see your fastball hasn't gotten any faster there, old buddy," said Ricky Lee as he walked up behind Odell.

Odell didn't say anything, but he threw the next practice pitch as hard as he could. It slapped into Mitchell's mitt with a loud smack.

"Ooooh, I'm skert now," laughed Ricky Lee.

Odell caught the return throw before rotating to his old friend. Ricky Lee had his patented grin plastered on his face and his cap perched on the back of his head. He was chewing a big wad of gum.

"We meet again," said Odell.

Ricky Lee stepped closer and inspected Odell's face, "Looks like you've shaved. I was going to help you out, but I guess I'm too late."

Odell rubbed his chin self-consciously. He had removed his sparse whiskers yesterday taking special care of the ones that normally populated the small mole located there.

"What have you been doing all summer? You didn't play in the last game and I was ready to kick your ass," said Odell.

"In your dreams, Slow-dell," Ricky Lee replied through his big teeth. "Went on a family vacation or I would've led us to victory like I plan to do today. You'll be crying like a baby when we finish off your little punk team."

Odell could feel his face starting to flush. Ricky Lee was trying to push his buttons and was succeeding. Odell knew that he needed to keep cool in order to keep his emotions in check.

Odell laughed and hoped it didn't sound fake or nervous to Ricky Lee as it did to himself. All he wanted to do now was to start the game and show this butthole who was the best.

"We didn't lose a game during the regular season, and y'all lost as many as you won. So, I guess my 'little punks' are better than yours," sneered Odell.

Ricky Lee walked to his side of the field and blew a huge bubble with his gum. Pointing toward Odell first, he then took the same finger and burst the pink orb before sticking the glob back in his mouth.

He then yelled to Odell, "Gonna bust your bubble today, Slow-dell!"

Odell hadn't ever been in a mind game like this. At this point, Kat had gone to another recess in his brain and beating Ricky Lee was all he could think about. The only way to get rid of negative feelings was to humiliate him.

Johnny walked over to Odell as he stewed over Ricky Lee's actions and remarks. There was a look of concern on Johnny's face and he squeezed his hands together over and over making squishy sounds.

"I don't think they've got enough eligible players, O. That guy you were talking to, he rode in the car with the other one. His name is Randy and, in my class, so I know he's got to be at least sixteen. He can't be on the roster filed with the league. We need to protest to the umpire before the game starts," Johnny said.

"You're sure?" Odell asked.

"Ninety-nine point nine per cent sure."

After thinking about it for a second, Odell responded, "I don't care. I want to play. We can still beat them. I'm not worried about the other guy."

"O, listen. Don't let your ego keep us from being guaranteed the championship game next week. If we play and lose without filing a protest, it's over. No more chances."

"Winning by forfeit is like kissing your sister, even if I don't have one. I want to win on the field, and I want to shut up that smartass Ricky Lee once and for all," said Odell as he stalked to their dugout.

The more Odell watched the other team warming up, the more heated he became. Ricky Lee kept puffing out his cheeks to produce pink balls from his mouth as he threw some practice pitches. Odell assumed he was going to pitch and studied his unorthodox windup.

Right away, he recognized it would give most of his team trouble. His opponent was sneaky fast and could alter his delivery several ways. Odell remembered the two of them tossing balls back and forth last year testing each other's speed and ability to make pitches curve.

Yeah, this will be a pitcher's duel, old friend.

Odell turned to his teammates. Most were loose and not paying any attention across the way. Mitchell was doing impersonations of tv characters, and a couple of the younger boys were playing rock, paper, scissors. They had gotten used to winning this summer, and Odell knew they depended on him to get them through today.

"Okay, listen y'all. Ricky Lee, their pitcher, is probably the best ball player we've been against this year. He'll be hard for most of you to hit what he throws. We need to do what we've done in a couple of other games," Odell began.

"Everybody take the first pitch, at least, if not the first two. Billy, you and Dewey, try not to swing at anything and you just might get on base with a walk. If you're not scared to, get a little closer to the plate. He could even hit you with a pitch, if you crowd it just a bit."

"I will, Odell. I don't mind getting hit," said Billy.

"Me, too," chimed in Dewey.

"Okay, but if either of you get on base, don't try to steal. I expect this to be a low scoring game, and a run or two might very well win for us. Mitchell, if you or Sandy can lay down a good bunt, do it. Since both of you are our fastest runners, if either of y'all get on base, steal second if you get a chance."

The salty old umpire who had been behind the plate for most of the games called the captains to the plate. Odell and Ricky Lee walked to where he stood. Not a very nice-looking guy anyway, he was even less so with a wad of chewing tobacco in his right cheek. The overweight ump spat a wet splotch off to the side causing Odell to wonder how anyone could put the nasty stuff in their mouth.

Odell had to admit to himself that looks, habits or manners didn't matter as long as the guy in charge of enforcing the game made the right calls. Since Odell had thought the other games were called fairly, he could overlook any other personality defects.

"Alright, you guys have seen me in action more than once. Y'all know what I expect. No cussing or any unsportsmanlike conduct. Any questions?"

Odell looked at Ricky Lee first and then at the ump. "If I suspected the other team had an ineligible player, what would I do to protest?"

Ricky Lee's eyes narrowed, and Odell could see he had touched a nerve. The umpire cocked his head from one to the other teens.

"What do you mean? Do you have some proof?"

"I guess it would be called hearsay since it is based on what I heard from somebody else. I don't have direct knowledge," responded Odell.

"That's bullsh--, crap. You're just scared you're going to get beat, Odell, and you know it," blurted Ricky Lee.

Odell now thought he'd turned the mind game in his favor. He smirked at his friend who was blushing.

"You know what I've said about using profanities on this field. I could disqualify you for that right now and give the win to the Renegades," the ump said and paused.

Ricky Lee hung his head and muttered, "Yes, sir. I'm sorry."

He studied Odell and asked, "If you've got some reason to file a protest that you feel like you can prove, tell me now and then tell the scorekeeper. Otherwise, we need to get this game started."

"It's okay, Mr. Ump. We're ready to play," said Odell while staring at Ricky Lee.

"Let's play ball then. You're the home team, so take the field."

Odell walked a little lighter on his feet back to the dugout. It had felt good to get under his obnoxious friend's skin. He was ready to play and didn't give a flip that there may be a sixteen-year-old on the other team. This was a chance to gain bragging rights that he was not willing to squander.

"Let's go get 'em, boys!" Odell called out and the rest ran to the field.

Johnny approached Odell and seemed upset. "Why didn't you protest?"

Odell shrugged and said, "I guess you're right. My ego won't let me."

CHAPTER 39

Kat sat in her new friend's car, riding to the park where Odell was playing baseball. She had called Sue after her mother had given permission before going to work. Kat had told a couple of little white lies about Sue, telling her mom that they were friends from school and that they would be going to the library. Nevertheless, Kat had been surprised by her mother allowing her to go and attributed her consent to Kat's recent melancholy mood.

Odell had been on her mind constantly since the day before. She needed to talk to somebody else about the feelings she was having about him, and the first person she thought of was Sue. Kat really didn't feel close enough to anyone else to have such a conversation.

When Kat called her, Sue had offered for them to get together to do something, and a plan had been hatched to ride around and maybe get some lunch. To support at least part of the falsehood, the two girls had gone to the Washington Library earlier, and Kat had checked out a couple of books. Going to watch Odell play had not been on the agenda until Kat remembered that he'd told her about it.

The two girls chatted about their lives so far, and Sue listened to Kat as she told her new friend of her hopes and fears. Kat explained how the family had moved around since she was a kid, and now it appeared they would be moving again in the very near future.

"I'm telling you, Sue, I think I'll die if we move to Brunswick. I looked it up on a map and it's a long way from Macon. I know we've only lived in our current place for a year, but I've liked it better than anywhere I've ever lived. I'd have to start all over again and wouldn't know anybody. Maybe I wouldn't feel quite this way if I hadn't met Odell because it's never bothered me very much in the past," Kat said.

"I can tell it's emotional for you. The new school year is only a couple weeks away and the thought of moving to a town that you've never been to would scare the hell out of me, too," replied Sue.

"It's all messing with my head, Sue. My parents try so hard to protect me, sometimes too hard. They deserve to be happy, and I know being close to the coast would be a dream come true for Mom. I'm sure they believe moving down south would be good for all of us," Kat said and paused.

"This summer has awakened something inside me that I can't tell them about. Odell and I haven't gone too far, but I have to admit I've wanted to. I don't mean to be overly personal. I thought maybe by talking to you I could get some advice about what I should do," finished Kat.

Sue had a hearty laugh and replied, "That's funny if you think I'm someone to give guidance about life. You don't know how screwed up mine has been. I'll tell you this, being fifteen was the hardest year of my lifetime, at least so far. Until I met Mike, I was so insecure about everything. Even though he's a year younger, there was something about him I liked almost immediately. Believe me, you'll get through this period, and maybe Odell is the one to help you like Mike did for me. He seems like a good guy and must be since my boyfriend really likes him."

"The problem is I might not have enough time to find out. I do think Odell and I could help each other grow up some and get through these tween years," said Kat sadly.

"Yeah, I guess if you two were a couple of hundred miles apart your budding love life would be pretty much shot to hell. I can only imagine if I was in your shoes. I'm sorry, Kat," she said shaking her head.

"Thanks, Sue. I just don't feel like I have any control at this point. I must admit that I'm more than a little jealous of you. Besides being old enough to drive and having your own car to get around in, you seem to have yourself together, know what I mean?"

"Okay, guess I've got you fooled. Look, Kat. I know I'm pretty lucky. It hasn't been long ago that I was feeling a lot of the same things you're going through, except for maybe moving away. I don't have it all together, I wish I did. Just because I'm sixteen and old enough to drive doesn't mean crap. Maybe I know how to jack off my boyfriend and you don't, that doesn't mean anything either. There's a lot of stuff we don't know. Don't get bogged down, girl. I hope it works out with Odell, but life won't end if it doesn't. I like Mike, a lot. But, you know what? I don't think he'll be my forever love. Maybe you shouldn't think the same about Odell."

"So, you don't think you and Mike are in love?"

"Well, maybe a version of it. I guess when you've never experienced close feelings about somebody else, it's hard to know. Yeah, I have really strong feelings about Mike, and I think we'll be together a while. My head tells me that we're too young to know what love is, so truthfully, I don't know. There's a big world out there, a lot bigger than Bloomfield, Macon and even Georgia. I want to experience all of it. All I'm saying is that you shouldn't give up or restrict yourself," Sue said.

Sue parked her car near a few others situated adjacent to the ball field. The girls had their windows down, and Kat recognized some of the voices urging Odell to strike out whoever was batting. Rather than immediately walking down to the field, the girls continued their conversation.

"I guess you're probably right, Sue. I read a lot of books and magazines, and they can take me to faraway places that I've dreamed about, but since I've gotten to know Odell, he's all I think about. It's a little scary when we get close. I think about doing things with him. I want to, really bad. I just don't know enough about sex. Anything you can tell me?"

For the next fifteen minutes, Sue obliged by telling Kat everything she knew on the subject. Kat listened with rapt attention to the tips Sue imparted. Every question posed to the older girl was answered to Kat's satisfaction. They were laughing about various names given the male anatomy when Kat heard a collective groan from the field. Even from the distance away, she could tell something bad had just happened in the game based on Odell's body language.

CHAPTER 40

Odell was not pitching a bad ball game, although he didn't have his best stuff today. Through the first three innings, he'd only given up two hits. However, he'd gotten to a full count with several batters and was fortunate not to have walked anybody yet.

The first time against Ricky Lee, the bubble gum king had hit a double off Odell much to his chagrin. He had obnoxiously hooted at Odell while standing on second base behind where he stood on the pitcher's mound. His continuous badgering continued through the next two batters. The saving grace had been Odell's ability to keep him from scoring by getting the next batter to pop up and then striking out the next one. The only other hit by Pine Forest had been a squibbler down the third base line that Ken was unable to throw out. Their sixteen-year-old player had been a non-factor striking out twice so far.

The Renegades hadn't been able to score either. To this point, none of them had gotten a hit, and Odell had been the only runner after walking his first time up to bat. Ricky Lee was obviously pitching around him, and there was nothing he could do about it.

It was the top of the fourth inning and the nothing-to-nothing score was feeling a little ominous. This was the first time all summer the Renegades were this far into a game without the lead. Odell was sweating profusely on the mound and not feeling as confident as he had before the game started. To make matters worse, he had looked on top of the hill and thought he saw Sue's car. Surely, she wasn't there, but he had a moment of doubt when he thought he saw Kat inside the vehicle.

He couldn't let himself think about that right now. Ricky Lee was at bat again blowing bubbles and grinning like a maniac. Odell knew he couldn't give him anything good to hit.

Mitchell called a timeout and jogged to the mound. He looked up at Odell and smirked before saying, "O, you haven't tried throwing side-armed in a while. Why don't you try it with this butthole?"

Odell thought it might just work. It sure couldn't hurt since Ricky Lee seemed able to hit his regular delivery easily enough last time at bat.

"Yeah, let's try it. Let's go hard inside corner, hard outside corner and finish with curve outside," replied Odell.

The plan worked like a charm. The first two pitches had Ricky Lee's timing off as he took two strikes without swinging. The third produced a weak swing that resulted in an easy grounder back to Odell that he tossed to first base without Ricky Lee even trying to run. The scowl on his face made Odell smile and hopeful for victory.

In their bottom of the inning, the Renegades finally got a break when Mitchell coaxed a walk and was able to steal second. Sandy struck out, but Kenny was able to get Mitchell to third with an infield hit. With runners on the corners and only one out, Ricky Lee would have to pitch to Odell so as not to load the bases.

Before stepping into the batter's box, Odell called Johnny over from the third base coach's area. He had an idea that might work but would need Mitchell's speed and awareness.

"Tell Mitchell I'm going for the suicide squeeze play on the first pitch. Ricky Lee will never expect me to bunt," whispered Odell.

"Are you sure? You probably won't get another chance like this for him to throw anything you can hit," Johnny whispered back.

"Yeah, I'm sure. A run can win this game. Let's do it," replied Odell.

Johnny jogged back to his place and spoke privately to Mitchell while Odell took his place in the box. He nodded toward Ricky Lee and slowly swung his bat back and forth with as much menace as he could muster.

Ricky Lee went into his stretch looking at the runners on each base before staring at the catcher behind the plate. He shook off a pitch before throwing a low ball on the outside corner. At the last second, Odell squared off in the box as Mitchell broke toward home. Odell deadened the ball with his bat as it dribbled straight toward Ricky Lee.

The pitcher was fooled just enough. He was able to run forward and grab the slow-rolling bunt, but by then Mitchell was sliding into home plate. All he could do was throw the ball to first to easily get Odell out as the Renegades scored the first run of the game. Cheers rung out from their side as Odell turned to Ricky Lee and gave him a big grin. It was a highlight, and he loved the moment as much as any he had ever experienced on a ballfield. Ricky Lee actually nodded to Odell touching his cap momentarily in acknowledgement.

The fifth inning went by uneventfully although Odell walked two batters. He couldn't remember being that wild in a while and attributed it to his elbow starting to hurt. During their half of the inning, he sat on the end of the bench rubbing it constantly.

If there was any consolation, Ricky Lee was looking a little tired, too. He walked Billy who was the worst batter on the Renegades. Billy was ecstatic standing on first base and kept dancing on and off the bag as if he were contemplating a steal of second.

A mantra rose from several of the guys on the bench. It sprung from the team knowing Billy's predisposition to try and run when in that position and knowing it never worked.

"Don't steal, Billy. Don't steal, Billy. Don't steal, Billy!" several of the boys shouted in unison.

Odell watched in disbelief as the pigeon-toed slowpoke took off toward second base against the advice of his teammates. The

Pine Forest catcher caught the pitch and fired it to their second baseman reaching him in plenty of time. The fielder with ball in glove was waiting on Billy when he started his slide way too soon. Billy's foot never came close to touching the base as he was tagged out.

Odell could only shake his head at the stupidity. Billy jogged back to the dugout bragging falsely of how close the play had been while Bruce berated him for trying.

As the inning ended, Odell grabbed his glove and walked slowly out to the mound. He couldn't remember being this hot and tired in a long time. His elbow felt so tight that he didn't know if he could throw another curve ball. He didn't even try to make any warmup tosses and waited for the other team's first batter.

Come on, O. One more inning, three more outs. Get through this and we'll win the championship next week, he said to himself.

Odell watched as the lowest end of the other team's batting order stepped up to the plate. Ricky Lee was not due up until fifth in the inning, so Odell knew he only needed to get three of the next four out and his nemesis would never even have another opportunity. He couldn't let that happen with only a one run lead.

From his first pitch to the equivalent of their team's Billy, Odell could tell it was not going to be easy. His normal pinpoint control had left him. The batter never swung his bat as the count went to three balls and two strikes.

Sweat ran into Odell's eyes and his glasses kept sliding down on his nose. He took them off and mopped his face with the short sleeve of his shirt that was wet with perspiration as well.

Finally, he wound up and threw the payoff pitch that lacked Odell's usual velocity. It crossed the plate a tad low and the batter never lifted the bat from his shoulder. The ump didn't call the pitch for an uncomfortable second, but finally raised his right hand calling, "Strike three, you're out!"

Two more to go, thought Odell as the infield tossed the baseball around. When it was thrown back to him, he faced their leadoff hitter.

Odell knew their next few batters pretty well. They were all decent players, but he hadn't had any real problems with any of them except Ricky Lee who still had three more ahead of him in the lineup.

Just throw strikes, Odell repeated through his brain.

The first two pitches he threw to the smallish hitter were high, and now he crouched more in the batter's box. Odell knew he couldn't let the guy get on base because the boy was quick and would be a real threat to run. Mitchell didn't have the best arm either.

Odell finally got a strike on the next pitch with the hitter still not swinging the bat. He became convinced the guy wouldn't even try to hit anything and since Odell's elbow was burning with every throw, he made no effort to put any speed on the following pitch. Odell was surprised when the batter hit a bouncer toward the hole between short and third that took a bad hop over Ken's glove. His brother Kenny did catch it backhanded but had no chance to throw out the runner.

Things were suddenly not looking good. Odell had to get the next two batters out or he would have to face Ricky Lee. He had real concerns about his arm and the fast baserunner, too.

Odell went into his stretch and stared at the runner on first. Dewey straddled the base holding his glove out in front of him. Odell thought briefly about throwing over to him. However, he was worried that Dewey would miss it letting the runner advance.

Again, the first two pitches were off target by Odell. On the third one, the runner broke from first and the batter laid down a perfect bunt on the right side of the infield. Odell tried to get to it but couldn't. The result was Pine Forest had runners on first and second with only one out. Unless a double-play miracle occurred that hadn't happened all year, Ricky Lee would get a chance to bat.

Mitch asked for time and ran out to the mound as Odell's brain tried to process his options. The young catcher had his mask sitting on the top of his head and showed his nervousness by chewing on his bottom lip.

"How are we gonna get out of this mess, O?" he asked.

"Good question. My arm is pretty much gone. I don't know if I can throw a curve, and my control is about gone, too," replied Odell.

"How about if you try side-armed again? It worked the last time you tried it."

"You might be right, Mitchell. Maybe it'll take a little pressure off the elbow. Let's try it on this guy. Of course, Ricky Lee is up after him and he saw the delivery last time, so I don't know how that'll work.

Odell knew the batter was their second-best hitter on the team behind Ricky Lee. His name was Andy, and he took his position in the box with a look of determination on his face.

Odell wiped the sweat off his brow with his glove and went into his stretch. He arched his body to the right as he threw the ball with a three-fingered grip from the side. Odell actually thought it was thrown well as it had good speed and tailed from the center of the plate more to the right edge.

Whether it fooled the batter enough, Odell couldn't tell because Andy hit a bouncing grounder toward Kenny playing shortstop. Odell turned and held his breath as his brother fielded the baseball a few steps toward second base and stepped on the bag. Andy was running hard to first and only a few steps away when Kenny fired a throw to Dewey on first.

It was a bang-bang play, but the throw beat Andy to the bag for what should have been the end of the game. There was a problem, though. Dewey dropped the ball.

Groans from the small crowd and other members of the team were very audible. Dewey picked up the ball hurriedly and stepped on first base again as if that would make a difference. Andy wore a big grin on his face as he made it back to the base after running safely by. Dewey hung his head in shame before flipping the ball back to Odell.

Odell slapped his glove repeatedly against his leg showing his disappointment and displeasure as the umpire called timeout. He could feel the tension building again as he walked back to the mound. They still led the game by 1-0 with two outs in the top of the last inning. However, Pine Forest had runners on first and third with Ricky Lee now waiting to hit. The Renegades would get another chance to hit if their opponents scored, but Odell wasn't thinking about that.

As he thought about what tact he could take with Ricky Lee, Odell noticed Kat and Sue approaching the field. It gave him new, albeit faint, hope that maybe this game would work out.

CHAPTER 41

The two girls left the car and hurried down the hill to the baseball field. Kat had been enjoying the conversation prior to hearing the noise from the game and seeing Odell's movements indicating something was amiss. Her thoughts had shifted to him, and she wanted to get closer to see what was happening and maybe offer encouragement. Sue went with her to give support also.

Odell gave Kat a nod and a weak smile as she stood near the sideline close to the Renegades' dugout. She thought he looked tired as she called out to him standing on the pitcher's mound.

"You've got this, baby!"

The small crowd had become subdued and was quiet when Kat's reassurance rang out. The batter, who Kat didn't know, turned toward where she and Sue stood. He appeared to appraise them and then puffed out his cheeks before blowing a pink gum bubble. He then sucked it back into his mouth and grinned at them.

Before stepping into the batter's box, the guy talked to Odell loud enough for everyone in attendance to hear. "Yeah, baby. Show me what you've got."

Kat watched intently as Odell took a deep breath and then exhaled. He stepped on the pitcher's mound, hesitated for a moment, then reared back and threw a pitch. It came close to hitting the batter and caused him to almost fall down while getting out of the way. When he stepped back to the plate, the guy was grim faced and didn't mock Odell again.

This was a side of Odell she hadn't seen before. He had the appearance of an extremely pissed-off individual, and the focus shown on his face transcended everything else in that moment.

The next pitch was thrown so hard that she heard Odell grunt when he released it. The batter swung and missed. When the ball got back to Odell, she noticed him bending his right arm back and forth like it was causing him extreme pain. A grimace had frozen on his tanned face. He gave a brief glance in her direction. She tried hard not to show the concern she felt for him but didn't know how successful she was.

Please help Odell, she said in a silent prayer.

***

Odell saw something in Kat's gaze. He couldn't believe she was here, much less what she was feeling at the moment. Odell had gone somewhere deep inside himself when he first saw that she was watching him. Calling him baby had brought new strength to his resolve. Ricky Lee's smartass remark added even more.

Mitchell gave him the sign for another fastball on the outer edge, but Odell shook it off. He didn't know if he could throw much longer. Since the Renegades really didn't have another alternative pitcher, Odell knew the game was in his hands.

Odell hadn't tried to throw a curve ball in the inning and was afraid to do it now. However, Ricky Lee had just seen a fast pitch and might be fooled by a breaking one. When Mitchell gave him the sign, Odell nodded up and down. He gripped the baseball inside his glove with his index and middle fingers close together on the seams.

The ball came out of his hand spinning toward the plate. It was breaking, but not enough, and hung in the air above the strike zone. Ricky Lee's timing was not off by much as the baseball launched off the sweet spot of his bat high to left field.

Odell's initial thought was the pitch had been the hardest hit of any in his career. Everything in time seemed to slow down at that moment as he turned to watch the flight of the ball.

He felt sick in the pit of his stomach as the ball began sailing over Sandy's position in left field. The diminutive fielder hadn't seen many flies over the course of the season, and Odell had to remind him from time to time to be ready. On a few occasions, the youngster had been seen throwing his glove in the air while the game was underway. Odell wished he had told him to be ready this time.

Sandy must've remembered because the swift kid turned his back and started running. As the ball started its downward trajectory, Odell watched Sandy stretch out his short-armed gloved hand while continuing to run at full speed. Reminiscent of the great Willie Mays' highlight, Sandy caught the ball over his shoulder in the web of his glove at the very last second.

Time sped up again and noise erupted everywhere. Odell watched as the grinning hero jogged back from deep left field. His cousin, Bruce, who had been watching the play from his center field position ran over to join him and slapped him on the butt as they approached the infield.

All of the team gathered around Odell on the mound whooping and hollering at the top of their lungs. Sandy tried to give the ball to Odell.

"Here's the game ball, O."

"No way, Pooch. You deserve it," Odell replied.

A couple of the guys hoisted Sandy on their shoulders as others starting chanting, "Poochie, Poochie, Poochie."

Odell walked away from the group and headed toward Kat. Before he could get there, Ricky Lee approached him from where he had been running the bases moments before.

"Hell of a game, O. Congratulations. Can't believe that little s.o.b. caught that ball," Ricky Lee said shaking his head back and forth like a dog shaking off water.

He stuck out his hand and firmly grasped Odell's. The two teens didn't say anything for a few seconds silently acknowledging each other.

"You blasted that pitch. I can't believe he caught it either," Odell finally replied.

"Oh, well. Just a game. See you at school in a couple of weeks and make sure you shave," said Ricky Lee as he turned and walked over to the rest of his team.

Odell continued the trek over to Kat. She was beaming at him and kissed him fully on the mouth when he arrived.

"Get a room," said Sue laughing.

"Maybe one day," replied Kat.

Odell was speechless. *What a day,* he thought.

CHAPTER 42

A couple of days passed before Odell was feeling like himself again. His elbow had been iced with a homemade compress off and on during the time that he spent mainly inside at home sipping cold drinks and reading.

The game had taken something out of Odell, and his mother had instructed him to stay inside for a while. Her father had suffered from a heat stroke when he was a young man causing her to worry about anyone being in the hot sun too much.

He had talked to Kat a few times over the telephone, and they had planned to get together today. Odell was disappointed to find out her mom didn't have a work shift, so the potential for intimacy was out of the picture.

Something was bothering her for sure as she hadn't sounded quite the same. They finally decided to take the bus to Westgate Mall and just walk around. Odell had an idea of a present he wanted to get for Kat, and the trip would at least give him that opportunity.

They strolled down to the bus stop together holding hands. He felt as if they hadn't really been together in forever despite their telephone conversations.

"I can't believe summer's almost over," said Odell.

"Yeah, me either. A lot's been going on the last couple of weeks, and for one reason or another, I feel like we haven't really talked lately," said Kat.

"I know what you mean," replied Odell.

Kat walked with her head down. Odell could tell there was something on her mind.

"I really need to talk to you about what's going on at home," said Kat as they arrived at the bus stop.

The couple sat down on the bench with Kat displaying a tortured look in her eyes. Her lips quivered for a moment before Odell slid a little closer to Kat's side.

"What is it? Are your parents fighting or something?" asked Odell.

"No, nothing like that. It's, I think we might…," she said before starting to cry.

Odell didn't know what to say or do. He hadn't seen Kat be this emotional and couldn't imagine what was causing it. He always felt uneasy when people cried and didn't know how to make things better. Finally, Odell put his arm around her which only made her sob harder.

They sat there for some time without speaking. Odell kept whispering everything would be okay without knowing what was happening and whether what he was saying was the truth.

Kat finally slowed down her crying and wiped tears from her eyes with her bare hand. She looked deeply into his and said something that made his heart want to explode.

"I'm pretty sure we'll be moving soon."

Odell's world was rocked. He opened his mouth and his response squeaked out, "No, no. That can't happen."

She nodded her head slightly, and he thought she might start crying again. If she did, Odell felt he might start, too. He couldn't let that begin, so he tried to put a positive spin on the news.

"Hey, don't worry. I'll be sixteen in just a few months, and I can drive to your house even if it's across town," Odell said trying to smile.

Kat sniffed, but no new tears appeared. "You might have to drive farther than that."

The hits keep coming, he thought before asking, "Farther than Macon?"

"Yeah, Mom and Daddy are talking about Brunswick. It's supposed to be a good job opportunity for him. They're really excited about living there."

Odell felt like he had been punched in the gut. The possibility of Kat moving from the neighborhood was bad enough, but the distance between Macon and Brunswick would be insurmountable. He could see the bright future he had envisioned with Kat being smashed to pieces.

"Oh," he said swallowing hard.

They sat in silence while Odell tried to come up with some way to fight his growing grief. He realized Kat must've been dealing with the possibility that this could happen for longer than the few moments he had to process the issue.

The bus rolled to a stop and the swishing sounds of the door opening interrupted his thoughts. When the couple didn't immediately get off the bench where they were sitting, the driver asked if they were getting on.

"Uh, yeah, sorry," said Odell as he stood and gently pulled Kat up.

"Let's enjoy the day, Kat," he said softly to her.

***

The two of them meandered around the mall stopping at some window fronts to look at displays. Neither seemed very interested in buying anything until Odell steered Kat to Friedman's Jewelry. In their window case among more expensive diamond sparkles was a simple 10K gold-plated heart on a dainty chain. A small sign indicated engraving was free.

"I want to get you that, if you'll let me," said Odell pointing to the heart.

"Really?" she asked gazing at him and then looking back inside the window.

"Yeah, I do. I've been planning it for the last few days. I just didn't know if you'd like it," he said with a hint of uncertainty.

"I love it, Odell. If you're sure it's not too expensive."

They went inside and after Kat inspected the piece, Odell paid for it. He knew it was the priciest gift he'd ever purchased, but he hoped it would convey his feelings for his girlfriend. They decided to put their initials on the back of the heart contained within vertical and horizontal lines with OS over KN. The sales lady promised to have it ready in an hour.

Kat squeezed his hand as the two walked to Hefner's Bakery. She seemed happy wearing a big smile which made Odell pleased with himself. The uncertainty over their future was temporarily on hold.

The smells coming from the bakery preceded their arrival. All the freshly baked goods were delicious, and they had a hard time choosing before getting a couple of doughnuts that they ate while continuing to walk around. They took turns wiping glazed sugar from each other's mouths when they finished the pastries.

"That was good and sweet as you are, Odell," said Kat.

He blushed and then replied, "Thanks, I guess I have my moments."

"No, really. You are the sweetest guy, and this summer has been great. God, I hope we don't move," she said sadly.

"I feel the same, but we agreed to enjoy the day, okay? Let's go get the necklace because I probably need to get home soon. Daddy's rotated to second shift and will be getting up to go to work, and Mama might need some help cooking dinner."

After returning to the jewelry store and picking up the purchase, Odell placed it around Kat's neck as she held her hair up. She studied herself in the mirror on the counter, and then he was surprised when she turned quickly and planted a light peck on his lips in the middle of the store. The sales associate smiled as the couple exited the store holding hands.

CHAPTER 43

Phillip was feeling restless again. The summer had been such a bummer and the thought of another school year was even more depressing. Here it was another Friday night, and he had nothing to do. As he combed his blonde hair into place, he thought of the options available for the evening.

He didn't have a steady girl although he'd been looking for one ever since that bitch Kat had dumped him months ago. Phillip thought that event must have messed up his vibes some kind of way because it seemed girls acted differently around him now. It couldn't be his fault because he was a good-looking guy with a hot car. Maybe she had told everybody lies about him. That made him mad to think about.

He also had similar feelings about the punk she was seeing. Phillip couldn't understand why she would even think about dating the guy. First, what a screwed-up name he had.

Odell, what the hell, he thought and then laughed.

Second, the guy wasn't even old enough to drive, so he knew they couldn't be parking. At least that made him a little less jealous because he couldn't bear to think that four-eyed idiot would've gotten further with Kat than he had. Remembering feeling her up aroused him, but then Phillip got pissed all over again thinking back on how she slapped him on that last date.

I shoulda gone ahead and done what I wanted that night.

Phillip had asked around the skating rink trying to find out as much as he could about Odell Sterling since he ran in different circles. They lived in different parts of the city, went to different schools and had totally different interests. The information Phillip had gleaned about him only added to the growing aggravation.

Phillip didn't care much about school and cared less about eggheads who did. That was one of the things he had found out concerning Sterling. What was nerdier than being the president of Jr. Beta Club? He wondered what made that attractive to Kat.

Sterling was evidently a decent baseball player according to what one of his friends told him. That meant nothing to Phillip because he'd never been interested in the sport. He had to admit to himself that Sterling looked to be in pretty good shape, but Phillip was a couple of inches taller and at least ten pounds heavier. He was confident he could beat Sterling's ass anytime he wanted and felt like that time was coming real soon.

That might just bring Kat running back to me, Phillip thought.

He finished getting his hair in place and stared at the image in the mirror. For a few seconds he second-guessed what he'd been thinking about. He should just let it all go and move on with his life. For some reason, he couldn't.

**

Durr's was even more crowded than usual for a Friday night. Odell couldn't skate fast at all on the floor but really didn't care since Kat was at his side. She wore a blouse that allowed the heart to be displayed against her summer brown skin. He watched happily as she occasionally touched the pendant he had given her.

The rink was noisy, and it occurred to Odell that the crowd appeared younger than usual. Maybe he was just getting too old for the activity. Odell realized at that moment he probably would stop coming here after turning sixteen. He still had hopes about him and Kat having better times somewhere else although his mind had been constantly bothered since learning the news about a possible move.

Because of the raucous atmosphere the couple could hardly hear each other when they spoke. Odell thought it far from an ideal scene since he wanted to talk with Kat and find out if she had heard anything else from her parents about future plans.

As they continued to go around in slow circles, Odell tried to tune out the music, constant chatter and hundreds of wheels clacking against the wooden floor. In his mind was a checklist that he went over.

Okay, it's Friday, August 18, 1967. That means Labor Day is two weeks away and school will start the Monday after that weekend. If Kat's family moves, it's got to be before then in order for them to get settled. God, I hope she doesn't have to go. I've got

to spend every minute I can with her. I've only got one more
ballgame next Tuesday, but that's all I have to do. Maybe we could
go downtown or the mall again. Or, how about a movie? I wonder
if our parents would let us go on a real double-date with Mike and
Sue. That would be a lot of fun.

"What's going on in that brain of yours," Kat said into his ear.

"Sorry, it's so loud in this place. I can barely hear my inner voice," Odell replied bending down to her ear.

She nodded and said, "Let's step outside for a minute."

As soon as they got to the front rail separating the skating area from the limited seating, Kat pulled Odell's hand to the door leading outside. They had to walk rather than skate since there was a large floor mat near the counter beside the entrance. Odell knew it was frowned upon to go outside with skates still on your feet, but since they both owned theirs, he thought it might be okay.

They stepped outside and stayed near the doorway. The noise level dropped several decibels in the evening air. Kat placed herself against the wall facing Odell. He was a little unsteady standing on the skates and placed one foot behind him with the toe stop down to better secure himself.

"So, have your parents said anything else about moving?" Odell asked.

Kat nodded, "Yeah, Daddy is taking me and Mom to Brunswick early tomorrow so we can see the area. The company he's been working for down there has gotten us a reservation at some swanky hotel on St. Simon's Island for tomorrow night and Sunday night. I won't be back until Monday," she replied.

Odell could hear the sadness in her voice. He tried not to reveal his own by responding, "Well, that sounds like an adventure," but thought it came out much too flippant.

She hung her head down and a lengthy sigh came from deep inside. Odell thought Kat seemed even more vulnerable than she had the other day, so he took her hand in his and gave a gentle squeeze.

"I don't want to go. It just seems so unfair, but I can't say anything, Odell. I feel like my life is falling apart just when everything is going so great," she said sniffing.

"I know. I feel the same way, Kat."

"Well, shit. Ain't that sweet? The two love birds," came a sarcastic voice from behind Odell.

Odell turned around to see a blonde-haired guy he didn't recognize at first. He had a cigarette drooping from his sneering mouth. There were two other smirking boys standing on both sides of him also smoking. Then a memory triggered, and Odell thought about the guys he and Mike saw at the Dairy Queen a few weeks ago. It was the same one who had given him the finger after calling Odell and Mike turds.

Kat spoke in an angry tone before Odell could say anything. "Phillip, this is a private conversation. You need to leave."

Odell looked back at Kat and was confused. Things started clicking in his head, and he suddenly knew this was the guy she had dated before.

Phillip laughed, "It's a free country, girl. So, this is your new boyfriend, huh? He don't look like much to me, but you lookin' fine. How 'ya been?"

Odell felt anger creeping inside and didn't like the feeling. He could see that Kat was less than thrilled with the situation, too. He kept his mouth shut, though.

"It's none of your business. Like I said, you need to go and leave us alone, Phillip," she said through clenched teeth.

Phillip took a deep drag from the cigarette and then blew it in the couple's direction. He gave another creepy laugh and said, "I love you, too."

"Hey, I don't know you and we don't want any trouble. Maybe you should just move on," said Odell as he sized up the guy and closed his right hand into a fist.

"I'll do whatever the hell I want to," Phillip said while puffing up and moving closer. He had a menacing appearance in his eyes, and his friends followed close behind.

Before further confrontation, Kat took Odell's hand and moved him toward the front door. Odell resisted at first, but then followed her as she took a few steps. He turned his head and watched the three boys to make sure they didn't rush him.

The couple entered the rink as Phillip said, "I'll be waiting on y'all when you come back outside. We ain't finished, yet. Ready to kick some punk ass."

When they got back inside Kat spoke to Odell with a sense of urgency. "There's something wrong with him, Odell. You need to be careful."

"I know about bullies, Kat. They're really cowards. That's why he's got his friends with him. I'm not scared, just mad."

"Please, baby. Don't get in a fight with him. I don't want you to get hurt. Maybe we can tell Mr. Durr or call your parents to come pick us up."

Odell calmed a little as she used the term of endearment. He had started to feel some sort of rage building while outside. He'd only been in a couple of shoving matches in his life and had always thought fighting was stupid. He had wanted to punch the guy a minute ago, however, and was thinking like his father had told him. Make the first one count if you're going to end up in a confrontation.

"Okay, I'll call Daddy to come pick us up a little early," Odell said.

He went to the front and asked if he could use the phone. Dialing the number, Odell wondered what to tell his father. He knew Daddy had a quick temper and was very protective of his family.

"Uh, hey, Daddy. I was wondering if you could pick up me and Kat a little early. I think there's a guy here who wants to get in a fight, and I'm trying to avoid it. I'm only worried because there's three of them."

"I'm on my way," his father replied before hanging up abruptly.

"Okay, Daddy's on the way. Let's get our shoes on."

They went to the bench area where their shoes were stored and sat down. Both started unlacing their skates with Odell maintaining a watch on the front entrance. He was immediately wary when he saw the boys swagger through the doorway. Kat showed her uneasiness by chewing on her bottom lip.

"I should've warned you about him, Odell. I thought everything was over after he tripped you and that he'd leave us alone. I never thought he was this crazy, but he must've been following us for a while. It had to be him who egged our houses. I should've told my parents," Kat said.

Odell quickly removed his skates and put on his freshly polished bee-bops. As he tied the knots on his shoes he thought about the referenced events. His anger was building again at the stupidity and callousness of this guy he didn't even know. Odell had never felt this way about anybody. It was one thing for Phillip Jackson to be jealous. It was quite another for him to cause personal injury and damage to property. His compulsion to confront the guy was overtaking reason.

"Don't worry about it. He'll get what's coming to him. I'll be back in a minute," replied Odell.

He got up and headed toward the trio at a deliberate pace. Kat was involved in the removal of her skates and didn't have time to react to Odell's departure. As he closed in on them, he heard her call his name, but he didn't stop moving.

Phillip and his friends turned and left the building just steps in front of Odell. As soon as he got outside, the three of them surrounded him and got in his face. Earlier when he had on his skates, Odell had thought they were about the same height. Now he could tell Phillip was taller by at least two or three inches.

"You ready for an ass whooping?" said Phillip.

"What's your problem? I don't even know you. I'll tell you this, I'm not scared," Odell responded.

Phillip seemed a little surprised. He paused as if thinking about a response.

"You ought to be. There's three of us," Phillip said.

Odell studied all of them as he took off his glasses and put them in his pocket. He decided his first punch would be to the throat after kicking Phillip in the shin with his thick soled shoe as hard as he could. They would be unexpected and hurtful blows. After that, he didn't know what would happen.

***

Phillip had not expected the punk would come outside and challenge him. He was now unsure of his earlier actions because he never expected that reaction. His hesitation was causing his friends to back off, and one of them said, "Come on. Let's go."

Phillip said, "Wait, we need to teach this guy a lesson."

"Naw, like he said, I don't know him, and I ain't got no beef with him either. Let's get outta here before we get in trouble," said his friend.

The other one agreed and they started walking off. Phillip was left standing alone with Odell staring at him. There was something about the way Odell stood in front of him that caused Phillip to swallow involuntarily.

"There's really not a good reason for us to fight," the other boy said.

His eyes were squinted like he couldn't see Phillip very well, but there was something else showing as well. It was like the kid wouldn't back down no matter what. He might even hurt Phillip.

What could even be worse would be the embarrassment of getting his own ass kicked.

Kat appeared and ran to the teens. Her eyes pleaded for peace.

"Phillip, please leave," she said touching his arm.

For the first time in a while, Phillip listened. His second thoughts brought a moment of clarity. He realized violence at that moment wouldn't solve anything. Whatever problems he might have he'd need to work out in some other way, or he'd end up in jail or worse. He didn't want that. Not right now, anyway.

To make matters even worse, a grownup showed up. He must be the guy's father and had the appearance of someone you wouldn't want to mess with. He wore a sleeveless undershirt and was smoking an unfiltered cigarette. If he was the punk's dad, he might have taught him how to fight. He thought maybe that's why Sterling didn't back off.

"Odell, what's going on?" the man asked while blowing smoke out of his nose.

"Just working out some differences of opinion, Daddy," Odell responded.

"Well, finish up so I can take y'all home."

Phillip glanced at the man and back at his son. This was definitely a no-win situation.

"Sorry about the misunderstanding," Phillip muttered before turning his back and walking to his car. He was through with that shit and felt relieved for the time being. He thought maybe he'd just learned a valuable lesson.

CHAPTER 44

After finally finishing the story, Odell put down the book he had been reading all weekend. *Catcher in the Rye* by J. D. Salinger was a novel that he had wanted to read since summer began, but he hadn't made time to get to it until Kat's trip with her parents to Brunswick. He knew that the book was on some advanced reading lists for school and although considered controversial by some educators, Odell wanted to experience it on his own before anyone else might influence his opinions.

It was early on Monday morning, and he was relaxed in his father's leather recliner. Thinking about the book, particularly some of the themes he could relate to, gave his life some new perspective. The main character's persistent obsession with sexuality certainly gave Odell cause to pause and think about his near constant preoccupation over the same subject. His brain began processing.

Like Holden Caulfield, Odell was confused by aspects of the feelings he had on the issue. But unlike the protagonist of that tale,

Odell didn't think he had near the depth of despair displayed by the character personified in Caulfield.

Odell couldn't help but feel some of the same anguish as others his age. He was smart enough to understand that he was not unique, and books like he had just finished helped him to some degree understand the growing pains associated with being fifteen.

Just because Odell recognized his plight didn't necessarily make it easier to solve those problems. He wondered how and when the difficulties he faced would be resolved.

The most pressing problem was one he shared with Kat. Past conversations with her had shown that she was at least as upset as he was about the likelihood that her family would soon be moving. No matter how much Odell told himself that their feelings for each other were strong enough to somehow keep the relationship intact, his head told him otherwise. Mixed in was the growing sexual tension between them.

She was supposed to be back home sometime later today, and he guessed he'd find out for sure if Kat would soon be out of his life. *What will we do?* thought Odell.

There were competing interests between raging hormones that made him and Kat feel tight and somehow unfulfilled, and the more emotional desires that came from connections of their spirits. Odell was convinced the two of them were on similar wave lengths both ways, and he believed that had to be some form of love. He understood, however, that being so young and inexperienced could make his beliefs misguided or even false. He needed more time with Kat to figure it all out.

He wondered how time could go by so fast and yet so slowly at the same time. Odell had heard grownups say things like, "Just wait until you're my age. You'll wish you stayed the age you are now."

Odell couldn't imagine that he'd ever think that, and to use a descriptive term from the just completed book, it sounded "phony." He was tired of not having control over his life, and part of him could imagine going on a questionable behavioral spree like Holden Caulfield.

Nah, he thought. *I might be flawed, but not nearly as much as that guy.*

Part of his nature that Odell had discovered was his ability to self-analyze and be critical when he found a fault. He thought he had been doing that for at least the last year or maybe two. So, what weaknesses did Odell think he saw in himself?

First and foremost, at least until this summer, had been what Odell considered as awkwardness around girls. He attributed this to not being near that many of them in his early formative years and being unsure how to react when attracted to one. Kat had changed him dramatically in that regard and as much as he didn't want to lose her, Odell thought that he could see himself being less uncomfortable in future interactions with the opposite sex.

He also found that he could be judgmental sometimes. Odell really didn't like others who were that way, so why was he? He guessed it had something to do with having some amount of intelligence and the ability to research a topic when he didn't know much about it. When Odell studied and thought through something, he tended to believe his opinion was superior to someone else's even if he didn't verbalize the belief. In that regard, he was struggling not to judge Kat's parents for wanting to move the family and upset their daughter.

Being respectful of his elders required that Odell couldn't say anything about feeling that way. It was similar to the problems he felt at church when the preacher's sermon or the Sunday school teacher's lesson didn't make sense to him and caused Odell to question what was being said. Most of the time he would just keep his mouth shut, but sometimes he couldn't which only led to him being judged by the adult in an unfavorable way.

He had begun to realize that being grown up didn't necessarily make you smarter and that human beings were fallible. Anyone could make a mistake, even parents. Experience was a great teacher, if and only if, you learned from it. He had read somewhere that Einstein said something to the effect that making the same mistakes over and over and expecting a different result was the definition of insanity.

Odell remembered Kat saying her family had moved multiple times. Wasn't that making the same mistake over again? He thought it could be but was not in a position to judge.

His mother closed her bedroom door and headed to where Odell lounged. She was already dressed in her work uniform and patted him on the shoulder as she passed by going to the kitchen.

"Good morning," she said cheerfully.

"Morning, Mama," he replied.

He put the book on the bar that jutted from the wall separating the den and kitchen and sat at the stool nearest a small window directly across from the stove. The opening was often used to pass food to those eating at the bar and provided a way for Odell and his mother to have a conversation.

She had begun the morning ritual of making dough for biscuits, and Odell for at least the thousandth time watched her work. Mom seemed unusually happy for a Monday and was humming some song.

"You really make that look so easy, Mom," said Odell.

"Just takes practice. Like most things, you have to repeat the process to get better. You know, kinda like you pitching a baseball," she replied without looking up from her work.

"Well, yeah, I guess so. But just because you might practice something and really try hard to get better, you've got to have some talent to make it all work. Just like those perfect biscuits you could make in your sleep, every time I try, I screw them up. I don't think I'll ever be able to do them like you."

She smiled and kept patting out the dough into greased pans. "Thanks, Odell. I think you'll do just fine."

Odell admired his mother in many ways. One of the things that always lifted his spirits was the supportiveness he got from her. He knew he couldn't speak freely about some of the doubts he was going through because they were too embarrassing especially when it came to desires felt over Kat. He thought she could provide some insights, however.

"Mom, can I ask you something? Did you have boyfriends before Daddy?"

She smiled to herself and briefly glanced at Odell before continuing rolling scoops of biscuit dough between her hands.

"One or two," she finally said and paused with a distant look in her eyes. "There was a boy who lived across the street when I was growing up. We used to call each other sweetheart. His name was Joe."

Odell had never heard anything about a boy named Joe. He was immediately curious and wanted to know more.

"How old were you then?" asked Odell.

"Oh, about your age, I guess. He lived in our neighborhood for a few years until he moved to Twiggs County. Joe and I were friends from grammar school through the ninth grade. I never saw him again after that," she said wistfully.

"That's sad. I never knew that you had a friend like that. It sounds very similar to the situation I'm in with Kat. It looks like she's going to be moving away, and I don't know what to do," Odell replied.

His mother stopped and her eyes glazed momentarily. There was a sympathetic exchange without words spoken, and Odell thought for a second that they both might start crying.

"I was young, just like you, Odell. In the end, everything worked out fine. You've got a good future ahead. Don't forget that. I'm a believer in what's meant to be, will be. Life has a way of sorting itself out," she said with a smile.

"Thanks, Mama. I'll try to remember that."

CHAPTER 45

About mid-morning Odell took the lawn mower up the road to Kat's house. He could tell that the family had not returned from their trip yet and figured to have the yard freshened when they returned. Maybe if they saw the place looking as good as possible, they might want to stay, at least that's what he thought. Odell knew he was grasping at straws, and it was just wishful thinking on his part.

Neither his mind nor his heart was into the work and about half-way through the job Odell shut off the engine and sat down in the tree swing. Gently swaying, he remembered sitting with Kat and drinking lemonade in the same place the first time. He could almost feel her presence now as they stole glances at one another during the nostalgic memory. Little did he know back then how the relationship would grow.

The mounting melancholy was a depression that he didn't seem capable of ridding himself. Odell was trying desperately to be positive in his own thoughts as well as in his outward appearance and wondered if he was succeeding at all. When he had viewed himself in the mirror before heading to the Normans' house, Odell thought he could detect sadness in his blue eyes. No matter what was going on inside, he resolved that he shouldn't let it show to others. He kept letting the words his mother had told him earlier form a mantra in his mind.

Life has a way of sorting itself out.

Odell glimpsed over at the front of the house where he had helped Kat and her mother clean the eggs off the siding. You really couldn't tell very much of the mess that had been there. It made Odell think of the confrontation with Phillip a few nights ago, and he automatically applied the words to that situation. That had worked out okay, and he had to trust the same would happen with him and Kat.

He closed his eyes and suddenly felt tired. The weight of all the emotions Odell had been going through added to his lack of sleep. It finally caught up with him, and he snoozed.

Odell fell into a dream state as his head drooped toward his chest. There was a comforting breeze blowing under the tree and over his body. He was at peace.

In the vision he was older. Not by many years, but Odell could tell he was probably at least a college student. He seemed more filled out as he watched the scene like a movie. Maybe he was not quite an adult but close to it. Looking inside his older self, Odell saw a more confident person. Maybe it was due to the fact there were no glasses on his face. *Contacts,* he wondered.

Walking toward him was an older Kat. Her hair was different, but the smile was the same. She had filled out, too. *Damn, what a knockout!*

They embraced as friends and lovers. He never wanted that feeling to end, and in the dream it didn't.

How long he was out of reality, Odell wasn't sure. When he awoke, he was a little disoriented but had harmonic feelings about the future.

After a few minutes, Odell returned to cutting the grass. He finished about the same time Kat's family drove up.

***

Kat had been quiet on the ride back to Macon while her parents discussed everything they had seen. She reflected on the past weekend that surprisingly had not been as awful as she thought it would be. The King and Prince had been the best place she had ever stayed in, and she especially enjoyed walking on the beach. Kat wished Odell could have been with her during those times because she knew he would've found the setting peaceful as she had.

She also thought it would have been nice to have Madi walk with her, too. There were other folks with their dogs running free on the packed sand or on leashes sporting happy doggie grins. Unfortunately, Madi had stayed in Macon with one of Kat's friends, so she had been unlucky like Odell.

The time at the hotel was peaceful and relaxing, and the meals had been delicious. She also had to admit spending time with her parents in the upscale environment had been pleasant as well. They had gone to view a house in nearby Brunswick that was located in a suburban neighborhood and definitely appeared to be a step-up from their current residence.

The place was at least one and a half times the size of the rental home in Macon. Her proposed bedroom seemed huge and there was a private bathroom suite dedicated to Kat. Her mother went on and on about the modern kitchen, and her father pointed out the fenced-in backyard where Madi could roam. The real estate agent mentioned it was not far from the school Kat would attend. She also told them that Dad's employer had already approved moving expenses and assistance with closing costs. Expedited closing was also possible through established relationships between a local mortgage company and the employer.

Everything over the course of the weekend must have been meticulously planned by the company Kat's father had been working for the last three years. The main office was in Atlanta, but they wanted to open a satellite branch in South Georgia because of the amount of work in the area. Kat had to admit, they must really like her dad's work as the presentation to the family was first class. For him to become the "go-to" supervisor in the region would certainly increase their financial status.

Until she had seen everything up close and personal, Kat couldn't come to terms with why her parents were bursting with excitement over the prospects of moving yet again. Now there was no denying that the opportunities presented were probably once in a lifetime.

She knew there was no way to get out of it, and the only remaining question was when the move would take place. The school year would begin right after Labor Day, so there was little time left in Macon.

Kat tuned back into her parents. They had been chatting non-stop and Kat had not been paying close attention.

"So, when exactly are we moving?" she asked.

"Kat, where have you been the last three hours? We've been talking about plans since we got on the road," her dad replied.

"Sorry, Daddy. I guess I was deep in my little world."

Kat's mother showed concern on her face as she said, "You did enjoy yourself on the trip, right? You do understand the opportunity for a fresh start, I'm sure."

"Yes, ma'am. I get it."

"Well, I've got to turn around and get back to Brunswick as soon as I get you and Mom home so I can get all the details worked out. Y'all can start packing up stuff that you're able to take care of. I'm not exactly sure when the movers will put us on the schedule, but I would think no later than the first of next week," said her father.

"Okay, Daddy."

Kat retreated again as her parents continued their conversation. *A week at the most. I've got to find some time to be alone with Odell before it's too late,* she thought.

As they pulled into the driveway, Odell was pushing his lawn mower in their direction. He was smiling, and all she could think was how much she would miss him and that smile.

***

Odell stopped near the Norman's vehicle, and Kat popped outside running to him. He had not expected the reception she gave him especially with her parents right there with them. As she hugged him fiercely, Odell didn't reciprocate in the same fashion but did pat her shoulders as he would a relative. He found himself becoming embarrassed at the public show of affection. No words were spoken between them.

She backed away from him and then ran toward the house with her head down. Mrs. Norman followed quickly behind Kat pulling her keys from her purse. Odell watched as they both entered the house. Mr. Norman walked slowly to the teen and wore an inscrutable look on his face.

"Well, it seems that Kat was happy to see you. I couldn't tell if you felt the same way," Kat's father said.

Odell swallowed involuntarily as he tried to understand what had just happened. Mr. Norman stood with his hands in the pockets of his trousers. His thin lips were pressed together in not quite a frown.

"Uh, yes, sir. I was, I mean I am happy to see her, too," Odell finally stammered.

The man nodded slightly and relaxed his posture. He looked around the freshly mowed lawn, and then removed his wallet from his back pocket. Taking out a five-dollar bill, he handed it to Odell.

"You've done your usual good job. This will be the last time I'll need you to do it for us," he said.

Holding the bill, Odell now had no doubts that the Normans would be moving. He wanted to protest but knew he couldn't. All he could do was to stare at Abraham Lincoln's face. The money felt worthless at that moment as all hope faded. He was undergoing some kind of weird feeling like an out-of-body experience. For some reason, Odell remembered from his studies the greatness of that president.

"Thanks," Odell said when he finally drifted back to reality. He folded the bill in half and placed it in the pocket of his shorts.

"I know you and Kat have gotten close this summer, and I'm sure she's going to miss your friendship. I wanted to tell you I appreciate what you've done to help around the house while I've been gone. You've been respectful, and as far as I can tell, treated my daughter well. Since we'll be moving soon, I might not have another chance to tell you that. Thank you," Mr. Norman said as he stuck out his hand to Odell.

Odell returned the gesture and gripped the calloused hand of Kat's father. He felt a little guilty as he remembered intimate moments spent with Mr. Norman's daughter. If Kat's father knew about that, Odell was sure the very hand that was now shaking his could inflict serious hurt.

As the handshake ended, Odell gathered himself. This was a time he instinctively knew provided an opportunity to spend some time with Kat before she was gone.

"Mr. Norman, I'll never forget this summer because I've gotten to know Kat. She's a great girl, and I'm going to miss her, too. Before y'all go, I hope I can maybe have a chance to spend a little more time with her. I understand y'all might be really busy, but if it's possible, we could do something together. Of course, that's if you and Mrs. Norman will allow it, and if Kat wants to," Odell said hopefully.

"I don't have a problem with that. I'll be going back to Brunswick, so you get with my wife and Kat with your plans."

"Thank you, sir. I will," said Odell before the two separated, and the teen headed home with thoughts of a way to say good-bye to his girlfriend.

CHAPTER 46

There was still one more ballgame to play before Kat went away and school started again. Odell thought it inconsequential at this point. It was funny, but not funny ha-ha. When the summer started, winning the championship of the fifteen and under city recreation league was primary in his mind. Now, that thought had shifted way back in his priorities.

Baseball had been one of the most important and dominant influences in his life for at least the last five years. He had wanted to be the next Mickey Mantle, Clete Boyer or Whitey Ford, if he was left-handed. The Yankees were all his favorites mainly because they were featured on tv every week.

Well, he liked other things, too. Reading was up there near the top. There were so many good books yet to read. *Catch-22* was going to be the next one. He enjoyed a good John Wayne or Clint Eastwood movie, also. Johnny Carson was the best on television, no doubt about it.

Nothing compared to Kat, though. She filled all his senses. Especially those that appealed to his basic instincts.

Since he'd talked to Mr. Norman, Odell's mind had been in hyperdrive. His life had changed. Odell didn't know what the future held, but he was optimistic about it. First, he needed to figure out his situation with Kat.

Maybe after the championship game. He couldn't forget about that.

The game was set for today. Odell flexed his arm spending time with his elbow. It was definitely better, but still felt tight. He knew he could pitch, but he hadn't tried to throw since the last one against Ricky Lee's team.

This might be my last game. No way, we're going to lose this one.

Odell thought for a minute. No matter how much Kat influenced his brain, he had to win this contest.

He walked down to the field tossing a ball into his glove. There was a calming factor that came over him from the ritual of gripping the seams and then releasing it in the webbing. The smacking sound was music to his ears.

All of his teammates were near the dugout and seemed loose. There was good-natured banter taking place as Odell arrived among them.

Mitchell jogged to Odell and already had on the shin guards protecting his lower legs. His usual dimpled grin was plastered on his face.

"How's the arm, O?" he asked.

"I'm not sure, but I think it's okay," replied Odell. "Let me throw a few and we'll see."

The two of them went to a spot away from the others where Odell began by softly lobbing the baseball to his catcher. When he didn't feel any discomfort after a couple of minutes, he indicated to Mitchell for him to squat down, and Odell started throwing increasingly harder pitches.

The real test came when Odell gave Mitchell a head nod and a twisting wrist motion indicating he would try a breaking pitch. Odell felt only a slight twinge in the elbow when he threw the curve and then tried a few more for good measure. The arm seemed fine, but Odell promised himself to try and keep from throwing as many of those pitches today.

"Alright, I'm ready," Odell said to Mitchell.

They walked over to where the rest of the team had gathered as Odell told the younger boy what he planned to do. Mainly, the pitcher would rely on speed and control of his pitches and save breaking balls for the moments in the game when their best hitters weren't expecting them. He wanted to protect the arm as much as possible.

Johnny was already trying to pump the team up. Odell thought their coach was maybe more excited than the players getting ready to take the field.

"Guys, this is what we've been playing for all summer. Look at the box of trophies at the scorer's table. We win, we get one. There are none for the second-place team. We've already beat this team once, so y'all know what to do," he said in a mounting voice.

Odell glanced around at the other boys. He took in the scene as he imagined an author would. There was nervousness on Wayne's face as his younger brother chewed on his bottom lip. His other brother, Kenny, was chomping on bubble gum and didn't seem too concerned. The Smith brothers were picking at each other as usual and weren't paying attention to what Johnny had said. Sandy was sticking out his tongue at his cousin Bruce. Ken was tight-lipped and silently thumping his fist in his glove.

It was Odell's team, and he wanted them to always remember this day in a positive light. That was enough reason to win and wanted to verbalize the feeling.

"Listen up. I'm betting one day we'll be a lot older. This game will only be a memory. It's up to us whether that will be a good memory or a bad one. I say, let's make it a great one. Go, Renegades!"

They all yelled the same imperative and ran on the field to their positions since they were the home team. Odell walked slowly to the plate where the umpire and the other team's captain already stood.

Odell almost felt like the ump and he were friends at this point. The over-weight guy who liked to chew tobacco gave him something approaching a grin causing a little bit of the brown liquid to seep out the corner of his mouth. He took a nasty-looking handkerchief from his back pocket to clean the mess.

"Not going to give a big speech to you captains. Y'all know how I operate and what I expect. Congratulations on making it to the championship. Let's play ball," the umpire said.

Odell shook hands with the Boys' Club representative and then got the brand-new game ball from the ump. It felt good in his hand. He walked to the mound as Mitchell took his position behind the plate.

He threw only a few warmup pitches and then watched as the infielders tossed the ball around him after Mitchell made a throw down to second base. When the ball was returned to him on the mound, Odell took a couple of deep breaths before stepping on the pitching rubber. It occurred to him this could be the last time he ever pitched, and a calmness came over him.

***

The team sat in the stands behind the field with a few remaining spectators. The joy of the moment was obvious from the loud celebration as the Renegades were relishing their win. Odell grinned as he watched the other guys hoot and holler.

In some ways, the game had been anticlimactic. It was obvious that the other team couldn't hit Odell's pitches even though he didn't have his best stuff. On the offensive side, the Renegades scored runs in just about every inning with even the youngest guys getting in the action. The final score was 8-1.

A recreation department employee also acting as the scorekeeper asked for quiet. It took three requests before the noise dissipated.

"Okay. Before I get started handing out team trophies to the Renegades' players, I have one other individual award to present.

As y'all probably know already since it was in the paper over the weekend, the leading hitter of the fifteen and under league this year goes to one of your players, Odell Sterling. He batted .533 for the season. Please come down, Odell," said the official.

Cheering and clapping started as Odell walked down the aisle between the metal bench seats to the table that was set up. He shook the rec department representative's right hand with his own and took the trophy in his left. It was somewhat an awkward exchange as Odell initially tried to stick his left hand underneath the shake rather than over it.

"You might as well stay here and let me give you another one for the championship."

Odell took the other prize so that he had one in each hand. He studied both and read what was inscribed. The first and biggest had a batter standing on a pedestal with *Leading Hitter* on the top line and *15 and Under League* on the bottom. The other one had the same batter on a smaller base and simply read *Champions 15 and Under League* on top and *Macon Recreation League* on bottom.

As he heard some of the teammates chant his name, Odell held up both trophies triumphantly before returning to his seat. The other guys went down one by one to get their mementos while he zoned out.

CHAPTER 47

Kat packed another box of stuff and tried not to think about Odell. Too bad that it was a losing proposition. She couldn't stop herself and hadn't been able to for at least the last few weeks. The pending move made everything so much worse.

She had wanted to go to his game today, but there was so much to do getting ready for the move. Kat and her mother had been working hard for the last couple of days and had made a lot of progress. At least most of the personal items were in boxes.

Her father had called earlier this morning to let them know that his employer had assisted in expediting the purchase of the new home. The closing was to be next Wednesday exactly one week from today. A professional moving company had also been arranged and was set to pick up their possessions the next day. Kat couldn't believe the speed at which everything was happening.

Kat had not really spoken to Odell since returning from the weekend trip. When they got back, she had hugged him without saying anything because the emotions were so overwhelming that she was afraid it would end in an embarrassing crying jag. Kat knew from talking to her dad afterwards that Odell wanted to see her, and she wondered if she could keep it together when they met again.

Part of her wanted to give herself to Odell without reservation. Somehow, she thought that might bind them forever. She knew in her heart of hearts, however, that couldn't happen.

Kat would have to bide her time. She thought about the future. While not sure what lay ahead, Kat had wondered if she could become a teacher. She liked helping others and had tutored other students in the past. Mercer University had a program for teaching, and she could come back to Macon for advanced learning after high school. Maybe she and Odell could be in school together.

Who knows, we could even get an apartment together, she thought.

Thinking about the next three years until that could happen didn't seem realistic, though. That was a long time to be apart.

Every scenario she could imagine for them to remain connected was failing. Kat felt as if she was falling into an abyss and there was no escape.

***

Odell thought the healing for his wounded spirit might have begun. Maybe it had something to do with the Renegades winning the championship. That had been against the odds, and he thought part of the success had been due to his firm beliefs from the start that he could help make it happen.

Similarly, he felt hopeful of a future with Kat although the odds were against him again. He thought if he believed hard enough, faith in his abilities would see him through.

After giving a great deal of consideration to a last date before Kat left for Brunswick, Odell called his friend Mike. After swapping the usual greetings, Odell pitched his plans.

"I was hoping that maybe you and Sue would take me and Kat on a double-date Friday or Saturday night," Odell said trying not to sound like he was begging.

"Hmm, feeling desperate, buddy?" asked Mike.

"Maybe a little. No, that's a lie, a lot. This whole situation is tough. I finally find a girl who I really like, and I think she feels the same way about me. Just when things are looking up, I find out she's moving away. It sucks that I can't drive, and we're so limited in ways to be alone."

"I get it, O. Yeah, I'm sure Sue would be up for getting together. Whatcha got in mind?"

"I was thinking maybe we could go to a drive-in. It's not an ideal way to spend some time alone, but I was hoping y'all could walk to the snack bar for a little while during the night. It would at least give me a few minutes to talk with Kat."

"Talk, yeah right," laughed Mike.

Odell felt his face turning a shade of crimson as he replied, "Okay, mainly talk."

"Okay, lover boy. You firm up the details, and I'll call Sue."

Odell hung up and got the newspaper to see the options playing at the theaters. Not that he cared much about any of the movies, but Odell needed to be able to tell his and Kat's parents about the plans and hoped they would approve.

CHAPTER 48

It proved harder to get permission than Odell had expected. Since neither Odell nor Kat had ever been on a double date before, their parents wanted to know as much as possible about the other couple. Odell's mother knew Mike because he and her son had been friends for several years. That was a little problematic as Odell's mom was somewhat suspicious of Mike's character anyway, and when she found out that Sue was a year older, she became even more so.

She finally relented when Odell offered to bring Mike and Sue inside the Sterling home on the evening of the date so that she could meet them. His mother kept insisting that she trusted Odell but didn't know anything about Sue. Since Sue would be driving, his mom wanted to eyeball her and form her own opinion rather than relying on Odell. Of course, Odell couldn't tell his mother that he'd already ridden in her car and thought she was a safe driver.

A contributing factor to obtaining the necessary approval for the date was the pending Norman family move. Odell had pushed his mom hard because this would be the last opportunity he could share time with Kat, and he knew she was sympathetic to Odell's feelings.

After several phone calls between Odell and Mike, Odell and Kat, and even the two mothers, it was agreed that Sue and Mike would pick up the other couple from Odell's home on Friday evening. Odell would walk to Kat's house and bring her there before Sue and Mike's arrival. If Odell's mother had reservations about anything after meeting the other couple, she could call the date off.

Everything worked out despite Odell's worries that it wouldn't. Mike and Sue showed up a little early and were charming. By the time they left the Sterling house twenty minutes later, the two couples were laughing about the ordeal they had just experienced.

"O, your mom is a trip. I felt like a bug under a microscope," said Sue laughing.

"She was definitely checking you out. It's a good thing you didn't wear a short skirt with fishnet stockings," snickered Mike and paused. "Although I'd sure like that."

"Aww, she was just being a mom. I didn't mind her inspection, but I expect you'll get your chance to check me out like that one of these days, Mikey," Sue teased.

"I thought she was going to say that the whole Sterling clan would come to the drive-in once she found out the movie was *Hombre*. Paul Newman is her favorite actor," said Odell.

"That would be interesting to have them park next to us. Can you imagine that? I don't think you know how to behave that long," said Sue winking at Mike.

"Thanks for doing this, y'all. You two are really good friends to go through this much trouble," said Odell.

"No problem, buddy. You're awful quiet, Kat. You okay back there?" said Mike.

Odell glanced over at Kat sitting beside him in the back seat of Sue's Nova. She had been reserved the entire time since he walked her back to his home before being picked up by Mike and Sue. She had been polite and respectful to Odell's mother, but something felt different about her personality. Odell couldn't put his finger on the change.

"I don't know. To be honest, I'm fighting emotions right now. I love that we're getting to go out together, but I hate to think I'll never get to do this again. I'm sorry and don't want to bring everybody down," said Kat.

Odell took Kat's hand in his. She finally looked at him and gave a weak smile.

Sue looked at them in her rearview mirror and said, "I know what we need. Who's up for a slice of strawberry pie from Shoney's? We've got time before the movie."

"Ohhh yeah, me," replied Mike.

"Sounds good," said Odell still looking at Kat.

She had a glint in her eyes that Odell thought might be the formation of tears. Kat reached over and brushed her lips against his and then whispered in his ear, "You are."

Her closeness aroused him momentarily but didn't help the growing dread Odell had started to feel about Kat's pending disappearance from his life. He had avoided telling her of his own sadness because she seemed even more vulnerable than he felt.

Odell put his arm around Kat, and they slid closer together. She rested her head against his shoulder, and he smelled the faint odor of shampoo coming from Kat's recently washed hair. He inhaled gently and enjoyed the softness on his face.

I need to remember this, he thought.

***

Kat thought the evening had been perfect so far which only made her more emotional. She was trying desperately not to show the depression plaguing her but was unsure about the success of her efforts.

Mike and Sue were carrying on a quiet conversation in the front seat that couldn't be heard where she sat snuggled against Odell. The speaker providing audio to the picture on the drive-in screen was located in Sue's window and turned up loud enough to drown out other sounds.

She and Odell had made out for a few minutes earlier, and she could still taste the strawberries and cream from the signature Shoney's dessert. Kat thought she'd always associate the flavor with Odell for the rest of her life.

She was not into the movie because she didn't care very much about westerns and there were too many other things on her mind anyway. Odell seemed to be interested, at least. He was watching intently as Paul Newman's face showed on the screen. Kat had to admit the actor was a good-looking man, but she was happy being close to this boy who wore glasses and smelled of strawberries.

God, I'm going to miss this guy, she thought.

She liked being close to him. There were tingles in parts of her body that felt dangerous when she was against his. As they slouched, he began slowly stroking her arm with his hand. The touch was light but felt electric. Kat responded by brushing her fingertips against the hair on his arm.

Kat felt like she was melting into him. Her face was warm in the crook of his arm, and she wanted to let herself go. There was a deep breath that came out of her and relaxation followed. Kat closed her eyes. She was near dreamy sleep.

As she slid into an in-between stage of reality and fantasy, Odell's hand slid to her chest. The blouse she wore had a couple of buttons that he unfastened. His fingers crept inside and found her breast. His touch remained gentle as he pushed her bra up and began to fondle that part of her.

Mike said something and she briefly snapped out of the reverie.

"Sue and I are going to the snack bar. Y'all want anything?"

"Uh, maybe a Coke," said Odell.

"No, thanks," replied Kat.

"Alrighty then. Y'all behave while we're gone," said Mike.

The two of them got out of the car and were soon gone while Kat tried to get back to the real world. She felt self-conscious about her unbuttoned blouse and tried to straighten herself when the car light came on, and Odell quickly removed his hand.

For a moment, Kat and Odell didn't say anything. There was movie dialogue coming from the speaker, but it had no importance to them. Kat wanted to say something more meaningful.

"I'm going to miss you so much," she said.

"Me, too," Odell replied.

She started crying. She didn't want to. Tears were streaming now.

He held her stroking and patting her back. Odell's touch was reassuring.

"I'm going to write you letters, and maybe we can talk on the phone, too. Who knows, maybe I can get my parents to go down to Jekyll Island for the next vacation," Odell said.

"We both know that letters can't replace these kinds of moments, Odell. Neither can talking on the phone which will be expensive anyway since it'll be long distance. And vacations? Come on. At the earliest that's a year away," she said sniffing.

"It's not fair," Odell said shaking his head. "There's really nothing we can do about it."

"We can make it a night to remember," Kat whispered into his ear and then nibbled on his neck.

As she continued tasting the area, Kat took Odell's hand and guided it to her inner thigh. He flinched for a second and then slowly slid his fingers up her skirt toward her cotton panties as she helped him with her own touch.

Her breathing had become a little faster and she opened her legs slightly. The anticipated contact was abruptly halted by the sound of approaching footsteps on the gravel outside the car. Odell stopped and withdrew his hand.

"Crap," Odell said as they both sat up.

A guy with a flashlight was patrolling the last line of parked cars. She assumed he was an employee assigned to keep such activities as she had in mind from happening. The crunching footsteps didn't stop until he was near Sue's car.

***

Phillip got out of his car that was parked on the last line of vehicles at the drive-in theater. He carried a flashlight that was usually kept in the trunk with other tools but had been retrieved earlier in the evening. He thought he might be able to see what was going on in the backseat of the Nova he'd first recognized at Shoney's. The thought of Kat and the punk ass making out aroused him and made him sick to his stomach at the same time.

Since the confrontation with Sterling at the skating rink, his mind had been bouncing back and forth about whether he should take further action. Phillip felt more than a little embarrassed that the guy had gotten the better of him, and his two buddies had avoided hanging around him without explanation. It was like a festering wound that wouldn't heal properly, and he was left to deal with the problem by himself.

It was quite by luck that he'd seen the two couples at Shoney's. Phillip had driven to the location to see if there were any single girls who might want to go for a ride. He was feeling restless and was still hurting that Kat would choose Sterling over him. The surprise he experienced when they drove past his car and parked in a slot on the opposite side made him forget his original purpose.

He had slid down in his seat and watched as best he could. His vantage point wasn't great, but Phillip could tell they were laughing and eating something. They seemed oblivious to him, and anger bubbled up as he observed.

He sipped his drink through a straw wondering where they would go when they left. *Why should they be so happy?* he thought.

When they settled their check with the waitress and backed out of their parking space, Phillip made a split decision to follow. His curiosity was forcing him to do so.

Phillip stayed a comfortable distance behind the girl driving the car and pulled off the side of the highway before they rode into the theater. He waited there for about fifteen minutes as other vehicles entered the drive-in.

As the sunlight began to fade, he finally drove his car inside after paying for a ticket. It was easy to find the Nova and park far enough away to prevent detection but close enough to watch them. Periodically, Phillip would glance toward the other car plotting what he might do. Then he saw the other couple in the front seat get out and head to the snack bar. This was his opportunity for revenge.

Now as he walked toward the car where Kat and Sterling were in the back seat, Phillip was aware of the gravel grinding underneath his feet and didn't care that his approach was not stealthy. He switched on the light and saw the two heads in the back seat pop up through frosted glass.

***

Odell looked anxiously out the window that had become fogged up from his and Kat's steamy encounter. He could see a tall figure with a flashlight pointed toward their location. Though he didn't have a clear view, there was something familiar about the guy's stature.

Guessing that he was an employee of the theater, Odell thought he should get out of the car to address any problem as the guy got nearer. He had not been in this situation before and was unsure how to handle it.

"I'll see what he wants," Odell said to Kat as he opened the door.

Kat appeared nervous in the pale light of the car's interior. There was also a hint of frustration on her face that Odell was feeling as well. "Hurry back," she replied.

Odell stepped outside as the blinding light was shone directly in his face. He diverted his eyes from the brightness and heard the chomping gravel as the other person stepped closer.

"Uh, could you get the light out of my eyes, please?" Odell asked.

For a few uncomfortable seconds, there was no response as Odell glanced toward the source with his head turned slightly. Then from the voice he last remembered at Durr's he heard, "Like this?"

Odell reacted in a fraction of a second as he recognized Phillip Jackson's voice, and he saw the arc of the flashlight swinging toward the left side of his head. He saved his face from the blow by ducking backward, but his glasses weren't so lucky. They were knocked from his nose and flew away from him.

His vision now blurred, Odell crouched and then sprang forward while Phillip was off-balance and out of position from the mostly missed blow. Odell's father's advice to make the first punch count rang in his memory. Forward momentum helped his leveraged uppercut right fist hit Phillip squarely under the chin causing his teeth to rattle. Then the taller teen's legs crumpled beneath him causing Phillip to fall flat on his back. The flashlight rolled away producing moving shadows.

Odell quickly straddled on top of Phillip's chest with his knees pinning the prone boy's shoulders to the ground. Odell drew back his already sore fist to pummel the face further but stopped with his arm cocked like he was about to throw a fastball. Blood was seeping from Phillip's slackened mouth, and he looked unconscious with both eyes closed.

Odell's brain raged as he contemplated further injury to Jackson. He wanted to do what Phillip tried to do to him. It would be so easy right now.

Beat his face in. Break his nose. Knock out some teeth. Teach him a lesson he'll never forget.

In a flash, he thought of being tripped, having his and Kat's houses egged, being called names at the DQ and the confrontation at the skating rink. *He deserves this,* thought Odell, *but is this who I am?*

Kat had gotten out of the car and stood looking down at them. She shook her head up and down slightly and then from side to side without speaking. Odell and Kat stared at each other in the flickering light from the movie screen for what seemed an eternity while he contemplated his options. It was as if she was thinking what he was considering, too.

Slowly, Odell got up and walked to her. They embraced and the comforting hug seemed to erase the bad thoughts stewing in his brain. Odell knew that the magic moment he been experiencing with her just a few minutes earlier had passed, but this felt pretty damned good. It was much better than the hate that was slowly dissipating.

In record time, several people including Mike and Sue gathered around the scene, and the theater manager was summoned. A couple of people informed the man in charge that the now semi-conscious teenager still on the ground had started the fight.

Phillip groaned and sat up with his long legs splayed in front of him. The manager produced smelling salts that were waved under Phillip's nose to further revive the groggy teen. He assisted Phillip with his minor injuries and then informed him that he was no longer welcome as a customer.

Phillip seemed resigned as he got into his car with slumped shoulders. He drove away dabbing his mouth with a paper towel and never looked toward Odell and Kat's direction.

Later in the evening after Odell's glasses were found with the lenses scratched but unbroken, he recalled the events and what could have been. Maybe it was for the best, but Odell wondered if that was true. The violent encounter had ended a tender moment with Kat and left him with the realization that you could be forced into such a situation no matter what steps you might take to avoid it.

Again, he remembered his father's advice not to start fights. If you found yourself in that situation, though, you fought to win. He had.

A part of his innocence had been taken from him. Another part was still intact.

CHAPTER 49

It was Monday and the beginning of the last week before school started again. Odell had mixed feelings about that, but it was not the primary concern in his life by any means.

Since their date on Friday night, he had only talked to Kat briefly over the weekend. Odell had called her Saturday morning hoping that they might at least go skating that evening. Unfortunately, she couldn't go because her father was back in town and had planned a family outing. Odell's frustration that carried over from the night before had escalated.

Yesterday all he could do was mope around the house after church hoping for new revelations to his problems that never came. He was fresh out of ideas to try and see Kat one more time before she would be leaving.

Odell kept reliving the last date. It had been special in some ways, but not as much as it could have been. The excitement he had felt just before Phillip Jackson's intervention had visited his dreams again last night and almost caused another wet one. He hated to think that these constant thoughts would dwell in his mind from now on. Unrequited love was definitely a downer, and he saw no happy end in sight.

His parents were at work already, and the brothers were outside playing. He slouched on the sofa and really had no plans on what to do. Odell didn't have a book to read, had no desire to watch television or to go outside and see what anybody else was doing. He was totally miserable.

Odell's mind kept jumping from one thing to another even in the depths of his gloom. The summer had been memorable, but he was anxious to get on with his life. That required him to keep getting what he considered his card punched. Setting goals, meeting them and then setting more. Each goal reached was another punch on the life card. If he punched enough of them, he'd be a success.

Since life was going to continue even without Kat in it, Odell needed to move on the best he could. She would have to do the same. It was just another punch on the card, but this one hurt and didn't feel like a goal was being achieved.

He suddenly had an idea. Odell could at least memorialize the summer. He went to his room and found the Brownie camera given to him before going to Washington, D.C. in the seventh grade. It had been sitting on the small desk in his room since his mother had taken a few pictures of the Renegades before one of their games. Checking the counter on the camera, Odell saw there were still several unused frames.

The Kodak camera hadn't been used much over the last year, and Odell wondered if the film stored inside was okay. He couldn't remember the last time he had gotten any pictures developed, but it looked like he had at least three shots left on this roll. He looked through the drawer of the desk and found another unused roll of film. Odell stuck it in the pocket of his jeans and used the strap to place the camera around his neck.

Odell decided rather than telephoning Kat first, he would take his chances and go to her house. While he didn't consider himself a great photographer, Odell had learned how to operate the camera well enough to capture images he liked. He had a photo scrapbook containing well over a hundred pictures pressed onto the pages. Some were arranged in groupings like vacations, others more random. He planned to dedicate a new page to Kat with the photos he would take of her.

He rode his bike up the driveway to the small, framed house and wasn't sure if anyone was home. There were no vehicles there, and it caused Odell to doubt his just hatched plans.

Walking up the steps to the front door, the camera swung from side to side against his chest. He was just about to knock when the door opened, and Kat appeared inside the screen holding Madi in her arm. Her brunette waves were whipped up casually on her head. The dog acted as if she was happy to see him, but Odell couldn't discern Kat's gaze. It was a blank look that caused his heart to sink. He wanted a happy face to photograph.

"Hey, I've been missing you. I took a chance you'd be home and hoped I could take a few pictures," said Odell.

Kat's attempt at a smile was weak. At first, Odell wasn't sure if she was going to come outside, invite him inside or to even speak.

After an uncomfortable moment she said, "Sorry, Odell. I've been pretty busy the last couple of days. I've missed you, too. I'm not very sure I look good enough for any picture taking right now."

"You look beautiful to me, and you, too, Madi," Odell replied.

Madi barked at the sound of her name. Her tail had been wagging since Odell's arrival and now it went into overdrive. Kat opened the screen door stepping outside right in front of him. Odell took the dog into one of his hands and hugged Kat awkwardly with his other arm while the pet was squirming and trying to lick his face.

"Now this would make a funny picture," said Kat and laughed.

"I'm glad to hear you laughing a little. I know you're not happy and neither am I. We need to make the best out of a bad situation. I want something to remember you by. That's why I got out the camera. If I have a few pictures of you, I can at least have something I can look at when I get lonely," Odell said.

They stepped back from one another after the hug, and Madi calmed down a little in Odell's arm. He began stroking her furry back and Madi's pink tongue hung out.

"Okay, whatever you say," replied Kat.

She began walking toward the swing where the two had sat several times over the summer. Odell watched her sway as she walked. He wanted to etch that walk in his memory. It was innocent and sexy at the same time. Kat took a seat in the well-worn swing with one leg folded under the other. Odell followed behind observing intently.

When Odell reached the swing, he stretched down and let Madi out of his arm. She looked up at him for a moment and then started sniffing the nearby ground. Soon she was distracted by other smells and moved away from them.

Odell studied his girlfriend who was perusing him at the same time. Her right hand held onto the rope securing the swing to the tree. She was dressed casually in a pink patterned top that was puffy on her shoulders and scooped enough in the front, so the pendant was visible. Her shorts came about mid-thigh revealing her well-defined legs. She was barefooted. It occurred to Odell that she looked wholesome and a little like a cheerleader.

He raised the camera and looked through the viewfinder. The light was sufficient even though she was in the shade. She was just as he always remembered her, and he snapped a picture.

Odell looked up from the camera. Her eyes were locked in his.

"I don't know what love is, but this has got to be close," said Odell.

Kat smiled revealing slightly uneven but white teeth. Odell stepped closer and took another picture.

"Do you think we'll see each other again?" Kat asked.

"God, I hope so," said Odell.

Kat's mom drove their truck into the yard as the two of them gazed at each other in a romantic trance. The sound of the engine broke their concentration. Mrs. Norman got out of the vehicle with a brown grocery sack in her arms and came near them.

"Well, hey Odell. I see you are taking pictures. How about if I take one of both of you?"

Odell took the Brownie from around his neck briefly taking his eyes from Kat's. Somehow it seemed an appropriate moment to capture in a photo.

"Thank you, Mrs. Norman. That would be great, if you don't mind," he said.

She set the bag down on the ground and took the camera from Odell. He slid his arm around Kat's shoulders without thinking about her mother. Mrs. Norman's smile could be seen prominently underneath where she held the device to her eye before saying, "Cheese."

Odell didn't know how the photo would turn out but hoped it would be good. In his mind, it would represent a major part of the summer and the lives they were just finishing. Odell knew the two of them had grown during the season and wanted something to remember it by. No matter how much he wished they could keep their relationship viable, reality didn't seem to favor that proposition.

"That was lovely. Odell, you'll have to send us a copy of the picture when you get it developed," said Kat's mom while handing the camera back to him.

"I sure will, Mrs. Norman."

She retrieved the bag of groceries, and Madi followed her inside the house. Odell and Kat sat quietly on the swing gently rocking back and forth. After a moment, she rested her head in the nook of his shoulder where his arm was still stretched around her.

"Will you write me and let me know your new address? I'll need it so I can send you a copy of the picture," Odell said softly.

Kat sighed and said, "Yeah."

"Are y'all still planning to leave in a couple of days?" asked Odell.

"No later than that."

"We could still do something together then. Maybe a movie or just go downtown again, if you'd like."

"Thanks, Odell. I just think it would make it worse for me. It's almost been too much to deal with already. I think it would be better for both of us to leave things as they are now. I hope you understand because you really mean the most to me," Kat replied as she turned to look into his eyes.

The fact was that he did understand. His limited knowledge of the feelings they shared dictated her response. His heart was breaking, and Odell didn't know if he could keep from showing his emotions.

Guys aren't supposed to do that, right? He thought.

CHAPTER 50

Moving day arrived and Odell debated whether he should travel up the road to say good-bye. He was in such a funk that he felt like he was suffering from the flu. He wished he had some parting gift for Kat but had nothing. The roll of film had been delivered to the store for developing and was not scheduled to be back until the following week. Otherwise, he could've at least taken her a picture or two. Instead, Odell guessed he'd have to mail her a copy when he got the new address.

This was by far the saddest experience in his young life. He was fortunate not to have lost a loved one, yet. Odell supposed losing Kat was akin to the death of a close family member, but he had no frame of reference to judge by. His brain told him she was not dying, and they still had a chance in the future to be together again. His heart just wasn't buying the concept.

Odell went to the telephone and dialed Kat's number. It never rang and gave a weird tone. He realized the family must have disconnected the service before the pending move.

It was like some force was leading him, and he made the decision to try and see her one last time despite Kat's earlier expressions that she didn't want to do that. Running out the back door, Odell kept moving as fast as he could around the house to the road in front. His arms pumped in rhythm with his legs and feet as they pounded the asphalt.

I hope I'm not too late.

Odell slowed down as he reached the Norman home and saw a large moving van in the driveway. There was a ramp running from the back that two muscular-bound men were using to haul furniture onboard. He also noticed that Mr. Norman's pickup truck was parked nearby and contained some items in the back bed.

He was breathing hard as he walked from the roadway toward the front of the house. The doorway stood open with the screen door propped by a brick. Kat emerged cradling a record player that was packed in its case and stopped in her tracks when she saw Odell.

She had the same sad, droopy eyes from their last encounter. Her mouth quivered slightly but said nothing before she continued her journey to her dad's truck.

Odell hesitated and then walked to the location. She was looking at the other stuff packed in the back as he arrived.

"I'm sorry. I know you told me the other day that I shouldn't come back today, but I couldn't help it," said Odell.

Kat had her back to him and finally seemed to settle on a place to set the small record player case in a corner of the truck bed. When she turned toward him her eyes were glistening.

Without speaking, she walked the few steps to where he stood, and they wrapped their arms around each other. The hug was warm and calming. Odell didn't want the moment to end, but Kat broke it in an even better way when she looked up and kissed him sweetly on the lips. None of the sexual electricity he had felt on several occasions when they had shared time together was present. Instead, he was enveloped in a cocoon with her that shut out everything bad.

They separated a step or two away from each other and she took his hand. Odell thought the smile that appeared on her face was almost angelic. With her free hand, Kat reached into the pocket of the pants she wore and pulled out an envelope.

He saw his name written on the front of it. She spoke for the first time since seeing her in the front doorway.

"I told myself this morning when I was still in bed that I hoped you wouldn't listen to what I said the other day and come by one more time. I don't know if I was praying to God, or just wanting it to happen to prove to myself we have powers that we don't understand," she said pausing.

"And, here you are. I don't know what that means except maybe there's hope for us in the future. Who knows? I guess maybe we'll find out sooner or later. I wrote this a few weeks ago when it started looking like this day might happen. I wish I had something else to give you other than these words from my heart," Kat finished by handing him the letter.

"Thanks, should I read it now?" croaked Odell.

"No, wait til later when you have some quiet time. Now, I really want you to go home. I don't want to see you standing here waving when we leave. I promise I'll send you the new address so we can stay in touch. Okay?"

"Okay. I just want to say thank you for everything. I believe you know how I feel, so that's all I can say," Odell said and swallowed the rest of his emotions.

"Yeah, I know, and you do, too," she said and kissed him lightly one last time.

She turned and walked back toward her house. Odell put the letter in his back pocket and began the slow tread to his own house.

Later that afternoon, Odell watched from a distance as the moving van left following the pickup truck. He strained trying to see if he could get one more glimpse but never did.

This was not the end he envisioned to the story.

CHAPTER 51

The tenth grade held promises as the third week of classes was coming to an end. It was good to be around some of the old friends not seen since the last school year, and Odell had also made a couple of new ones. The stinging loss of Kat was still on his mind, but he was busy enough that it didn't occupy quite as much of his time. It was hard to believe that it would soon be October meaning cooler weather was on the way.

Once again, routines were the order of the day. He would get up early, eat breakfast, gather his books, go to school, attend classes, bullshit with friends, go home, take care of homework, watch a little TV, sleep, start over again. Maybe it was kind of boring, but his mind needed occupying and the routine helped.

Odell had gotten the developed pictures he had made of Kat along with the one taken by her mother of the two of them together and placed them in his album. There were several of the Renegades, too, that he placed on a separate page.

He thought about having the one of him and Kat together enlarged and maybe putting it in a frame to set on his desk. Odell hadn't done that yet and wondered if it had anything to do with the fact that he hadn't heard from her since she left. It was a sweet photo and always brought good memories, but not hearing from her left him unsettled.

Two competing sayings kept going through his head. One was, *Absence makes the heart grow fonder.* The other was, *Out of sight, out of mind.*

The letter Kat had given him on that fateful last day was stored in his cigar box with his other collected valuables. The words she had written on stationary were a reminder of the summer that could never be taken away even if they went their separate ways and didn't see each other again. As the English teacher was droning on about literature, Odell reread the letter in his mind.

Dear Odell,

If you are reading this, my worst nightmare has happened. I kept hoping somehow it wouldn't. I told myself that if we didn't move, I would burn these words without you ever seeing them. Sadly, I didn't get to strike that match.

Even though my heart is torn into pieces at this moment, I just wanted to tell you how much you have meant to me over the summer. I think you know already because you've also expressed similar feelings.

The fun times we had and the closeness we felt cannot ever be erased despite time moving on or the distance between us. I believe our paths crossed for a reason.

I've learned that a guy can be smart and athletic. Sweet and tough. Funny and serious.

As we've talked about, the age we are now has got to be the hardest time to go through growing up. You've helped me and I believe I've helped you, too. I sure hope so.

Going forward, I wish you all the happiness in the world. I'm sure you will hope the same for me.

ILY, Kat

"Mr. Sterling are you listening?" asked Mrs. Sherwood.

Odell felt himself coming back to reality. He wasn't sure what if anything he'd missed from the lecture.

"Uh, yes ma'am."

"I'm not so sure. I was just saying that I have graded the writing assignments on the topic of what y'all did over the summer and yours was exceptional. I'm not going to embarrass you by making you read it to the rest of the class, but I wanted to acknowledge your achievement."

She passed out the respective papers to all the students in the class showing red markings for errors and a grade in the top right-hand corner. Odell heard grumblings from several of the guys as they received theirs. When the teacher laid his in front of him, he saw *A+* written along with *Good Work!*

He had titled the essay *Renegade Summer,* and the twin themes were centered around the encountered experiences of playing baseball and meeting a special girl. Odell had kept certain details private and not included in the paper but tried to express the emotions faced over the summer vacation. He was pleased that the teacher found his descriptions worthy of the good grade.

***

When he got home that afternoon after school, Odell stopped by the mailbox and retrieved the mail. He had been doing this daily since Kat moved hoping there would be a letter from her. Shuffling through the usual stuff and about to give up again, there was the same kind of envelope as the one in his cigar box. His name was written in Kat's cursive, and he noticed right away there was a return address.

Odell hurried inside and went to his room. He sat down at the desk and tore open the envelope that smelled faintly of Kat's perfume. He read:

Dear Odell,

I'm sorry it's taken me so long to write you. Things have been incredibly busy since we got to Brunswick. I bet you've been pretty busy with school starting, too.

I really can't believe this is the first home that belongs to us. It's so nice!

Daddy loves his new job, and Mom loves being close to the beach. We have gone twice already on the weekends. I have a feeling we'll be going a lot more.

School is alright and my schedule is not difficult. I've met a couple of girls in my class who live near me and are pretty cool. They're both on the junior varsity cheerleading squad and talked me into trying out. Would you believe I made it?

Anyway, I wanted you to know I'm feeling better. I could tell by looking in your eyes that last day that you were worried about me. That's the last thing I wanted, so I decided to try and make the best of my life.

I still hope that one day we'll see each other again. Until then, take care and please feel free to write me if you like.

Yours truly,

Kat

Odell smiled as he finished reading the letter. He was happy to hear that she was adapting to her new surroundings and even happier after seeing the last paragraph.

He didn't have any fancy stationary, but he took out a sheet of paper from his notebook. While everything was fresh on his mind, Odell penned a letter.

Dear Kat,

I was so glad to get your letter today. I have been missing you and wondering how you're doing. From what you've said, everything is looking up, and that makes me happy. Special congratulations on making cheerleader!

After reading the one you left me that last day, I was sad but hopeful. I still am and now even more optimistic, thanks to you.

I've had time to think about us as I'm sure you have. I believe, despite our age, we are more mature than we may realize. I feel like we're both going to be fine and succeed in the future.

Yeah, I've been busy with school, too. I'm taking an extra course instead of study hall, so I have lots of homework. I've joined a couple of clubs and got chosen for student council as well. I'm trying to keep my mind occupied, I guess.

Like you, I'm not ruling out that we'll see each other again someday. I wouldn't bet against that happening because of the connection we felt together.

I'm enclosing a copy of the picture your mother made of us in the swing. It turned out well. I've probably looked at it and the others I made of you a thousand times. They will always be my reminder of the bittersweet summer of '67.

XO,

Odell

He finished writing, placed the photo in the middle and then folded the letter over it. Odell stuck it in an envelope and then sealed it with his tongue. He was careful to address it correctly and would drop it in the mailbox before tomorrow.

Sitting back in the chair, Odell thought that maybe he had been wrong a few weeks ago when the moving van was disappearing from view. Then, he believed it was the end. Now, he believed it might be a new beginning.

The End

Acknowledgements

As with my first three novels, I have had assistance from some wonderful people who helped me complete this latest book. I appreciate each of them more than I can adequately express.

First, to my wife, Donna. Thank you, my love, for being the first to read the manuscript. Your edits and suggestions are always spot on, and you probably don't realize how much I depend upon your insights. You have kept me grounded for over forty years, and I don't know what I'd do without you.

Second, to the rest of my beta readers. Darryl Bollinger has been a good friend since junior high school. His writing experience remains a huge influence on my writing as it has since my first book. I urge fans of my stories to try some of his novels if you haven't already. Thanks, buddy for all your help and advice.

Next, two members of my former profession were also invaluable contributing readers. Misty Peterson is a brilliant attorney who helped correct structural writing errors and also provided good ideas about the story. Likewise, Cindy Adams, who is another excellent lawyer, author, friend, and former colleague provided similar guidance. These two women assisted with the feminine perspective as well as with other technical issues. I consider them indispensable whenever I undertake writing a new novel.

My last reader's assistance is also special to me. To my daughter, Mandy, forgive me for ever doubting what you would accomplish with two advanced degrees in English. I am proud to have you as my daughter and marvel at you taking the time from your busy life to help me with my writing.

I have to acknowledge my family for being inspirations in my stories as well as in my life. My parents, Otis and Shirley, imparted the work ethic that my brothers and I always tried to emulate. They, as well as my departed youngest brother, Lynn, are never far from my mind. Some of our family experiences tend to pop up fictionally in all of my books. I am glad that I still have two brothers, Kenny and Wayne, to help recall those times.

Finally, many thanks to the readers of this novel for your support. Hopefully, I've brought you some enjoyment, at least for a little while. I always love hearing from you whether in person, via e-mail, through a written review, text or some social media post. You make my day when that happens, and I hope you'll keep spreading the word.

Any mistakes remaining are mine. Peace.

Made in the USA
Columbia, SC
29 January 2022

55022810R00172